So Twisted

So Twisted

A Bad Behavior novel

MELISSA MARINO

FOREVER
YOURS

New York Boston

Copyright © 2016 by Melissa Marino
Excerpt from *So Screwed* copyright © 2016 by Melissa Marino
Cover design by Elizabeth Turner
Cover copyright © 2016 by Hachette Book Group, Inc.

Forever Yours
Hachette Book Group
1290 Avenue of the Americas, New York, NY 10104
forever-romance.com
twitter.com/foreverromance

First published as an ebook and as a print on demand: November 2016

Forever Yours is an imprint of Grand Central Publishing. The Forever Yours name and logo are trademarks of Hachette Book Group, Inc.

The publisher is not responsible for websites (or their content) that are not owned by the publisher.

The Hachette Speakers Bureau provides a wide range of authors for speaking events. To find out more, go to www.hachettespeakersbureau.com or call (866) 376-6591.

ISBNs: 978-1-4555-6952-6 (ebook), 978-1-4555-6962-5 (trade paperback, print on demand)

To L:
Thank you for lifting me so high I could catch
my dreams.
All my love, M.

So Twisted

So Twisted

Chapter One

CALLIE—

Is anyone else getting a wedgie from these damn things?" I shouted to the other females I was working with. I hurried to the other end of the bar as I adjusted my hot-pink bloomers that were under my extra short patent leather skirt. Our new uniforms were about as functional as wet toilet paper.

"Hey beautiful, how long does a guy have to wait to get a drink around here?" I turned and saw a barely legal guy at the other end of the bar, clearly not needing another cocktail.

Luckily, the DJ had decided that was the perfect time to crank the music, and like that, the cries of the drunken were silenced.

It was eleven o'clock and the night was young. The bar was packed, which was good for my bank account, but bad for my dignity. Every hour that went by at Venom, the downtown Chicago club I bartended at that catered to the newly twenty-one crowd, lowered the IQ of my customers.

"What can I get you?" I asked the dude heckling me.

He leaned in. "You can get me a double vodka, sexy."

"Is that it?" I said, making his drink.

"No," he slurred. He leaned in further, practically drooling over himself. "You can get me your phone number."

I rolled my eyes. "Sorry, sweetie. I don't date customers."

"Who said anything about dating? I just want to see that skirt on my bedroom floor in the morning."

"Ain't gonna happen. Anything else?" I said, handing him his drink.

"Yeah, I want those shiny, knee-high boots wrapped around…"

I cut him off before I could hear the rest. "Twelve dollars."

He reached in his pocket and pulled out a handful of crushed bills. He picked out a few and handed them to me. Something was crunchy in that wad of cash. Something damp, too. I wanted to vomit.

"There's more where this came from," he said with a wink.

Fuck my life.

"Wait just a second," Frat Boy Slim babbled. "You look familiar."

"Probably because you're looking right at me. Crazy how the mind works, huh?"

I attempted to step away, knowing that continuing a conversation with this guy would be as enjoyable as a two-day-old pulled pork sandwich that had been soaking in curdled milk, but he wouldn't let up.

"Wait!" he said, jumping and spilling half his vodka on his pink Lacoste shirt. "Aren't you in that um…math class…the one for teachers with me?"

"Mathematics in elementary school?" I asked.

He snapped his fingers at me. "Yes! That's the one. I knew I recognized you from someplace."

There was seriously no hope for our future if this was the kind of moron teaching our children.

"That must be it," I said. "Okay, then. I have to get back to work."

"Hold up. Do you live off campus? No way you still live in the dorms."

"No. I don't live in the dorms because I'm too old for that shit, and I only go part-time. Anything else?"

"Pfft," he spit, waving his arm around. "You ain't old. You can't be older than twenty-four or so."

I touched my nose, letting him know he got it right. "Einstein."

He nodded and snorted simultaneously. "Yeah. I'm pretty smart. And I think you are, too, so why don't you just tell me what time you get off so I can get you off?"

I wasn't sure if it was my disgusted look or the distraction of having a drink thrown in his face by the girl standing behind him who was listening to our conversation, but like magic, he disappeared.

I rubbed my temples, feeling the pain of a headache coming on. "Fuck my life," I said aloud before placing a smile on my face as fake as the skirt I was wearing before I approached the next customer. "Hey there. What can I get you?"

By the end of the evening—actually three o'clock in the morning—I was totally spent. As I walked out the back door, I stopped and unzipped my knee-high boots with the four-inch heels. I crossed the parking lot barefoot, and even though it was March in Chicago, the feel of the icy ground numbed my aching feet. After getting into my car and waiting a few minutes for it to heat up, I drove home. The streets were empty except for a few drunken stragglers, their arms draped over a new friend who will soon be a lover or maybe even an old lover who was never a friend. It hardly mattered which one it was because I was jealous all the same. Logically I knew half of them would be alone by morning, but for the night, they had someone close. They had deep kisses and warm bodies. All I had was hot chocolate and Garrett's Popcorn waiting for me at home.

Exhaustion hit me the moment I began the climb up the stairs to my apartment. My head pounded with pain, and every muscle in my legs screamed for rest. I dropped everything, except my phone, at the front door and dragged myself to the couch, where I collapsed. My bed would've been much more comfortable, but my room might as well have been a mile away at that point. I had just enough sense to set the alarm on my phone for seven a.m. so I had time in the morning for a quick shower before class. Hot chocolate and popcorn was going to have to wait.

* * *

I heard voices but refused to open my eyes. It would be admitting morning had arrived, and that couldn't be possible when I had just closed my eyes. The faint sound of my alarm grew louder and louder as I continued to deny the time.

Strong steps against our hardwood floors approached me, but then stopped abruptly and reversed. With a sigh, I peeled my eyes open—which were stuck together from the glue of my false eyelashes and leftover makeup I hadn't bothered to wash off. I slapped my alarm off and cursed the sun for being, well, the sun.

"What is your problem?" Evelyn said, her voice raising. "I thought you were leaving?"

"Someone is on your couch. A woman, and she's in her underwear," an unfamiliar man voice answered.

"Will you knock it off? I told you I had fun and that I'd text you later," Evelyn said.

"It was fun, wasn't it?"

"Yes." She sighed. "So, see you later."

"But what about the girl in her underwear?" he asked.

"I'm not in my underwear," I shouted, opening my eyes.

Evelyn's head popped out of her bedroom door. "Oh. Yeah. Definitely not underwear."

A tall blond guy wearing a wrinkled white button-down and blue pants turned. He gave a quick nod and side smile, clearly hiding his embarrassment over his mistake.

"Hey there," he said, swinging a suit jacket over his shoulder. "I was just—"

"Leaving," Evelyn said, nudging him.

Evelyn's one-hit wonder began his walk of shame, but stopped in front of me. His eyes drifted down my body, stopping at my skirt.

"Yes?" I asked, sitting up.

His head tilted and he smiled. "You work at Venom?"

"For shit's sake," I said, standing and stomping to my room.

The last thing I heard before getting into the shower was Evelyn telling him he was an inconsiderate jackass with a small dick.

I love that girl.

While I was normally not a morning person, I was even less so when I'd only had three hours of sleep. I practically cried through my five-minute shower, but when the smell of coffee hit me, my spirits lifted slightly. When I came out of the bathroom, in my ratty robe and hair up in a towel, there was a cup waiting for me on the counter in the kitchen. She even put the right amount of my favorite peppermint mocha creamer in it.

I sat at the kitchen table, going through my class notes, when Evelyn came out of her room and breezed into the kitchen like the breath of fresh air she always was. Her long blond hair was curled into perfect waves, while her cream-colored blouse was tucked neatly into her black pencil skirt. I was lucky if I managed to leave the house wearing matching shoes.

"Thanks for the coffee," I said, yawning.

"No problem," she said, slipping on her black heels. "Everything good?"

I nodded. "Mm-hmm."

"You sure?"

I set my notes down and looked at her. She was nervously biting down on her lower lip, messing up her red lipstick. Something was up. She never ruined her lipstick unless she was nervous (which she hardly ever was) or she was getting lucky with a dude (which happened on a fairly regular basis).

I stood and crossed the kitchen. "What's up?"

"Nothing," Evelyn said.

I rolled my eyes at her as I poured myself another cup of coffee. "You're a terrible liar."

She twirled a lock of her hair and pressed her lips together tightly. "I'm worried about you."

"Worried about what?"

"Cal, you can't keep working like this." She moved and stood in front of me. "You're so exhausted between working these late hours and with school."

I took a sip and shrugged. "I don't have a choice right now. At least I'm not working two jobs anymore."

We had this conversation so many times before, and while I knew it only came from a place of concern, my situation wasn't by choice. Sometimes I wondered if she realized that.

"Look, you're sweet to worry, but we've been through this already. My student loans are through the roof, and while I know I can defer, it'll be more of an issue in the end. If I thought I could still pay rent and everything else by any other means besides bartending, I would, but that isn't happening. I'm just taking a larger course load now so I can finish next year."

She took hold of my hands. "Look, I was thinking I could ask Bridget if you could do some help around the office. With the wedding season coming…"

I shook my head. "Me, working for wedding planners? Seriously? Plus, I'd still be making more a few nights a week at Venom. The money is too good."

"I'm not trying to piss you off," she said. "I think that…"

I pulled my wet hair back, looking up at the ceiling to blink away the tears. "Ev. Please," I pleaded.

"Oh," she said, putting her arms around me. "I'm sorry. Please don't be sad."

I sighed and put my coffee cup down so I could hug her back. "You worry too much."

She shrugged when we pulled away. "Sometimes, although worrying is usually your specialty. But I know how hard you work, both with school and the bar, and I love you so stupid."

"I know. I love you, too, Blondie."

"I have to run." She walked over to the table and picked up her purse. "See you later?"

"Probably not. Work tonight."

Work. Work. Work.

* * *

I sat at a café by campus, the late afternoon sun glaring off the table's surface, reviewing material from my earlier class. I was on my third coffee of the day, but while the caffeine from my triple-shot latte was giving me just enough energy to keep my head up, it wouldn't last. My eyelids burned, and there was a serious nap in my future if I got everything done before work.

I returned to my notes but was interrupted when my phone rang. I dug it out of my purse, checking the caller ID. EVELYN.

"What's up?" I said.

"Hey, are you busy? I've got some news I think you might be interested in."

"Studying. Something going on?"

"Okay. Before I tell you anything, you have to promise me you won't get mad first."

"Why would I be mad?"

"I can't tell you that. You might get mad."

I put my pen down and took a sip of my mocha. "Fine. Go ahead."

"So, you're promising not to be mad?" she asked.

I didn't like where this was headed. Evelyn only asked me not to be mad at her when she did something I told her specifically not to do. The last time she pulled the "promise you won't be mad at me" bit, she came home with a ridiculously expensive handbag I'd admired when we were shopping together.

I knew I had to give in if I was ever going to find out what she was up to. "Okay, I promise I won't get mad. Tell me."

"I think I found you a job."

"Huh?"

"Hear me out. Okay, a few days ago I was at the office, and a client, Leslie Matthews, came in. She's hosting an event for the Junior League of Chicago. While we really don't do party planning, just weddings, Bridget does this yearly event for promotional purposes. I got to talking to Mrs. Matthews, and she was telling she was having knee replacement surgery in a few months."

I yawned. "Uh-huh."

"She told me she was worried because her son, Aaron, who's a single dad, really depends on her for when he's working. I met him at last year's event and recognized him as an owner of some of the clubs and boutique hotels we do weddings at. Anyway, he's looking for full-time help since

Mrs. Matthews is going to be out of commission."

She paused, waiting for a response, but I had none.

I sighed and looked at the clock on the wall. *Come on, Evelyn, spit it out, I have a nap waiting for me.*

"Okayyyyy," I said. "Are you getting to the point?"

"Yes! Aaron needs a nanny, a live-in nanny," she said.

I thought for a second before responding. "This is really fascinating, Evelyn. I hope you alerted the *Tribune* to this development."

"Am I talking too fast for you?" She paused and sighed. "You could be his nanny."

"What? Why would I want to do that?"

"Because you can live in his house, which is amazing, rent-free and make more than what you're making at Venom."

I tapped my fingers on the table as I processed what she said. It wasn't totally crazy, considering I'd worked for several families over the years as a nanny and was studying to be a teacher. Plus, when my father died, my mom had to work multiple jobs, leaving me to care for my two younger sisters.

"Okay, okay, I know what you're thinking." She interrupted my thoughts. "I know you too well not to know that you're considering all the 'what ifs,' but seriously I think this could really go your way. Today, on the way to work, it just popped in my head. So, I called Mrs. Matthews, and long story short, I told her all about you, that you were an education major, still in school, and had been a nanny in the past. She got in touch with Aaron and he was thrilled. Remember when you had asked me to help you with your résumé a while back? I still had it on my computer so I sent it to him."

"You did what?" My voice soared an octave.

"He e-mailed me and asked if you were available for an interview tonight at seven. I said yes."

"Evelyn!"

"Nope. No getting mad remember?"

I could almost hear her smiling on the other end, proud of herself for putting this plan all together. If I was being honest, it did sound appealing. I loved working with kids; it was the whole reason I wanted to be a teacher. Plus, the idea of making more money so I could quit the hellish hours of working nights lightened the weight on my back.

"I don't know, Ev. What about my hours during the day for school and the rent for our place? There's a lot of things to consider."

"He knows you're still in school. I was clear with him about your need for flexibility. And as far as our rent, we'll cross that bridge when we get to it."

Was this something I could do? Was it something I *wanted* to do? I ran through a bunch of variables, considering worst-case scenarios and all the reasons why this probably wouldn't be a good idea. Evelyn was quiet, knowing I was processing it all. The possibilities were too enticing. An interview with this guy wouldn't hurt.

"First," I said. "Thank you. Second, I'm definitely interested, but I have to be at work at six, so I don't think I can meet him tonight."

"Callie, this is a huge opportunity for you. I think Venom will survive if you're a couple hours late."

She was right. If this played out as desirable as it sounded,

I could throw my patent leather skirt in the Dumpster of that dreaded bar. "What should I do now? Should I call him to confirm?"

"Nope. I assured him you would be there."

"What if I'd said no?"

"You've forgotten who knows you best."

Again. She was right.

By the time I left the café shortly after, something inside me felt lighter. The feeling wasn't fleeting or riddled with uncertainty. It was just…promise. As I climbed the steps to the "L," I sent out all the positive vibes I had that this went well.

At seven o'clock on the dot, I stood outside the exquisite brownstone where Aaron Matthews and his daughter lived. A black wrought iron fence surrounded the brick house, while circle-topped windows decorated the front. I looked at the roof, adorned with hanging vines bare from the winter, but no doubt gorgeous in the summer. The vines intertwined through tall, thin pillars that ran the length of the roof.

I rang the doorbell and waited while I continued to admire the outside of his home. To the right of the door, I noticed a small Disney princess figure. I bent down to pick it up as I heard the door open.

"Hello there. Calliope?" a deep voice said.

"Hi." I lifted my face to look at him.

Then I almost fell over.

Oh. Hell. No.

Nope. Can't work for this guy.

My eyes scanning over him created a multi-visual experience, every bit of his presence capturing me all at once.

He was tall, very tall, with an athletic build and dark hair that curled slightly at the edges. He smiled, a smile that accentuated his perfectly straight teeth and full lips. When my eyes reached his, the real trouble started. They were blue, the color of the light, aqua edges of forget-me-not flowers, and piercing against his dark hair and features.

Forget-me-not. It was unlikely to happen.

"Are you all right? You look a little pale," he said, concerned. He moved from the doorway, stepping closer to me. "Do you feel faint?"

I took a deep breath and stood up. "Mr. Matthews, yes, I'm Calliope. Or Callie. Whatever. I'm so sorry. I'm just getting over a little cold and not quite myself yet."

Nice save.

He extended his hand to shake mine, gripping it tightly. "Nice to meet you, Calliope. And please, call me Aaron. Thank you for coming on such short notice, especially now that I know you haven't been well. Are you sure you're up for the interview?" he asked.

"Oh yes, of course. Ah. Here," I said, shoving the Disney princess at him.

He smiled and nodded, taking it from me. "Everywhere. They're absolutely everywhere. Thank you. Well, why don't we go in so we can talk?"

I followed him inside, desperately trying not to stare at his ass along the way and failing miserably. I reminded myself there was nothing wrong with a basic human reaction. We were animals by nature, and admiring another animal you found attractive was normal. Although…from where I stood, there wasn't much normal about the way he looked.

I unbuttoned my coat and looked around the exquisite home. Marble flooring lined the hallway and extended throughout as far as I could see. I trailed behind him down the large foyer, which connected to a narrow hall leading to the rest of the home. To my right was a formal dining room with a long glass-topped table and several high-back chairs.

If offered the job, it would've been far and away the most beautiful home I'd ever lived in. My meager background didn't lend itself to such expensive surroundings. It almost made me uncomfortable.

"Please sit down," he said, motioning to the table and chairs. "Can I get you something to drink?"

"No, thank you," I said, hanging my coat on the back of the chair. I looked across the table and saw a copy of my résumé and references that Evelyn had e-mailed earlier. I noticed a few notes in the margin.

"So, Calliope, why don't you tell me a little about yourself?"

"Well," I said, taking in a deep breath. "I'm a third-year elementary education major. I've been going part-time so I could balance work along with it, but I hope to graduate next spring, so I've taken on more classes this semester. I work nights at a downtown club, but that's been temporary. My goal has always been to work with children."

"Which one?"

"Which children?" I asked confused.

"No," he said, laughing, his bright smile lifting the corner of his mouth into a handsome grin. "Which club?"

"Oh. Right. Duh. Um, Venom? It's near Rush—"

"And Division. Yes, I know it well."

"You do?"

"Don't act so surprised. I'm not that much of an old man at thirty-one."

"No," I said quickly. "Of course not. I didn't mean to insinuate."

He held up his hand, continuing to smile. "You were right to assume it isn't my type of crowd, but I used to be part owner of it. I sold off my piece some time ago, but it's good to know it still has some wonderful employees there."

He paused, his eyes running across my face, as his smile faded. There wasn't a sound surrounding us, but the energy in the room more than made up for the silence. The quiet sound of something brewing. Shivers rushed across my body.

"Have you always lived in Chicago?" he asked.

"No, but I never want to live anywhere else. I love it here."

"Agreed. Best city in the world."

He paused, glancing down at my résumé. "Your résumé is very thorough," he said, running his finger down the margin where his notes were. "I really asked for the interview to see if we'd be a good fit, or if rather, you'd be a good fit for us."

I nodded, waiting for him to continue.

Or maybe I was fixated on the fact that the way he said *fit*, a normal, everyday word, sounded so sexy.

Or maybe I realized my ogling was going to get me fired before I was hired.

"Why don't I tell you a little bit about us now?" He ran his hand through his hair and smiled. "I'm sure Evelyn has explained my situation. My mom's having surgery this summer, and I'll need someone full-time to help with my daughter."

As the word *daughter* left his mouth, his entire face lit up.

"What's her name?"

"Delilah and she's four. She's very smart and very high-energy. I love the idea of having someone with an education background. I'd love for her to go to the museums, take classes, and things like that."

"Absolutely."

"And I'm sure as is the case with many four-year-olds, she's very stubborn and isn't afraid to let her opinion be known."

"It's very common. Testing boundaries and all that."

"Well, she can definitely win top prize in the most dramatic tantrum competition. But she's sweet, and while I'm sure I'm biased, I think she's the most beautiful little girl, inside and out."

"Is she here? Can I meet her?"

"I thought it best that I meet with any candidate when she was not here. She's actually spending the night at my parents' tonight."

"Well, she sounds like a remarkable little girl."

"I think so," he said with a nod. "I understand you'll need some flexibility with your hours?"

"Yes. Three mornings a week I have class, but that's only for the next six weeks until summer. Obviously I'll be completely available then during the summer."

"It wouldn't be a problem. Even though my mom has been watching her while I worked from home, Delilah has been used to having me here. I wanted to ease her into someone new for the first few weeks. She's really only been looked after by family, so as you can imagine, she has one overprotective Daddy."

The way he said "Daddy" was so endearing I melted a little.

"Totally understandable," I said.

"So, in the fall, you'll be in your final year?"

"Yes."

"That's wonderful." My eyes glanced over the white collared shirt he was wearing and to the small patch of chest hair that peeked through.

He slipped a piece of paper out from under my résumé and pushed it across to me. "Would this be acceptable to you?"

I looked at the paper and the number on it referring to the weekly salary he was offering. It was more than I'd made in a week at any job ever. My eyes looked it over again and again, as he tapped his pen on the table. This was in addition to the free room and board. My mind was blown.

"Very," I responded as calmly as possible. "Thank you."

"Of course that includes room and board, meals and such. I'd like to check out your references and verify the background check before we go any further. However, I do promise to call you by Monday with my decision regardless of what I decide."

"Great. Thank you."

We stood and I grabbed my coat from the back of the chair. He walked me to the front door, and as he opened it for me with one hand, his other hand brushed against my back. His touch, as light as it was, sent a shiver through my body. "Thank you again for coming on such a short notice."

"My pleasure."

I stepped outside and walked down the stairs as I buttoned

my coat. I stopped at the bottom and turned. He still stood in the doorway, watching me. I smiled and waved.

He returned the smile, and even in the chilly temperature, my body grew warm all over. If offered this job, it might be the best employment opportunity ever or a mistake of epic proportions.

I went to work that night and the following, thinking of not much else besides Aaron. I worried that if I did move in, my infatuation would only increase and cause me to screw up one of the best jobs I might ever have. I mean, a child was involved with this. Plus, one bad reference from a prominent Chicago figure could jeopardize my future teaching career.

I spent Sunday mulling things over and decided to relax until I heard from him. He may not even offer me the position, and in that case, all of this was for nothing. From working and worrying all weekend, I was exhausted. After a long shower, I put on my most comfortable pajamas and climbed into bed.

Sleep came fast and hard, and I didn't wake until my phone buzzed on my nightstand the following morning with an incoming call. Groggy, I tried to identify the number on the caller ID, but it was no use.

"Hello," I said, my throat full of morning phlegm.

"Hi, Calliope? It's Aaron Matthews."

I shot up, clearing my throat. "Oh, Hi. How are you?"

"Good. I'm sorry if I woke you, but I wanted to catch you before you went to class."

"Oh no," I lied. "I've been awake for ages."

"Well, the reason I am calling is that I would like to offer you the nanny position. Pending the rest of your references coming through as glowing as the others, of course. Plus, I'd like you to meet Delilah beforehand as well."

"Really?" I said excited. "That's—"

Fantastic?

Yes. I wanted to say it was fantastic. It was, but it was something else, too. The emotions I had when we met, the way my body responded, was not only out of character, but frightening. With my focus being solely on school and work for so long, I didn't have time to date, let alone even be completely attracted to someone. What would happen when we were living together day in and day out? That was a recipe for a very volatile situation.

"What do you think, Calliope? Will you be our nanny?" he asked eagerly.

I had a choice. Either I could turn down the job, fearing my initial emotions would filter into my daily life. Or I could stop worrying about what might happen, take hold of this amazing opportunity, and know I could handle anything that came my way.

I mean, was there really a choice?

"Yes, of course, Aaron. I'm thrilled to be your nanny."

Chapter Two

AARON—

She said yes.

It was the answer I'd wanted to hear, but had hoped she'd say the opposite. I wasn't sure what I was doing. I wasn't sure what I was feeling, but like I'd done for the last four years of my life, I put one thing before everything else. Delilah.

Callie was perfect. She was smart, energetic, and driven, all the things I'd been looking for in a nanny for the past month that no other candidate had possessed so completely. Her spirit had filled the room, and I knew before she even left after the interview that I had to have her.

Had to have her.

"Daddy?" Delilah said, entering the living room, her worn bunny lovey in hand. "Who are you talking to?"

She rubbed her blue eyes, her blond hair wild from sleep. My sweet baby girl. There wasn't a morning that went by when my heart didn't feel like it was so going to explode looking at her.

"I was on the phone, sweetie," I said. "Come here."

She walked over to me and climbed up on the couch. Once she sat, I pulled her into my lap and hugged her. Her hair smelled of the lavender shampoo I used on her from her bath the night before, a scent that reminded me of her whenever I caught it anywhere.

"How did you sleep?" I asked.

"Good," she said, pulling the bottom of her pink Disney princess nightgown over her legs. "Is Nana coming over today?"

"She is, but not until a little later. I'll have you all to myself until then."

She laid her head on my chest, snuggling close, and I soaked up every second of it. It was only a matter of moments before she'd break from her sleepiness and be up and running with newfound energy.

"What should we have for breakfast?" I asked.

Before she could answer, the doorbell rang, an odd occurrence this early in the morning. Delilah hopped off the couch and began running down the hall.

"Maybe it's Nana now," she said.

I chased after her, but she had reached the door before I could catch her.

"Delilah Leslie," I shouted. "Don't you dare open that door. We need to make sure it's someone we know, right?"

She sighed and rolled her eyes, a behavior she'd recently acquired that made me fear for the teenage years. "I know, Daddy. You tell me every time."

She stood to the side, as I looked through the peephole and

saw my brother Abel. "Huh," I said, opening the door. "What are you doing here?" I asked.

"Uncle Abel!" Delilah said.

He stepped in and shoved a Stan's Donuts and Coffee bakery box and two coffees at me without a word. "Hey squirt," he said, picking her up. "What's shakin'?"

"You came to surprise me?" she asked.

"Yup. And to bring you a surprise, too."

I peeked inside the box, and there were an assortment of pastries and doughnuts. "He sure did," I said, holding the box up for her to see.

She gasped. "Can I have three?"

"Ah. No," I said. "You can have one. Come on. Let's go sit at the table."

Abel gave her a quick squeeze before setting her down. Delilah ran ahead of us, as I handed one of the coffees to Abel.

"What the hell are you doing here so early?" I asked again.

"Do I need an excuse to visit my brother and my niece?"

"When it's before eight on a Monday morning, I think it's only right to assume something's going on," I said, entering the kitchen.

"Just getting an early start on the day," he said, sitting down. He unzipped his coat, revealing his white button-down work shirt underneath.

I raised my eyebrows. "You been home yet? Or did you accidentally fall asleep at work?"

"Maybe you need a nap, Uncle Abel," Delilah said. "That's what Daddy makes me do if I'm too tired."

"Don't worry. I didn't fall asleep at work, squirt," he said, winking at me. "I had a sleepover at my new friend's house."

I rolled my eyes at him, and shook my head. Abel was eight years younger than me and had the emotional maturity of a piece of toast. If I was being fair, I was the same way at twenty-three. Fresh out of college and didn't have a care in the world. The extent of my decision-makings was what bar I was meeting friends at and what woman I'd bring home.

"Daddy?" Delilah said. She stared at the pastry box I was still holding.

I set the box down in front of her. "Sorry. Which one do you want, sweetie?"

I stepped away to get plates, and when I returned she was still looking over her choices, biting her lower lip in concentration before pointing to a rainbow-sprinkled doughnut.

I picked up the doughnut and put it on her plate. She took no time in shoving a huge bite in her mouth. "What do you say to Uncle Abel?"

"Thank you," she said. She quickly covered her mouth, knowing I'd tell her not to talk with it full before swallowing to say, "Sorry, Daddy."

I looked at Abel. "Thank you, Uncle Abel," I said.

"Mom said you got the nanny thing squared away. Is she hot?"

"Seriously? What's wrong with you?" I asked. "Delilah, you can go take your plate and watch television while you eat."

"Okay," she said, rushing out of the room with her breakfast.

Abel waited until she was out of the room before returning to harassing me. "I take that as a yes."

"Ah. No. You can take that as a warning not to talk like that in front of Delilah. You know she repeats everything, to everyone. She doesn't need to hear you say that, and then tell Callie."

He poked at the different pastries. "Callie, huh?" he said.

"Well, Calliope, but yeah." I paused, watching him press his finger into the confection. "Abel, you picked them out. Do you have to touch everything in the box?"

He held up an apple fritter, pointing it at me as he talked. "I love how you keep avoiding the question."

"I'm avoiding it because it's ridiculous. I can't believe that was your first question."

He took a bite and waved his hand at me. "Never mind. I can tell by how you're acting she was hot."

I shot him a dirty look. "Even if she was, that has nothing to do with why I hired her."

"I know it wasn't, but I'm not wrong, right?"

Abel knew me better than anyone else. If I kept denying, he'd see right through me and badger me relentlessly. On the other hand, the thoughts I'd been having about Callie were in such bad form for a person I'd hired to live in my house and be a caregiver for my daughter.

"Don't say a word," he said. "I see it all over your face."

Like a fucking open book.

I picked up my coffee, swirling it around gently in my hand. "I don't know what you're talking about."

He snorted, a mouth full of food. "Sure," he mumbled. "If she was a Granny Nanny, or hell, freaking Mary Poppins, you would've said."

"I know it's hard to imagine that I don't walk the earth leading with my dick like you do, but when it comes to serious matters, like Delilah, it's totally out of the question."

"Hey, I'm not judging you. In fact, you noticing an attractive female makes me worry about you less."

"I notice attractive women. I am human."

"Could've fooled me. When was the last time you had a date?"

I felt anger rising inside of me, the question that made me the most defensive. Abel damn well knew this, too.

"I don't need or want to date. My whole life is wrapped up in that little girl," I said, pointing to the living room. "Now, did you really come over here to give me a hard time about my lack of a love life?"

He brushed his hands off over the table. "No. I came here because I need you to fire one of the cocktail servers."

"Abel," I said slowly. "I've told you to talk to Marshall, who is your boss, about anything to do with the bar."

"Yeah, but you're the owner. Plus, you're my brother."

"Why would I fire…? Wait…what did you do?"

"Okay. You don't have to fire her. Can't you move her to another one of your places?"

I took a deep breath and closed my eyes. "What did you do?"

His head dropped, and he stared at the floor for a moment before cautiously looking up at me. He had done the same thing ever since he was a kid. I knew I'd be saving his ass for something because that was what I always did.

"I didn't know she was married," he whispered. "Now she's gotten all clingy and weird."

"Was this the one you had a sleepover with?" I asked, making quotation marks with my fingers.

"Yeah. But that was only because she took the breakup really hard."

I ran my hands through my hair and stopped myself from screaming at him. "When are you going to grow the hell up?"

He shrugged. "Any day now. So?"

"I'll talk to Marshall later, but I swear to hell if you so much as look at a coworker too long, I will kick your ass from here to Milwaukee."

He looked at his watch before standing. "Thanks. I gotta go. See you later, squirt," he shouted to Delilah.

"I'll be thinking of you when she's bouncing off the walls in an hour from the early morning sugar rush," I said, punching him in the arm.

I was following him to the front door when he stopped and turned to me. "Aaron? A little piece of friendly advice?"

"What?"

"Lighten up. Life is too short to worry about a little sugar."

Chapter Three

CALLIE—

I'm so happy for you, Callie," Evelyn said. "I'm going to miss you something awful, though."

Candlelight reflected off the floor-to-ceiling windows of the cocktail lounge where we were celebrating my new job on Saturday night, my first Saturday night off in ages. Everything, from the crystal glasses to my smile, sparkled.

She lifted her champagne glass as I raised mine. We clicked our glasses together and took a sip. "Thanks," I said. "I wish you'd reconsider letting me help out with the rent for a little while longer."

"It's no biggie," she replied waving her hand around in dismissal. "We agreed already anyway. I don't want to hear another word about it from you."

"It still makes me feel bad, though," I said. "You've always picked up my slack."

She rolled her eyes. "It's not now, or was it then, slack.

You're my best friend, and if I needed any help, of any kind, I know you'd do it for me."

I shrugged my shoulders knowing she was right. I would do anything for her. It didn't make my situation any easier to swallow. Evelyn was everything I was not—successful career, gorgeous, and a personality that lit up a room. I was basic, a natural beauty I supposed, who had worked so hard, for so long, that there were many days I couldn't believe I was only twenty-four.

Evelyn picked up one of the oysters from the plate in front of us. She tilted her head back and let it slide in. "So, I heard you talking in your sleep this morning. I probably should've warned you Aaron was a looker."

And she also knew the most perfect moment to change the subject.

Heat warmed my face, but I tried to hide it by digging through my purse.

"Are you blushing?" she asked.

I took a compact out and flipped it open. "No."

"Aha."

"What?" I snapped.

"You're full of shit, and I can hear everything you say in your sleep."

"What are you talking about?"

"I heard you mid-dream begging him to give it to you this morning. You want him—you know it, and you should stop pretending like you don't."

"You're such a liar."

"No, I'm not. I heard every word."

"I can't believe that you think that you heard—"

Wait.

Did I?

I covered my mouth in shock when it all began to come back to me. Yes. There was a dream. I was in an unfamiliar room when he'd quietly snuck in. Words were exchanged briefly before he crawled up the bed, began placing kisses up my leg and thigh. Just before he dipped his head down to lick his tongue between my legs, he'd asked for reassurance. I didn't reassure him. I *begged* him for it.

I shook my head out of my dream recollection before rolling my eyes. "Okay, so he's attractive for an older guy, but he's going to be my boss. I'll be living with him, and thinking about what you're insinuating is inappropriate and unprofessional," I said, tossing my compact back in my purse.

"He's not that much older."

"Again. Inappropriate and unprofessional."

"Whatever," she said with a snort.

"What's that supposed to mean?"

She wiped her mouth with a napkin and took a sip of her champagne. "You need to loosen up a bit."

"Not loose enough to sleep with the guy I work for and live with, Blondie."

She picked up another oyster. "Who said sleep with?" She swallowed the oyster and waved her hand around. "You're right, though. It's totally wrong."

"I could never…I would never…do…things like that with my boss," I stuttered. "I mean, he's attractive, and maybe if he wasn't my boss, I'd consider…"

We were silent for a few minutes when our waiter came back to us. "Would you like another round, ladies?" he asked.

"Yes," we replied in unison.

She put her hand on mine. "You've had two boyfriends, neither of which lasted longer than six months. You have slept with, what, four guys? The last of which was that dude you brought home from Lounge and that place has been closed for two years. There's nothing wrong with wanting. It's human nature."

She was right. I was a healthy, red-blooded, twenty-four-year-old woman who had wants and desires. There was nothing wrong with that.

Nothing at all.

Right?

Right.

It was only wrong if I acted on it, if I crossed a professional, moral line, and I had no intentions of doing that. Plus, this was only assuming he had any interest to begin with. I was certain Aaron Matthews's taste in women leaned more toward the sophisticated, refined side. At the very least, someone older.

The next morning, I nursed a massive hangover and tried to pack up my room. I was grateful Evelyn said it was okay for me to leave all my bedroom furniture so I wouldn't have to worry about it. All I had to do was pack up my clothes and other personal items. I was putting some books in boxes when I heard my cell phone ringing in the kitchen.

I raced into the kitchen and picked up my phone, not stopping to check the caller ID before answering. "Hello?"

"Hi, Calliope, it's Aaron Matthews."

With the sound of his voice, I felt butterflies, and perhaps even a rhinoceros, tumble around in my stomach.

"Hi, Aaron. How are you?" I asked as calmly as possible.

"Wonderful. I got your room all ready today. It was a bare room with a bed, so Delilah and I went to Bloomingdale's and picked out bedding and linens and such. She thought you'd like Cinderella bedding, but I convinced her otherwise."

"Aw. How cute."

"Well, I'm sure you're really busy getting ready for the move, but I was wondering if you'd like to stop by later and meet Delilah before you move in on Wednesday? I thought it might be a little less awkward for her and…"

"Of course," I said interrupting him. "I think that's a great idea."

"Great. Would you like to come for dinner?"

"Absolutely. What time works for you two?" I asked.

"How about six?"

"That's perfect."

"Sounds good, we'll see you then."

We said our good-byes just as Evelyn walked in.

I smiled. "Dinner at six with the new boss and his daughter. What do you wear for such an occasion?"

* * *

There was no parking in front of Aaron's house so I had to park a couple blocks away. I didn't mind, since it gave me a chance to shake off the nerves I had. Not only was having dinner with your new boss cause for anxiety, but also meeting the little girl who I'd be responsible for raised it to an entirely new level.

The lake breeze blew my hair around my face. My auburn hair was usually in some messy bun piled on top of my head, but for the night, it was lying in long, soft waves between my shoulders. I'd put on some mascara and lip gloss, which was more than I normally wore. Something told me that once I moved in, I was going to be adding in extra time to my morning routine.

Stop. He's your boss. A little girl is depending on you.

As I approached the house, I saw Aaron sitting on a small bench outside his front door. Chicago weather was unpredictable at best, but a temperature reaching into the fifties with April only days away was a nice welcome after a cold winter. I watched him for a moment as he was completely engrossed in the book he was reading.

"DADDYYYYY!"

A little girl, with white-blond, curly hair, jumped up from the side of the house, waving a Barbie around her head.

She handed him the Barbie, and as I approached them, they were carefully looking it over. Aaron's eyebrows were furrowed in concentration as he tried to adjust Barbie's clothes.

"But Daddy, it has to fit her. If it doesn't, her boobies will show…see," the little girl said, pointing to Barbie's exposed breasts. She sat down next to him, laying her head on his shoulder.

"I'm trying, Delilah, but this shirt is too small for her," he replied, trying to work a hot-pink tube top over Barbie's massive boobs. "Why don't you look in your case for a different shirt for her?"

I laughed and he looked up. "Oh, hi," he said, embarrassed. "We were just trying to…well…Barbie needed a more…a bigger…and…"

The fact he was trying to explain why he was dressing a Barbie doll, as he turned several shades of red, was enough to make me continue laughing. It was adorable.

I waved my hand while trying to compose myself. "It's fine. No need to explain."

He shoved the Barbie back at Delilah and stood up, smoothing his hands over his jeans. "It's nice to see you again."

"You, too," I said. I walked over to the bench and knelt down. "You must be Delilah."

She nodded while brushing her hair out of her face. She was beautiful, with blond hair and the most perfect curled ringlets pinned up on one side with a barrette. With blue eyes that matched her father's, she looked like a doll.

"Delilah," Aaron said. "This is Callie. She's the one I've been telling you about."

"Hi," she said softly, reaching for her daddy's hand. "Are you going to live with us?"

"I sure am." I sat down next to her on the bench. "I'm going to help out your daddy, and we'll get to do lots of fun things. What are your most favorite things to do?"

She bit down on her lower lip in concentration. "I like to play Barbie, and Daddy got me the Barbie Dreamhouse when I was brave when I had my tonsils out."

"Wow. I love Barbie's Dreamhouse. Tell me what else do you like to do?"

"I like to color and paint and go to the library."

I smiled at her. "Well, those are all my most favorite things, too, especially the library."

"Daddy?"

"Yes, sweetheart," he answered.

"Can we eat the lasagna now?"

He laughed. "Yes, now that Callie's here, we can eat. Make sure you have your Barbie and all her clothes."

We entered the house, and Delilah ran in ahead of us down the hall. The house smelled amazing, of garlic and tomatoes.

"It smells wonderful in here," I said, slipping off my coat. I laid it down on a maroon upholstered chair next to the front door.

"Come on. Let me show you the kitchen." I followed him down the hallway until the left side flowed into a kitchen fit for a chef.

"Wow," I gasped. "This is…incredible." Dark granite countertops surrounded stainless steel Viking appliances. Various copper pots and pans hung from a wire rack above the island.

"Thank you," he said as he went over to the stove. "I don't use it nearly enough, but my ex-wife liked to bake a lot so…"

He trailed off as he opened the oven and pulled out the lasagna. I walked over and stood next to him, eyeing the pan. "And you made this?" I asked.

He shrugged. "Delilah, come eat," he shouted. "Please, Callie, sit down."

I made my way to the beautifully set table, which was adjacent to the kitchen, and sat down. Table runner and chargers complemented the place settings. Water glasses were filled with sparkling water as lemon slices floated in the middle. A large vase of lilies sat in the middle of the table.

Delilah came running, a piece of white construction paper in her hand.

She plopped down in the seat next to me. "This is for you," she said, handing me the paper.

"You made this for me?" I asked. "It's awesome! I love the house and the sun and the pretty rainbow. Thank you."

Aaron set a plate down in front of me and then Delilah. "And I've been told to swear that she did it all by herself. No help from me."

"I did," she said, nodding. She picked up her fork and carefully stabbed a piece of lasagna that Aaron had cut into small squares for her.

I leaned over and looked at her in the eye. "You know what?"

"Mmm-hmm," she said with her mouth full.

"This is the best picture anyone has ever colored for me."

She was too involved with her lasagna to show much emotion, but what she didn't express, her dad more than made up for. Aaron stood, midstep, a plate in his hand, staring at us. A slow smile lifted his lips as he took in a deep sigh, letting it out quietly as I saw his shoulders visibly relax.

"Something to drink, Callie?" he asked, returning to his step.

"The water you put out is fine. Thank you," I said.

He sat in the empty seat with his plate. "So," he said, placing his napkin in his lap. "I thought we'd go over a few things. I know you don't technically start until Wednesday, and I won't be out of the house until Monday, but why not get a few things out of the way now, right?"

"Absolutely."

"She's usually up by seven in the morning," he said. "Bedtime is at eight. If it's any later than that, she's a bear the next day."

He paused, slicing into his lasagna and bringing it to his mouth. I watched his lips, the way they wrapped around the fork before pulling it out of his mouth. It took me a few moments to realize I was staring while I was locked in on my utensil porn. The bite of lasagna I tried to swallow lodged in my throat when it occurred to me utensil porn was probably a real thing.

"Does everything taste okay?" Aaron asked. His face frowned as his eyes glanced at my plate.

"Oh, it's delicious," I said, scooping up a cheesy piece. "I love all the basil in it."

"We got it at Eataly," Delilah said.

Aaron laughed and placed his fork next to the store-bought lasagna. "And as you've learned," he said, his cheeks red with embarrassment, "she can't keep a secret worth anything."

"Most four-year-olds can't," I said. "Furthermore, I love Eataly. You made a good call."

Delilah wiped the back of her hand across her marinara-covered lips. "We got chocolate pies for dessert. Three of them."

"Delilah," Aaron said. "Use your napkin, please. And it isn't exactly three chocolate pies. Crostatina."

"Crostatina?" I asked.

He took a sip from his water glass. "They're these little chocolate-filled tartes. Nutella, actually."

How *dare* he. He was playing dirty. Real dirty. Not only was he attractive, but he was also smart, successful, and a Nutella buyer. Was there no end to his perfection?

Yes, there was. It ended in the same place it began. The place where he was my boss and any impure thoughts about him, Nutella, or a combination of the two needed to be removed from my brain.

"Delilah, have you been to the Field Museum?" I asked.

She nodded. "They have dinosaurs there!"

"I know," I said. "Would you like to go there with me sometime? I haven't seen Sue the T. rex in a long time."

Aaron's eyes moved between Delilah and me as a slow smile spread across his face.

"Can I, Daddy?" she asked bouncing in her seat.

His gazed stopped on me. "Of course you can," he said.

* * *

"So good," I said after I swallowed the last bite of the Nutella-filled dessert.

A small drop of chocolate remained on the plate, and I resisted the urge to use my finger to scoop it up.

"Glad you enjoyed it," he said, standing and gathering his plate.

"Can I be done?" Delilah asked.

"Yes," Aaron said.

She ran from the table as I stood and picked up my own plate and glass.

"Let me help you," I said.

"That's not necessary. You're still our guest tonight. And even when you're not, you aren't responsible for cleaning up after us. We all do our share, okay?"

"I don't mind," I said, following him into the kitchen. "I prefer to always pull my weight."

I placed my things in the sink and went back to the table to clean up the rest. Standing in front of the dirty dishes, I turned on the warm water and grabbed a sponge. He came up next to me, placing the last of the glasses under the running water.

"I rinse, and you load the dishwasher?" I asked.

He didn't answer me. Instead, he looked at me, tilting his head like he was contemplating something. I had no choice but to stare back. His proximity was close, almost too close, and I could smell his soap, a clean scent, along with a hint of his aftershave. He must've shaved earlier in the day because stubble was apparent across his jawline.

He shook his head and shut his eyes for a moment. "Yeah. Okay," he said. "Sorry. I was going to say—"

Delilah skipped back in carrying a large assortment of Play-Doh in a clear bag.

She held it up to me. "Do you like Play-Doh?"

"I love Play-Doh," I said. "Why don't I finish helping your daddy clean up, and then we'll play."

"It's okay. You go on," Aaron said, shutting off the faucet.

"Are you sure?"

"Absolutely."

"Okay," I said. "Delilah, let's go sit down at the table and do it there."

She ran over to the table and began to carefully take out

all the different colors and accessories. I sat down next to her. "What should we make?" I asked her.

"Flowers?"

"Flowers it is."

We sat at the table and rolled out different colored Play-Doh and used her little plastic cutters to make flowers. Aaron was busy cleaning up, but every now and then, I felt his eyes on me. When I'd turn to look at him, he would be staring at us. At one point he noticed I saw him, and his grin grew.

And it was the sexiest smile I had ever seen.

It was handsomeness and joy mixed with something endearing. My skin tingled and a pit in my stomach formed. It wasn't from nerves. It was from wanting something I knew I wasn't going to get.

After a while, Delilah started to yawn, a sure sign that bedtime was coming soon. Aaron walked over and stood behind his daughter. He kissed the top of her head, brushing her hair back. "It's almost time for bed, sweetheart, and Callie needs to get home. I think we've kept her long enough."

"I had a lot of fun with you, Delilah," I said.

"Are you going away now?" Delilah asked.

"Yes, but I'll be back soon, okay?"

She yawned and nodded her head.

"Let's clean this up and next time I'm over we can play some more."

By the time we packed up all the Play-Doh and cutters, she could barely keep her eyes open.

Aaron picked her up and carried her upstairs. After a few minutes, he came back down, and when he did, I was waiting in the hallway, at the bottom of the staircase.

"Is she okay?" I asked.

He laughed. "She's more than okay, she's out cold. I think the excitement really wore her out. I have to say, she seems quite taken with you, as am I."

His smile faded when he realized what he'd said, his eyes shifting from me to a large, ornate wall mirror hanging in the hallway. I'd expected embarrassment on my part, but there was none. I knew he didn't mean it the way it came out, but it was his reaction, the way he avoided my eyes that made me feel oddly vindicated. I wasn't the only one figuring things out.

But I needed to end his misery.

"Thank you for the amazing dinner," I said, putting on my coat. "I'll see you Wednesday, but if you need anything before then, just give me a call."

"Well...thank you...for coming."

I racked my brain trying to come up with something else to say, but the word *coming* kept replaying in my mind. There wasn't anything he said or did that I didn't automatically turn into something sexual.

"So," he said. He shifted on his feet awkwardly. "See you then?"

And there was nothing I said or did that didn't make me come off as a complete ass.

I nodded. "Yes. See you then. Good night."

With quick steps, I headed down the hallway and threw open the front door. I turned and gave him a quick wave as I bolted out the door.

I didn't turn around or look anywhere until I was closer to

the neighbor's house than his. Once I did, I saw him standing tense in front of the large bay window, rubbing his two hands together.

I needed to get a grip. I had until Wednesday, less than three days, before I moved in. Three days to get myself in check before we lived together.

Live together.

I barely remembered the drive home; my mind clouded with images of his face…his mouth…his body. All I could hear was the sound of his voice.

I entered a quiet apartment, calling out for Evelyn with no response. I set my coat and purse on the table when I noticed the light in my room was on. Strange, I never left it on when I was out.

I crossed the room to turn it off, but as soon as I saw what was on my bed, I covered my mouth to stifle a scream. My bed was covered with several open Victoria's Secret boxes, cotton shorts with matching tanks, and assorted other pajamas. I got closer to the bed, looking over all the beautiful things. There was an envelope in the middle. I opened it.

I thought you could use some nightwear instead of the ratty T-shirts and sweats you usually wear. Plus, you're going to be living with a man now. You should dress appropriately.

Xo-Evelyn

That girl. She was trying to stir up all sorts of trouble.

Chapter Four

AARON—

"Well, look who the fuck is here," Marshall, my best friend, shouted from behind the bar. "What the hell are you doing here?"

I slid into the leather high-back barstool in front of him. "Do I need an excuse to visit my own bar?"

WET was one of Chicago's most elite cocktail lounges, a speakeasy where the famous and successful came for privacy. It was one of my most profitable business endeavors to date.

"No, you don't need an excuse. You just don't ever do it," he said. "Scotch?"

I nodded. "Is Abel around?"

I watched as he poured two fingers of Macallan 18 into a faceted whiskey glass.

"And here I was thinking it was only my pretty face you wanted to see," he said.

He slid the glass across to me, and I brought it to my lips, letting the familiar burn run down the back of my throat. "To be honest, I'm not sure why I'm here. I think I just needed a breather."

"Oh yeah? Everything okay?"

"Yeah. It's good," I said, setting my drink down. I stared at the beveled edges of the glass, my thoughts running together like the colors reflecting off it from the candlelight.

Marshall leaned in. "You sure, man? Is Delilah okay?"

"Yes. She's perfect." I lifted my glass to take another sip. "Just a lot on my mind. I hired a nanny finally. She starts in two days."

His eyebrows lifted. "Is that so? She hot?"

"What is it with you and Abel? Can you think of anything besides your dicks?"

He pushed himself off the bar, retrieving a stack of napkins under it. "I don't think so. If I think of anything besides my dick, I'll let you know," he said with a smirk.

He twisted the napkins between his palms, fanning them out in a neat pile, before placing them atop the bar. It seemed like such a small touch, but those touches were what made or broke a business. Marshall wasn't just a bar manager. He was the one I trusted with the whole operation. In fact, I'd trust him with anything in my life. He's been through it all with me.

He was there the day I met Lexie, my ex-wife, at North Avenue Beach during one of the most intense heat waves ever recorded in Chicago.

And he was there the day I came home with a not even one-year-old Delilah to find Lexie gone. She wanted out of it all. The marriage and motherhood.

"Seriously, though, man," Marshall said interrupting my

thoughts. "It's nice to see you finally getting a hand around the house. You need to start living again."

"I know, but it isn't like I haven't been living. I've had other responsibilities."

"No doubt. You've made that little beauty your life. So much so that I think you forgot about your own."

I shrugged. I knew he was right. He was always right. Everyone—him, Abel, my parents—always told me the same thing. It didn't matter, though. Everything inside me broke when Lexie left, and the only choice I had was to put myself back together for my daughter.

Marshall wiped up a small puddle of booze from the bar before tossing the rag to the side. "I know you don't need to hear all this shit again, but Lexie was never it. She gave you Delilah and a mountain of grief. That's all. You've let her run the show for years even after she's been gone. Time to make peace."

Easier said than done, but I knew I needed to try.

After I finished my drink, I headed home. After taking care of the babysitter, I ascended the stairs and down the hallway to Delilah's room. I carefully cracked the door open before slipping inside.

My angel.

I knelt down on the floor next to her, brushing her tiny curls back so I can see her first. My chin rested on a knit blanket she slept with every night that my mom had made for her.

"How could she have left you?" I whispered.

I would never understand it. I was long over any love lost between Lexie and me. I wasn't even sure if much was there to begin with, but the devastation over how she left was still raw.

I gave Delilah a kiss on her forehead before sneaking out of her room. After retreating back downstairs, I paused, knowing what was coming.

It was always the time it came crashing down around me like shards of broken glass, stinging my skin and catching my breath.

The quiet.

The isolation.

All of it, on so many nights, was so excruciatingly palpable it was like I was being suffocated.

But for the first time in years, the fog that surrounded me lifted slightly.

The silence.

The solitude.

It was different.

Not since Lexie left had such a breath of fresh air blown through my home and temporarily eased my loneliness like it had when Callie was here.

I was left wondering, though: Was it because there was someone, anyone, who was going to be living in the house to have an adult conversation with? Or was it because it was Callie?

I didn't know if it mattered.

I walked into my office and flicked on the light. Papers were scattered across the large mahogany desk, but what I was looking for was hidden in a flat, silver safe in one of the drawers. I sat in my oversized leather chair and retrieved the safe from the bottom drawer. A place for important documents, the safe was also where I kept memories of my past life and reminders of what I was doing in my current life.

I lifted various things out, passports and financial papers, making my way to the plain brown manila envelope at the bottom, and all the memories of our first meeting came flooding back.

* * *

It's exactly what the weather forecaster said. A scorcher. The late morning sun beat down on my tan skin, but the heat only fueled my pursuit of a win.

"Ready, Matthews?" Marshall shouts, holding the volleyball in place to serve.

One more point for the win.

My feet push deep into the sand and I crouch down. "Go for it," I say

Marshall's serve is fast and hard as it flies over the net to our opponents, but they play back harder. After a bump and set, the dude closest to the net spikes it over. The tips of my fingers push it back over to the empty space between the guys. One dives for it, but misses. The ball lands in the sand. We win.

"Yes!" I say.

Marshall runs over, high-fiving me. "That was perfect, man."

Our celebration is interrupted by a group of four girls, spread out on large beach towels with tanning-oiled bodies, cheering for us from the sidelines. One, with long platinum blond hair, a tight body, and a smile brighter than the sun, catches my eye immediately. I think the feeling is mutual, but as soon as I wink at her, she rolls her eyes at me. Lucky for her, I don't give up easy, especially when I see something I want.

"I'll be back in a few," I say to Marshall.

"Or maybe not," he replies.

He knows me well. It's why he's my second-in-command at the bar, WET, I opened recently. I hear him chuckle as I jog over to the leggy blond.

"Afternoon, ladies," I say, nodding my head. "I think your presence was our good luck charm."

The brunette on the end slides her sunglasses down her nose. "Our pleasure. Watching you guys, especially your friend, is the best view we've had all day."

I look behind me to spot Marshall. "Hey," I shout, waving him over. "Come meet my new friends."

I turn my attention to the one I'm interested in and flash her my best, sure-to-get-in-her-pants smile. "Hi there."

She raises her eyebrows, looking me up and down. "Hi."

"Hot enough for you?" I ask, stretching my arms above my head.

She shrugs. "I can take hotter."

"Can you?"

I bite down on my lower lip and move to sit down next to her.

"Don't waste your time, lover boy," she says, laughing. "Those lines and the pretty boy face don't do shit for me."

Ouch.

"If my face or lines don't do it for you, what would?" I ask.

She shields her eyes from the sun to look at me. "Offer to buy me a drink. That's a good start."

I nod. "That I can do. The vodka lemonades at Castaways might put me in an even better position."

She stands and brushes off some sand that made its way onto her towel. Her tight stomach tells me she works out. Plus, the very little left covered by her bikini leaves even less to the imagination.

"Come on, Iceman," she says, pulling on a pair of shorts. "I'm thirsty."

We start walking toward Castaways, the North Avenue Beach bar, as a light breeze comes off the lake.

"Why Iceman?" I ask her as we near the bar. "No Maverick?"

She pauses and turns to look at me. "Iceman was way hotter."

She smiles and I know.

That girl is going to be in my bed by nightfall.

* * *

And she was. We started seeing each other casually at first, but then increasingly more often. With both of us consumed with our careers, the little free time we had we spent with each other.

Life always has a way of throwing you a curveball. A little more than a year after we started dating, Lexie found out she was pregnant. She took the news as if she found out she was dying. She was convinced her life, her career in finance, and the body that she loved were all finished. Everything from raging morning sickness, weight gain, and exhaustion only furthered her unhappiness.

While it wasn't in the cards for us in the beginning, the idea of becoming a father grew on me and I began looking forward to it. I tried to share my enthusiasm with Lexie in the hopes she'd find some happiness in it as well, but she grew depressed and despondent.

I knew what I needed to do. I hoped it'd be enough.

I asked her to marry me and she said yes.

I rubbed my temples, feeling the dull pain of a headache approaching. Retrospect was a painful bitch.

I picked up the manila envelope I'd set off to the side. The top flap was worn, no adhesive left over from the many times I'd sealed it and reopened it again and again. Every time I'd say I wouldn't do it again, but I always went back on my word. I pulled the stack of papers out, setting aside the small, folded sheet of stationery.

Marriage certificate
November 21, 2007

We were blissfully happy for a while, but it was short-lived.

The bigger her belly got, the more concerned I became that she wasn't going to be able to handle being a mother. While she wasn't careless, she acted like she wasn't pregnant most days. There was no joy associated with anticipation of the baby. She didn't want to discuss a nursery or all the other little things we were going to need for a baby. Even when it was time to take a birthing class, she found every reason she could to get out of it—work, sickness, and even forgetfulness. I knew what it was, though. Denial.

Delilah was born after several hours of difficult labor on

May 12. The moment I saw her, my heart soared. I'd never known a love like that could exist.

Lexie did her best to adapt and put on her maternal face, but she grew impatient when she couldn't immediately console Delilah or when she couldn't figure out what she needed. A lot of the times, I found it easier for me to take over, but the more and more I did, the less and less Lexie did. I thought maybe it was a case of postpartum depression, but deep down I knew it was more than that. I encouraged her to seek therapy. She said she did, but to this day I wasn't sure it ever happened.

Six weeks after giving birth, Lexie went back to work. She immersed herself in a giant caseload and worked ungodly hours. Aside from peeking in on Delilah as she slept, there was little interaction. My business was thriving as well, but I was the one who got up in the middle of the night with her, fed her, bathed her, and loved her as much as I could. I didn't know much about being a parent, but I was certain that Delilah had to be wondering where her mama was and missed her. If it wasn't for my family, especially my mom who watched Delilah while we worked, I don't know what I would have done.

Not only did Lexie pull further and further away from her daughter, she distanced herself from me. She would often fall asleep on the couch, surrounded by paperwork, and avoided joining me in our bed. Our sex life, which was once exciting and fulfilling, had become nonexistent. If she chose to do anything in the house, it wasn't with Delilah and me. It was in the kitchen, baking, until all hours.

I knew it was only a matter of time before the bottom

fell out, but I thought I'd at least have a say in the situation. Instead, shortly before Delilah's first birthday, Delilah and I came home from a day at the zoo to find most of Lexie's personal belongings gone and a note.

I picked up a folded piece of blue stationery and opened it. At the top was a monogram of her initials in fuchsia lettering. ACM. Alexis Catherine Matthews.

Aaron,

I just can't anymore. You and Delilah deserve better than what I can give. The papers from my lawyer should arrive later this afternoon.

I will sign over full custody to you.

I'm sorry.

Lexie

She left the note with her engagement ring, which was in a black velvet box in the safe as well. I lifted it out and slowly opened the top. The platinum three-carat round cut ring sparkled against the light, reminding me of when I picked it out. There wasn't a doubt in my mind at that time that things would go as badly as they did.

No talk.

No explanation.

Nothing.

It was like Delilah and I meant *nothing* to her.

My heart healed, not from love lost because I wasn't sure that was what Lexie and I had, but from a betrayal so great it changed me on the inside. I'd never know if it was me, Delilah, or both of us that made Lexie so desperate. All I knew for sure was the only time Lexie was truthful was when she wrote that note. The rest of it? All fucking lies.

I placed the note and marriage certificate back in the envelope, leaving only the divorce decree and a pile of legal documents where Lexie signed away her rights to anything to do with Delilah.

Anger rose all around me, not as crushing as it once was, but enough to serve its purpose. I shoved all the papers back in the envelope and placed it in the bottom of the safe. The ring was tossed in next to them. Once shut and locked, I returned it to the drawer where it would stay until I needed Delilah's birth certificate for something or I wanted to give myself any further reminders of what my life was.

I wasn't without blame, though. The string of choices I made, the desperate attempts to make Lexie into someone she wasn't, was all on me. Now, I paid the price with solitude for myself and an existence for Delilah that was full of everything I could give her to make up for the fact that her dad had fucked up, too.

I needed another drink. I stood and crossed the room to my bookcase. After pulling down on the brass knuckle of the liquor cabinet, I retrieved a crystal whiskey decanter and matching glass. I poured three fingers and brought it to my mouth. The welcome burn again. Two sips in and I knew I'd need something stronger. I closed up the liquor cabinet, took my drink, and made my way to the kitchen. On top of the refrigerator was a brown box of exactly what I needed.

There was one cupcake left from a playdate Delilah had earlier that day. I opened the top of the Molly's Cupcakes box and knew I'd made the right decision to set this one aside for me, the Cookie Monster cupcake with vanilla chocolate chip cake and a cookie dough center. Whiskey and cupcakes. My wild, crazy night.

I knew I would push myself in my workout the following day, but I didn't care.

Maybe Abel was right. Maybe there wasn't anything wrong with having a little sugar from time to time.

Chapter Five

CALLIE—

I looked around my empty room and was overwhelmed with emotions—sadness, uncertainty, and excitement to name a few. Most of my belongings were stacked neatly in the corner, ready for me to put in my car the following afternoon. Evelyn was kind enough to let me leave a few things behind, but aside from some furniture I had no use for while I lived with the Matthews, my life was packed away in a few small boxes and two suitcases. It wasn't until the night before I left that the full realization of the situation sunk in for me.

The fact was, I had met Aaron twice, and in those two meetings, I was more turned on by the sight of him than I was during an entire seven-month relationship with my ex-boyfriend, Cody. Cody's idea of foreplay consisted of a kiss, with his tongue shoved in my mouth, and two boob squeezes. I knew the guy needed work when he went down on me for the first time and looked like a Saint Bernard at a water fountain. However, just being in the same room with Aaron, hearing his voice and watching him move, did something that Cody never could. I didn't know what it was, but it made my Georgia O'Keeffe respond.

I knew I should've been only thinking about my job at hand, being a nanny, but thoughts of Aaron kept creeping in. No matter what, though, there was no way I was going to risk losing this job. Any funny business, naked or otherwise, couldn't happen. It was unethical, and furthermore, I knew what a good thing this job was. There was no room for me to mess that up.

"Come on, Cal," Evelyn shouted.

It was my last night with her, and we decided to go old school with our dinner, having our last one together mirror our first—pizza and Coronas.

I walked out of my bedroom and to the kitchen where she was getting plates and napkins. We dug into the pizza and grabbed a beer, settling down on the floor in the living room.

We ate and reminisced, remembering some of the funnier moments we shared living together.

As we continued with stories and memories, I knew there was nothing I wouldn't do for this girl. I was pretty sure the feeling was mutual.

"Ugh. Please tell me you're not bringing those ugly-ass shoes with you. I thought I told you to burn them," she said while pointing at my feet. She was referring to my beloved pink sparkly Toms I was wearing. They were worn out and completely tattered, but the most comfortable things ever.

"Listen, Blondie. These," I commented, holding up my foot, "are one of my favorite things in the world."

She sighed. "I'll have to take them when you aren't looking."

"Don't you dare!"

She downed the rest of her beer and stood up. "Next round?"

"Absolutely."

So, we had another. Then another. Then another. By beer number four, we were talking about our most embarrassing and unusual sex-related stories.

"Oh my God. Do you remember the time you brought that dude you met at Crimson home?" I laughed. "He wore white leather pants with black sneakers. Then the next morning, you found him sniffing through my underwear drawer."

Evelyn was doubled over laughing, remembering the infamous Leather Pants Lover of Days Past. "He claimed he was looking for the Bible," she said, barely being able to get out the words. "I was so traumatized I decided to have a deep, committed relationship with my Rabbit and no men for many months after."

Evelyn had talked about her beloved Rabbit vibrator for almost as long as I'd known her—the mind-blowing orgasms, the simultaneous clit/G-spot stimulation, and the overall awesomeness that was the Rabbit. A few months ago, and after reaching the pinnacle of a dry spell, Evelyn convinced me to buy one. So, technically I owned a Rabbit, but it was still neatly packaged in the plastic it was delivered to me in. I was a little scared to use it, truth be told. The enormous green length that resembled something like a large pickle, the deli-size kind, and multiple buttons frightened me. It seemed like so many things could go wrong.

What if it short-circuited? Was there a chance of a spark, leading to a small fire? I wasn't ready for the possibilities. For now, the Love Bunny was packed neatly away in one of my boxes.

We continued to laugh and drink until it was time to call it a night. I cleaned up after I sent Evelyn off to bed. When I was done, I stood in the quiet apartment and looked around. I'd miss the home I shared with my best friend and all the happy times we had, but that was all I'd miss. I wouldn't miss busting my ass, working at a bar for almost half of what I would be making with Aaron. I wouldn't miss the caffeine-induced days in which I drank coffee like a drug addict just to get from morning to night because I was so exhausted. I wouldn't miss worrying about how to pay for rent and all other expenses I had and still not let Evelyn know how bad the situation was. I wouldn't miss working so hard at school and work that I barely had a social life, let alone a man.

Shutting my eyes to shield myself from all the powerful emotions coming at me, I gave the home and the life that I'd grown to know so well a fond farewell.

* * *

I stood in front of Aaron's home for seven minutes, holding one of my boxes, deciding how I should proceed. I wasn't sure if I should just let myself in or assume I was still a visitor. I mean, I didn't even technically live with him yet, and yes, I did understand that move-in day was just that and I would be living there after that, but I didn't do it yet. It may have seemed completely irrational and stupid to the outside observer, but this was how my brain worked.

I didn't need to decide because the door opened and Aaron was standing there, all smiles, to greet me. It was the first day at a new job, and I was incapable of *not* making an ass of myself.

"Callie, are you okay? Your face is all red," Aaron asked, concerned.

It must have been the mixture of embarrassment and, well, embarrassment. While I stood there continuing to further humiliate myself and unable to talk, I completely disregarded the spots I was seeing and light-headedness.

I blew out a hard breath as Aaron rushed to my side. "Seriously. Are you okay?"

I nodded and tried to pull together whatever was left of my dignity. Considering I was probably getting fired, I hoped Venom would still take me back.

"Are you on any medication?" he asked.

No, but I should be.

I shook my head. "No, I'm fine. I was just…you know, the boxes and lifting…and then just got a little light-headed… Fine…I'm fine."

"You still don't look right to me. Here," he said, taking the box. "Why don't you come sit down for a minute?" He guided me inside, and sat me down in the chair closest to the door. "Does this happen to you often?"

"No," I replied, shaking my head. "I'm fine really."

He knelt down in front of me. "Maybe you should put your head between your legs and get some good breaths in. I heard it helps when you feel faint."

For your own safety, please do not kneel down in front of me like that unless you want me to knock you down and ride you like a jockey at the Kentucky Derby.

"I'm so sorry," I said. "Please don't think this is a reflection of who I am or that I'm hiding some mysterious fainting illness."

"Are you sure?" he asked.

"Just a little something came over me. I think a case of the nerves."

A slow, sexy smile lifted from his mouth. "Whatever do you have to be nervous about?"

God, he was so beautiful and he didn't even know it. Even in just jeans and a black V-neck sweater, he looked amazing. The sweater was snug enough that it clung to his tight chest, and the sleeves curved around his biceps muscles.

"Callie! You're here! I've been waiting *so* long." Delilah came running down the hallway and wrapped her arms around my legs.

"Hey you!" I said, kneeling down to her. She had on a brown corduroy dress and multicolored tights. Her hair was up in two pigtails, complete with Hello Kitty barrettes. "I love your barrettes."

"Thank you," she responded. "Daddy did the tails and barrettes, but my nana bought them for me."

"Wow. I love Hello Kitty."

"You do?" she asked, her eyes getting big. "I have Hello Kitty stickers and paper and markers. Do you want to see?"

"Of course," I said, standing back up.

Delilah grabbed my hand and tried to drag me to the stairs, but before she got far, Aaron stopped her.

"Sweetie, let me show Callie around and get her settled first; then I'm sure she would love to see all your Hello Kitty things."

Delilah pouted and stomped her foot. "I want to show her now, Daddy. You said she was coming to live here to play with me."

"No, I didn't," he said. "I told you she was coming here to live with us and help Daddy, not to play with you anytime you say so."

"Okay," Delilah said quietly.

"You can go watch TV while I talk to Callie and show her to her room." Aaron leaned down and placed a kiss on the top of her head before she ran off down the hall to the living room.

He shook his head at me. "I don't want to even think about the teenage years. Four years old and sassy like a pro."

"Well, we learn early," I said. "It's how we get so good at it."

"Must be in the double X chromosomes. Although her stubborn streak can be attributed to me, or so I've been told. Which, by the way, she'll use to her advantage any chance she gets. I'm sure you'll see soon enough, but just so you know, you have my permission to not take any shit from her."

"I'll write that down in my notes. Take no shit."

"All right then, let me help you with your things." He bent down to pick up the box he brought in, and I got the perfect view of his ass, all hard and perfect in his jeans.

"Mmmm," I moaned softly as I checked him out.

He had started to head toward the stairs but stopped and

turned around when he heard me. "Did you say something?"

"Mmmmmmarble floor…it's gorgeous," I said, motioning toward the floor.

"Thanks," he replied awkwardly before turning back around and walking up the stairs.

Once on the second floor, he entered the first room on the right, stepping to the side as I followed.

"Are you kidding me with this?" I said.

The cream-colored room was huge; three of my old bedrooms could have easily fit inside it. There was a king-sized, four-post bed made of light wood, along with a matching nightstand and dresser, that had contrasting deep burgundy-colored bedding on it.

After I walked in farther, I looked to my left, noticing my own private bathroom, complete with a lavish tub and separate shower.

"This is beautiful," I said. "I mean, really."

He smiled. "I'm glad you like it. My ex-wife did most of the decorating around here, but like I said, I bought the bedding recently. If you would like something different…"

"No," I interrupted. "It's amazing."

"So, you obviously have your own bathroom. Delilah's bedroom is next to yours, and mine is on the other side of that. Across the hall is the bonus room, which has a lot of Delilah's toys and such, but it's so disorganized. It was meant to be a bedroom for another child, but obviously that never happened so it kind of became the free-for-all room."

"I can definitely help you fix that up with organizing and such," I said.

"Yeah?" he asked. "I mean, that isn't really part of your job, you know? To clear clutter."

"Are you kidding me? I love to do that kind of stuff."

"Wow," he said, pushing his hands into his pockets. "You're really something else, aren't you?"

It wasn't what he said. It was the tone—quiet and with something else I couldn't quite put my finger on. It seemed like sadness. It made my heart ache a little, knowing I was coming into a home that had a lot of history, and from what I could gather, not all of it good. I tried searching for answers, looking across his face, but the part I needed to see was turned down. His eyes.

"Um," I said. "So, I guess—"

I stopped talking when his eyes, so blue in color it reminded me of my grammy's aquamarine ring, stared at me. You don't realize how seldom someone really looks you in the eyes until it happens. It made my heartbeat race, and heat rise throughout my body. It was that intense, this stare down, which neither of us were retreating from.

"Daddy," Delilah shouted from downstairs. "Can I watch *Tinker Bell*?"

And like that, the spell was broken.

He shook his head, clearing whatever it was that he was thinking of. "Yes," he called back.

He smiled, the subtle, warm gesture he usually had on returned. "Okay, then."

I followed him out of the room and noticed another set of stairs on the opposite side of the hallway. "Is that to a third floor?" I asked.

"That," he said, pointing, "is to my favorite part of the house. Come on, let me show you."

We walked down the hallway and up a flight of stairs. He typed a code into a keypad next to the door, and when it buzzed, he pushed it open. A gust of cold, early April air hit me, and I knew we were on the balcony I'd admired from the outside.

Following the similar theme throughout the whole house, the balcony was done in all white. A hot tub was covered with a brown cover, but I recognized the large square shape.

"You have the most amazing view," I said. "I can see why this is your favorite part of the house. I would live out here in the summer."

He chuckled. "I would, too, but Delilah gets bored easily. Sometimes I'll drag the little kiddie pool out for her so we can hang out." He looked around, taking in the view as well. "I want you to be comfortable here, Callie. Nothing is off-limits. Come out here whenever you want. The hot tub, or anything else in the house for that matter, is yours to use. In the winter, the heat lamps and heated tiles are on timers along with the tub, so it's ready to go whenever anyone wants to use it. I'll give you the code to get up here."

"Well, I'm sure that comes in handy when you are entertaining or having a guest over," I said, fishing for information. I'd been waiting for the right intro to see what his dating lineup looked like.

He shrugged his shoulders. "I don't do much entertaining. Usually the only people over are family and a few friends on occasion. Um, I guess I should mention," he said. He paused and looked down at his shoes. "There's no woman in my life, and I don't really date because…well… it's complicated, and with Delilah, I'd rather not add that into the mix right now. My social life will have to wait until she's little older."

I wanted to feel bad for his predicament. It would've been right to, but I didn't. He was single. He was staying that way, and while I knew nothing would be between us, I was glad I wouldn't have to see him with anyone else.

"Let's go get the rest of your stuff, okay?" he said.

Once everything was in my room, Aaron and I went back downstairs and he showed me around to the areas I hadn't seen before: laundry room, living room, and even though I'd seen the kitchen, he pointed out where everything was. On the other side of the kitchen was Aaron's office.

We were chatting in the kitchen when Delilah wandered in. "Callie, can I play with this?" she asked.

"Play with what?" I asked, trying to see what she was holding.

Both Aaron and I approached her, and as we got closer, my heart leaped to my throat when I recognized the box she was holding.

"Delilah, can I have that back, please?" I asked. I went to go take it from her hands before Aaron could see what it was, but she yanked her arms back, bringing the box closer into herself.

"Where did you get that box?" Aaron questioned

"Callie's room. She has toys in her boxes."

Luckily with the box held close to her body, Aaron wasn't

able to see what kind of toy it was. If he could, he would've seen his daughter was holding my Rabbit vibrator in her hands.

I was dying. It became harder to breathe, and I concluded all of my internal organs were shutting down. My body was trying to save me the humiliation of Aaron finding out I brought a vibrator into his house. I was going to get fired and kicked out at once for being a pervert.

"Callie's things are not for you to be going through, young lady," Aaron said sternly. "Now, go back upstairs and put that back where you found it right now."

"That's okay," I said. "I'm heading upstairs right now and I'll take it." I moved toward Delilah again to retrieve the box, but she jerked away again.

Then, to my horror, she turned the box around and held it up to Aaron. "But, Daddy, I don't have one of these. Callie has a toy cucumber, and I don't have one this big for my play kitchen. Plus, it has buttons to do stuff."

I was frozen in complete and utter shame. Aaron's eyes squinted at the box trying to identify what it was, and then once the realization hit, his eyes enlarged to the size of baseballs, possibly softballs.

"Give that back to Callie now," he shouted. Without waiting for her to decide, he grabbed the box out of her hands. He shoved it at me, crushing the box against my chest.

"Be right back," I said, running out of the room. By the time I reached the stairs, I heard Delilah crying and Aaron reprimanding her.

I hope the remains of my patent leather Venom skirt can be sal-

vaged from the Dumpster behind Venom because I'm going to be back behind the bar by nightfall.

Once in my room, I tried to find an appropriate spot to hide my "Kids Choice for Toy of the Year." I opened the closet door and hid the box on the top shelf behind an extra blanket. I sat on the edge of my bed and put my face in my hands, praying I would survive this.

A soft knock at the door brought me out of my thoughts. I turned and Aaron and Delilah were standing in the doorway. Aaron nudged Delilah gently.

"I'm sorry I went through your box and took out your toy cucumber," Delilah said shyly, her eyes rimmed red.

I smiled. "Thank you. Do you want to play with your Hello Kitty stuff now?" I asked.

"Yes, please."

I looked at Aaron, and with a silent understanding, we told each other we would never mention this to each other again.

I spent the rest of the afternoon and into the evening playing with Delilah and letting her show me all her favorite things. After dinner, I helped her take a bath and get ready for bed. Once I had her all tucked in, I called down to Aaron and he came in to read her a story.

I let them say their good nights in private, and I walked back to my room. I lifted one of my suitcases onto the bed and unzipped it, putting my clothes away, one by one.

"She's out like a light already. I think you wore her out," Aaron said, leaning against my doorway.

"Well, we have lots of plans for tomorrow. The park, *Strawberry Shortcake* movie, Easy-Bake Oven treats, and she wants me to paint her toenails, but I didn't know if that was okay."

"Yeah, it's fine. My mom has already taken her to the spa to have pedicures and stuff." He rolled his eyes and shook his head.

"So, I think I'm going to unpack and get settled, unless there's something else you need?" I asked.

"No, please make yourself at home. Like I said before, this is your home now, too, so watch TV, use the kitchen, whatever you would like." He looked at the floor for a second and shifted back and forth on his feet. "Um…thank you," he said.

"For what?"

"I know this probably isn't the easiest situation to come into and I appreciate your enthusiasm." As soon as he was done talking, his eyes shifted from the floor to me. For the briefest of moments, I felt like we were Aaron and Callie and not boss and employee. Two people wanting something more from each other, and not knowing what that meant. It was fleeting, but it made me wonder, *What if things were different?*

"I'm happy to be here," I said.

"Good night, Callie."

"Good night, Aaron."

He closed the door behind him, as I collapsed onto the bed from both physical and mental exhaustion. My body ached from tension from head to toe. I decided as soon as I was done unpacking, I was going to soak in the tub with the hottest water I could stand.

Or I could accept Aaron's invitation to make myself at home and hit up the rooftop hot tub. The thought made me unpack as quickly as possible while I searched for my bikini.

Once I found it, I slipped it on and grabbed a towel from the bathroom.

I tiptoed down the hallway and up the stairs to the balcony door. After keying in the password, I opened the door as gently and softly as possible. I gasped when I saw I wasn't alone. It looked like I wasn't the only one who had the idea for an evening hot tub dip. Aaron had beaten me to it and was already seated in the tub, his arms outstretched and his head back. The frigid night air hit me hard, and my body erupted in goose bumps. I wrapped the towel around my body and stepped out onto the balcony. When the door closed behind me, Aaron's head popped up.

Steam rose around him before disappearing into the darkness surrounding us. His face glowed under the soft lighting as I caught him off guard, his eyes fixated on mine.

Now or never.

"Um, hi," I said. I opened my towel and let it fall to the tile floor. "Can I join you?" I asked.

Chapter Six

AARON—

My eyes lazily raked over her body, from head to toe. I couldn't even stop myself from doing it before it was too late.

My tongue swept over my bottom lip. "Absolutely," I said, clearing my throat. "It's nice to have the company."

It was nice, but I wasn't sure how long I could stand being around her in that tiny white bikini. Small triangles of fabric covered her breasts, but her hardened nipples were visible, no doubt from the cold Chicago air.

She stepped forward, closer to the hot tub, as I remained still. I needed one more moment to take her in. Her body was insane, toned but not too thin, with legs on her five-foot-six frame that went on for days. I thought about how her smooth skin would feel beneath my touch.

And that ass.

Fuck.

Stop.

She works for you. She LIVES with you.

When she reached the hot tub, I sat up and offered my hand to assist her in getting in. As she sat on the edge of the tub, her legs swung around to the water and she eased herself into the tub. I released her grip, moving myself to the opposite side of the tub.

"Thank you," she said.

"Again, it's nice to have the company," I replied. "I'm always out here alone."

We were quiet for a minute, averting our eyes from each other to the view around us.

"You have a beautiful home, Aaron," she said, breaking the silence.

"Thank you." I shrugged my shoulders, unsure if I should continue. "My ex-wife wanted to live here, and you know, I wanted to make her happy. We moved in shortly before we married."

"Do you not like it here?" she asked. "I mean, it's none of my business, but how could you not want this?" She lifted her arms and gestured around.

"It's not that I don't like it here. I know how lucky I am to have such an awesome place for me and Delilah, but..." I trailed off.

I shifted uncomfortably, my body creating waves of water that moved around us. My eyes moved to above Callie's head as I decided how much or how little to tell her about my past.

"I'm sorry," she said. "I shouldn't have brought it up."

"No. It's okay. If you're going to be living with us and taking care of Delilah, these things are going to come up. There's no need to apologize."

I ran my hands through my wet hair roughly. "It's not a big deal, but I suppose I should explain to you about the situation with Delilah's mother."

"Oh no. You don't have to. I mean—"

"No," I said cutting her off. "It's important you know." I took a deep breath before continuing. "My ex-wife decided she didn't want to be a mother anymore shortly before Delilah turned one." I paused, looking up at the sky. "We got divorced and I got full custody. She didn't even want visitation."

I continued to avoid looking at her because I didn't want to see that sad, pathetic look she was no doubt giving me. It was always the same reaction when I told people. While I knew it was genuine, I couldn't help but assume it was *me* they viewed as pitiful.

"I'm so sorry," she said. "That's beyond messed up. It must've been so hard for you."

I held up my hand and shook my head. "Don't. Don't feel sorry for me. I can deal with it, but it's Delilah. She got cheated out of having a mother, and as much as my mom steps in, it doesn't replace what she lost," I said. After a moment, I continued. "I don't particularly like living here. There are too many memories, but it's the only home Delilah has ever known. I don't want to take that away from her."

"You're all that matters to her," she responded. "You could move to the North Pole, and as long as you were with her, she'd know all the love and stability a little girl could ask for."

I shrugged. "I suppose."

"You know, my family dynamic was different at best, but I never felt unloved or unsafe. Kids are smarter and stronger than we give them credit for."

"It's just really overwhelming at times. No one can understand the pressure I have to make sure that little girl has everything to make up for the fact that she had a mother that didn't want her."

She slid her body across the rounded bench. My body stiffened, and I sat upright as she got close, but my eyes never lost sight of her movements. She was getting too close, but wasn't close enough. A push and pull inside me grew until it scared me enough to force it away. I moved back over, creating the distance I needed.

"Listen, I'm no expert," she said. "I don't have kids, but what I do know is that no matter their upbringing, they'll take what they know and do with it as they want. Some kids wallow in their disadvantages; others use it as catalyst to do better. It's the reason I work so hard and have had a job since I was sixteen. I was that little girl at school with the hand-me-down clothes and taped-up shoes. I'd stand in the cafeteria line with my purple lunch ticket, embarrassed that everyone knew that the purple ticket meant I got the state-provided lunch. I wanted the yellow ones like my other friends had. The yellows meant their parents had enough money to buy them a proper lunch themselves. I didn't want to live my life holding the purple ticket."

Everyone had a story. She'd lived a lifetime before I'd even met her. No better, no worse, but different.

"It seems like you've been through a lot, too," I said. "I'm sorry."

"Don't be. You don't want me to feel sorry for you, so please don't feel sorry for me."

As our conversation stalled and we sat in silence, I snuck glances while she looked at the starry night sky. She was beautiful. There was no mistaking that. Her hair, which was the same color as my favorite Pinot Noir, was piled on top of her head, with a few loose strands falling around her face. My eyes drifted lower, to the tiny strings that held her small white bikini up and curved around the roundness of her perfectly sized breasts.

Shit.

I was hard just looking at her. Who the hell was I kidding? I was hard the moment she dropped her towel.

Maybe even before then.

This had never happened to me before. I'd been the boss to many people for many years. Of course, there were attractive employees, but that was a line I never considered crossing. Leading my life by emotions instead of logic was how I got in trouble with Lexie.

Her head turned, and like that, I'd been busted. Her green eyes didn't waver, though. It was like she knew and didn't care.

Of course she'd care, dickhead. You're her boss. She just moved in, and you're looking her over like a hungry animal.

These years of not having a woman, in any kind of intimate setting, made me lose any sense of decency.

"I think I better head in," I said.

I couldn't be around her anymore, not like this. As I hopped out, I heard her gasp.

"What?" I asked.

She swallowed and blinked rapidly. "Is that what I think it is?" she asked, pointing to my side.

I laughed as I grabbed a towel from the ledge and wrapped it around my waist. "Yeah, it's a tattoo from my wild and crazy days."

I rubbed my hand across the massive tattoo that went from my underarm all the way down my body and stopping above my right hip. It was an unrolled scroll, 3-D in design, with intricate edges to convey the old, worn edges of the paper. I'd had elaborate plans for the center, which was blank where words should be.

"How long have you had it?" she questioned, squinting her eyes to get the best look she could without much light to help her. I briefly thought about moving back toward her again, so she could look closer, but I knew I shouldn't push it.

"I got it when I was twenty-two and never finished it. My ex-wife wasn't crazy about tattoos, and then after we were done, I didn't even think about it," I said, picking up a terry cloth robe that hung over a chair. I put it on, my body shivering even with the heat from the lamps and floor. "It'll be finished one day. It was supposed to be the story of my life. I'm just not sure what that is yet."

I tied my robe and was trying to make my exit, when I noticed her staring, her mouth hanging open.

"It's...incredible," she said. "Like...yeah."

She looked around for a moment, and began to climb out

of the hot tub. Her entire body was wet, her bikini clung to her body…everywhere. As she moved to step on the floor, I rushed to her side.

"Be careful, it gets slippery sometimes," I said, taking hold of her arm. I held on until she was safely down.

"Thank you," she said, running over to pick up the towel she'd dropped earlier. She wrapped it around her shoulders like a cape, but before the oversized towel covered most of the top of her body, I saw something that made me tie my robe tighter.

She turned, looking confused. "What?" she asked.

"You, um…," I stammered. "Have…umm, a tattoo, too."

"Yes, I do. Just a small heart right here." She opened her towel slightly, pushing the bottom of her bikini down to expose the tattoo completely.

Jesus Christ.

My mind went to thoughts of touching it, licking it, and—

I turned around and leaned over the back of the hot tub. After opening a cabinet, I got another towel out.

"You're probably cold. Here's another towel," I said. Instead of handing it to her, I tossed it like a hot potato. And because she wasn't expecting it and I was a moron, it hit her in the face.

"Shit," I said. "Sorry."

"Thank you. Should we head in?" she said, rearranging the towel.

I nodded and headed to the door with her following close behind. Once inside, we walked down the stairs, being careful to be quiet and not wake Delilah. She passed me, quickly tiptoeing down the hallway, pausing in front of her bedroom door.

I had stopped outside my door as well, watching her. We stared for a moment, maybe two, before the sound of tiny cough from Delilah's room broke the spell.

"Good night, Aaron," she whispered.

"Sleep well…Calliope."

Chapter Seven

CALLIE—

I woke the following morning close to seven, and as I rubbed the sleep from my eyes, I was confused by my surroundings. After sleeping so hard, I'd forgotten where I was until I recalled I was in my new room, in my new home.

I glanced at the clock and had forty-five minutes before Delilah was due to be up. After a stretch, I made my way to the bathroom and took longer than usual to get ready for any normal day. I wanted Aaron to be under the impression I woke up flawless and free of morning breath and drool crust. It was like how I was at Venom, getting all dolled up for the job, but instead of impressing strangers, I was trying to impress my boss.

Yes. My boss. Impress. Nothing more than that.

There was a spark, though. I knew it. I felt it all over my body, an electricity that tingled from every extremity. I was unsure what it meant, though. He was *so* attractive. Besides the age difference and the whole boss-employee thing, I didn't know if a plain, college girl would be enough for him.

Hypothetically, of course.

I walked down the stairs of the quiet house. The morning sun was sneaking through the slats of the blinds and curtains, desperately trying to light up the darkened home. I stopped to peek out the window on the way to the kitchen. Most of the winter's snow and ice had melted and spring was going to start showing her face shortly.

Upon entering the kitchen, I realized this was another one of those things I was going to have to get used to. Yes, I was living in Aaron's home as the nanny, and room, board, and all meals were included as part of my employment, but I didn't feel comfortable rummaging around his refrigerator and pantry looking for Cheerios and milk.

After another few minutes of contemplation, I decided to make pancakes for all of us. It was a nice gesture the first morning I was here, and it gave me the opportunity to check things out in the kitchen. Pancakes were always a good reason to look through someone's cabinets.

As I moved around, I looked through the pantry and cabinets, gathering the ingredients I needed to make the pancakes. Once I had it all lined up, I began measuring and dumping into a stainless steel bowl. With a large whisk, I beat it together until it was the perfect consistency.

I looked above the island in the center of the kitchen to where numerous pots and pans hung. I could've used a regular frying pan, but going by how much Aaron liked to cook and use his kitchen, I was willing to bet that there was a griddle somewhere around.

I knelt down and looked in some of the cabinets on the side of the island. When I didn't spot anything, I looked up in a cabinet to the right of the large stove. Immediately after opening it, I saw the griddle that I was looking for. It was at the very bottom of a stack of platters. As I pushed and moved the platters aside, I placed my hand under the griddle to bring it out, but as I did, I felt and heard that I had knocked something small over inside the cabinet.

Once I removed the griddle, I set it down on the counter and plugged it in to heat up. I went back to the cabinet, straightening the platters and reaching in to find whatever I'd knocked over. I felt a small bottle, and when I brought it forward to put it back in place, I saw it was a prescription bottle. I turned it around to look at the front and the patient's name read: Aaron Matthews.

I heard a toilet flush, followed by footsteps running down the hallway upstairs. It startled me, so I shoved the bottle back in the cabinet and closed it quickly. The last thing that I needed was my boss finding me checking out his pharmaceuticals, even if it was by accident.

I didn't get a chance to see what the prescription was for, and I'd be lying if I wasn't curious. My mind began running wild. Was he sick? What if it was something serious? It could be anything…viral…bacterial…hair loss…restless leg syndrome…dry eyes…Oh no…what if it was…No…I couldn't even think about it…but…what if it was erectile dysfunction?

The thought was too horrible to even ponder.

"Come on, Daddy," Delilah shouted from upstairs.

I thought Delilah would like Mickey Mouse pancakes, so with a measuring scoop, I poured two small circles onto the griddle. I was attempting to make the face, but the thoughts of the possible penile medication invaded my mind once again.

I looked back to the griddle and saw that while I was praying, I forgot I'd poured the batter. The burned edges of the pancakes caused smoke to rise from the griddle and fill the air. I flipped the switch on the exhaust fan to clear the fog while I scraped off the ruined pancakes, replacing them with new batter. While I watched it bubble, I heard footsteps coming down the stairs and into the hallway.

"Callie! You're here!" Delilah ran into the kitchen and wrapped her arms around my waist.

I was flipping her pancake, and with my free hand, I patted her back. "I am. I promised I would be."

Aaron entered, looking sleepy in a wrinkled T-shirt and plaid pajama bottoms.

"Morning," I said. "I hope you don't mind, but I decided to make breakfast."

"That's nice of you," he replied halfheartedly without his usual smile or friendliness. "But it isn't part of your job description."

He brushed past me and to the cabinet next to the fridge. After grabbing a bag of coffee, he started fumbling with the coffeemaker.

Someone wasn't a morning person.

"Pancakes!" Delilah said.

"Do you like pancakes?" I asked, placing the Mickey Mouse pancake on a plate.

She nodded while jumping up and down. "I do!"

"Good. Here you go," I said, handing her the plate.

She took the plate with two hands, and when she realized what it was, she started bouncing again. "It's a Mickey. Daddy look what Callie made me."

"That's great, sweetie," he replied without turning his attention from the coffeemaker. "Make sure you say thank you."

Delilah looked up at me and smiled brightly. "Thank you, Callie."

Aaron slammed the top of the coffeemaker down and walked to the refrigerator. We reached it at the same time and grasped for the handle simultaneously. With just the tips of my fingers grazing the top of his hand, I stilled—the energy rose between us.

Or maybe it was just between me and myself.

My eyes darted to his, and for a quick second, his eyes held still on mine, until he snapped his hand away from my touch.

"Sorry," he said. "Go ahead."

I was taken aback by his attitude, which was seemingly so different from the man I'd sat with in a hot tub the night before. Perhaps he really wasn't a morning person, but if I was being truthful, I felt like it was more than that.

I poured Delilah her milk, and as I went to return the carton to the fridge, Aaron grabbed it from me instead. "Thanks, I'll take that."

I returned to the griddle and flipped the pancake that had started to bubble. "Aaron, how many pancakes would you like?"

He was stirring his coffee and staring off into space. "Aaron?" I repeated.

His head snapped to attention. "I'm sorry, what?"

"Pancakes. How many would you like?"

"Whatever is fine with me. Do you want coffee?" he said, reaching for another coffee mug.

"Yes, thank you, but I'll get it myself. Why don't you sit down with Delilah before the pancakes get cold?" I took the three pancakes off the griddle and placed them on a plate.

Aaron had seated himself next to his daughter, and as I placed the plate in front of him, the corner of his mouth turned up slightly. "Thank you."

"No problem. I like cooking and I don't get to do it often. Plus, with a kitchen like this, it's a pleasure."

I helped myself to a cup of coffee and grabbed my plate to join Aaron and Delilah.

I looked to Delilah who had dismembered her Mickey pancake's ears and was sporting a milk mustache. "Is it good?" I asked her.

She nodded her head. "Better than Daddy's."

Aaron and I laughed knowing four-year-olds don't have much need for tact.

"I'm glad you like them," I said.

Aaron took a sip of his coffee and turned his attention to me. "Do you want to come to the park with us?" I asked, clearing the table of plates.

"Sure. Let me just get showered, okay?"

"All right. I'll get Delilah all ready and we'll get going."

He nodded, and he took a final sip of his coffee. "Sounds good. Thanks again for breakfast."

He smiled, the smile that I was waiting for since he first

walked into the kitchen, and his entire demeanor lightened. I guess his mood was nothing a little coffee and pancakes couldn't fix.

* * *

We were sitting on a bench at the park, watching Delilah on the swings, silent. He lifted his phone from his pocket and started fiddling with it. I had a love-hate relationship with mobile phones. Of course, the convenience factor was a plus, but the way it was used to avoid interactions with people around you was the biggest negative. In Aaron's case, it was working to his advantage.

"Do you want some coffee?" I asked. "I can run across the street and get some for us."

"No, thanks," he said, without looking up from his phone. "You go ahead."

"That's okay. I was just seeing if you did."

He shook his head. "You were only asking for me?"

No. I was asking the other jackass sitting next to me.

I thought it best to not even answer him because if I did, I might say something I regretted.

"Callie!" Delilah called from the swing. "Come push me."

I ran over to her, and stood behind her. "Remember to use your legs like I showed you. Out and in, okay?"

I gave her a small push, waiting for her to start moving her legs, before pushing her more. Her soft voice was encouraging herself, repeating, "Out and in."

She begged for me to push her higher and higher, and once

I did, I stepped back to move in front of her. There was such pure joy on her face. I briefly wished that my life could be so simple as trying to reach the clouds on a swing.

I looked over and Aaron was nowhere to be found. Figuring he went to find a bathroom, Delilah and I moved from the swings to other areas of the park. I was standing close under her at the monkey bars when I saw Aaron approaching, carrying two Starbucks cups.

"Oh!" Delilah said, swinging to the last hook. "Is one for me?"

"No. But I got you a cookie instead."

I helped Delilah down, and she ran to meet Aaron. She grabbed for the small brown bag with her goodie in it, but Aaron yanked it away.

"We need to find some place to wash your hands, baby girl," he said.

She started to pout, kicking dirt with her rhinestone-toed sneakers. I pulled a travel-sized bottle of hand sanitizer from the pocket of my jacket and walked to them.

"Here, Delilah," I said. "Come use this and then you can have your cookie."

I squirted a small amount into her tiny hands, and when she had rubbed it in, Aaron handed her the cookie.

"You think of everything, don't you?" Aaron asked, watching Delilah run off with her cookie.

I shrugged my shoulders. "Keeping her free of dirt and germs, I think, is in my job description."

"Here," he said, holding out one of the coffee cups to me. "I wasn't sure what you wanted, so I went with a double-shot vanilla latte."

Okay. I take back the jackass comment.

I took the cup from him. "Thank you. This is actually my favorite drink," I said, taking a sip. "Changed your mind, huh?"

For the first time all afternoon he looked at me, like really looked at me. His eyes scanned mine while his expression seemed serious. "No. I didn't change my mind. I remembered sometimes what I want and what others want isn't the same."

He turned his head once again and didn't look my way again for the rest of the day.

After putting Delilah to bed later that evening, I closed the door to her room softly as I exited, sighing deeply as I leaned against it. Aaron had said his good nights to Delilah and retreated to his office.

He was avoiding me. I just didn't know why. A pit formed in my stomach from anxiety, wondering if I'd done something wrong or considering if the Aaron I saw now was the real Aaron. I went over and over our time together up until this morning. There was kindness and interest on his part. The previous night, in the hot tub, there was a…connection. I couldn't name it or articulate what it was, but it was there.

Or maybe I had imagined all of it.

I pulled the elastic from my hair that held it in a bun. My fingers dug through my hair so I could massage my head, trying to release the tension. No. I needed something more. I was feeling more and more depressed by the minute. I needed a distraction.

After I took a long bubble bath, I climbed into bed with a book, but my mind was still all over the place. What would it take to quiet my brain and relax me?

Well. There was always one way, but I couldn't. No, I couldn't in Aaron's house, not with both him and a little girl down the hall.

No.

Well. Maybe?

I rushed to my closet and reached for my Rabbit that I had hidden behind a blanket. As I situated myself on my bed, I briefly experimented with the buttons before feeling comfortable enough to give it a try. The moment the tip of the Rabbit ears met my most sensitive spot, a sensation so powerful and intense overwhelmed me.

"Evelyn wasn't kidding," I said to myself.

Aaron was my most taboo fantasy and I gave in. I submerged myself within the walls of illusion, the place where Aaron took my face in his hands and kissed me deeply.

The place where he'd moved his hands from my face to my hips, roughly pushing me into him to feel where he was hard.

The place where we'd barely make it to bed as we frantically removed each other's clothes.

The place where we touched and tasted each other's bodies, gripping tightly to the want we'd been so hungry for.

The mixture of mental and physical arousal was more than I could handle, and I became unaware of much else. My softened moans, whispered words, were all just for me to hear.

Chapter Eight

AARON—

I didn't mean to listen.

What a bullshit thing to tell myself. Of course, I did.

I heard her say my name as I passed by her room on the way to my own. When I stopped to listen for it again, I heard her moan softly, once…twice, followed by my name again.

It was everything I wanted and feared at the same time.

I didn't know what it was with this girl, but I couldn't get her out of my mind. After I stood outside her door for longer than I should've, like the perverted fuck I was, I rushed back to my room to take a shower.

Oh, and also to take care of the raging hard-on I got by hearing her say my name.

Christ, Aaron. What the hell are you doing? Oh. That's right. The same thing you did the night before.

I entered the shower, turning the knob all the way to one end to make the water as hot as possible. Once I was wet all over, I reached for the soap and started getting a good, strong lather going. If I didn't take care of the stiff one I had, I was concerned I'd cause permanent damage.

Once I was satisfied with the amount of lather, I placed the soap back on the shelf and brought my hands to my dick that was begging for a release. I intertwined my fingers and slipped my cock between the palms of my hands. As I released a muffled groan, I leaned my forehead against the marble shower, letting the warm water wash over my back while drowning myself in images of Callie.

Starting with slow but firm strokes, I worked my palms up and down my hardness, my fingers tightening to increase pressure. It didn't take long for me to immerse myself in the imaginary scenario, a scene in which I started at her toes and kissed and nibbled my way upward. My hands moved quicker, and I increased my rhythm until I was pumping myself hard.

The fantasy continued with my journey up her body, stopping at that little fucking heart on her hip. After giving her a playful bite on it, I worked the outline of the heart with the tip of my tongue. Her body squirmed with excitement, and she whispered my name.

I moved my tongue from her hip down to the inside of her thigh, taking my time. She lifted her head to look down at me before I went any further. My gaze held hers and I waited. Then, I waited more. I was going to wait until she begged for me.

My cock throbbed almost painfully for its own release, but my hunger for her took precedence.

All at once I was pulled from the fantasy and was back in

my shower, head still against the marble and my hands rapidly tending to my dick. I was moments away from my release when my mind gave Callie one last look. A beautiful sight of her body arching up off the bed and her orgasm taking her over. My cock pulsed and I came hard, my thoughts of her disappearing into the steam around me.

Later, I laid in bed, trying to get comfortable even though I knew sleep wouldn't come easily. Everything that had happened since I met Callie had been such a whirlwind, a flurry of overpowering emotions, that I had no idea how to separate them all. What started off as me simply hiring a nanny was turning into something much different.

When Callie moved in, she conjured up a plethora of feelings I hadn't had in years. Desire and want, the most basic elements of attraction, crashed down on me. Her smile and enthusiasm lit up a room, along with the energy she brought to the house.

There was so much chemistry between us, but I pushed it aside. I assumed I was out of the game for so long it could have been anyone that caught my eye, but as soon as she moved in, I knew I was wrong.

What the hell was my problem? I was her boss. She was living with me and my daughter. The thoughts I had of her were completely reprehensible and made me even more of a pathetic jerk.

I shut off my sexual desire when my only concern in life was Delilah, but in one fell swoop, Callie changed it all. Everything shifted after last night in the hot tub. That was the first night I got myself off thinking of her.

It was wrong—beyond wrong. It was completely reprehensible.

This morning, I was cloaked in guilt. In order to put it behind me and get Callie out of my mind, I did the only thing I knew how to do. I acted like a total jackass to her. I ignored and avoided her at every turn. It didn't mean I still didn't take notice of her, but I thought if I could separate myself from her as much as possible, the want would stop.

Sometime during my struggle to fall asleep, I must've dozed off because I awoke to my bedroom door opening slowly. Thinking it was Delilah wanting to sleep in my bed, I called her in.

"Come on in, sweetie," I said.

The door continued to open, but I soon realized that it wasn't Delilah. It was Callie. She was wearing a pink tank top and matching short shorts.

"Aaron," she whispered. "Are you awake?"

I wasn't sure. "Huh?" I asked.

"Aaron," she repeated. "I need you."

Was this real?

"I'm sorry to wake you," she whispered.

I sat up slowly, gazing at her, sleepy and confused. "It's okay," I said sitting up.

"Callie, what is it?" I asked. "Why aren't you saying anything? Are you holding a knob?"

"I...ah..."

I threw the covers off and got up in a hurry. "Callie?"

"I...," she said glancing down at the front of my loose-fitting pajama pants.

What the hell was going on? I looked down to my bare stomach, and further to see if there was something I was missing, something to explain why she was staring like she was.

"Calliope!"

"I broke your knob," she blurted out.

I was still baffled why she was standing there, holding a knob. "You did what?"

She held the metal piece out to me, and all at once she talked...and ran. "The toilet," she said, darting down the hallway. "I broke the toilet knob, and now it's squirting everywhere."

I quickly followed her, and when we reached her room, I could hear it. Then I stepped into the bathroom and saw it.

"Shit!" I said.

The water from inside the toilet was shooting up and out all over the bathroom like a fountain. I stood for a moment, surveying the situation, running my hands through my hair. "Shit," I repeated.

"I tried to turn that, well, this." She held out the knob to me until I took it. "And it broke and—"

"Run downstairs to the laundry room and shut off the main water valve," I said, cutting her off. "Do you know what that is?"

She nodded and started for the door, but I stopped her. "And grab a Phillips screwdriver from the toolbox in the laundry room, too."

What the hell did she do? I made my way through the spouting water and the accumulated puddles, getting drenched by water in the process. The knob I was holding was obviously from the water valve, but as I got closer, I realized the screw was missing. I looked across the floor and, after a few moments, saw a screw floating in a puddle next to the toilet.

But where the hell was the water shooting up from? I wanted to get a closer look, but I knew the water would be shut off any second by Callie. The water had soaked through my pajamas, which I realized in that moment was going to totally show that I wasn't wearing underwear.

"Fuck," I said to myself.

It wasn't like I knew she'd get me up in the middle of the night and I'd end up all wet. This was going to elevate my "creepy boss" status to an entirely new level. I glanced around the room, looking for a towel or something, but I knew there'd be no hiding it.

The water slowed and then stopped, letting me know she had located the water valve. I splashed over and looked in the back of the tank to where the water had been coming from. I almost instantly noticed that the top of the inlet valve thing was broken at the top.

I heard Callie panting as she ran back into the bedroom. She tiptoed into the bathroom, being careful not to slip, before handing me the screwdriver.

"I'm so, so sorry," she said.

"It's okay," I said, kneeling down to reattach the knob to the water valve "It's just water."

"I'll clean it all up. I just—"

I inserted the knob back into place and pushed the screw through the hole. As I turned the screwdriver to put the screw in tight, I turned to tell her again it was okay, that accidents happened.

But her heaving chest, her breasts pressing against the lace of her top stopped me. My hand slipped, and I had to refocus my attention on the task at hand.

Just screw the thing back in.

Screw.

Screw.

Shit.

I stood up, and as I did, Callie's eyes followed me. They were at my face, then my chest, stomach, and then she stopped where I knew she'd be able to see the outline of my cock through the wet bottoms.

Quiet filled the bathroom, the only sounds were sporadic drips of water and our breathing. We stood face-to-face, and without words, our bodies began inching together. I wasn't sure who was moving toward whom, but it was happening, like gravity. I swallowed hard, pushing down the improper thoughts I was having—thoughts of pushing her up against the wall, ripping her bottoms off, and fucking her senseless. Thoughts of yanking down the lace of her top, exposing her breasts, and licking, sucking my way across her nipples. Thoughts of kneeling in front of her, lifting her leg over my shoulder, and bringing my mouth to where she ached for me.

Our bodies, our faces, our mouths were getting dangerously close. I could smell her breath, sweet and minty. I wanted to grab the back of her neck, pull our bodies together, and taste her everywhere, but I waited.

"Calliope," I whispered.

"Aaron."

The sound of her voice, sexy and sweet, was enough to thrust me back into reality. I couldn't let this happen.

I took in a sharp breath and stepped back. "Can you turn the water valve back on before you go back to bed?" I said.

She retreated on her own, brushing her hand across her face. "Of course."

My eyes moved from her to something green laying on the edge of her bed. I squinted, trying to make it out, and…

It was…

A toy cucumber.

"What?" she asked.

I jerked my eyes back to her, trying to act like I didn't just see what I saw. "Nothing. Nothing at all," I responded. "I'm going to head back to bed. Good night."

"Are you—" she started to say, but it was too late.

I bolted from the room to my own, where I headed straight to the shower. My new shower routine brought new meaning to lather, rinse, and repeat.

Chapter Nine

CALLIE—

He bolted from the room as fast as he could, leaving me confused once again.

I was too exhausted to examine the entire situation any further. I wiped up the puddle with a towel and walked back downstairs again and turned the water valve back on. My eyes were tired and heavy by the time I made it back upstairs. I was about to climb into bed when something caught my eye.

Something green.

Lying next to one of my pillows was Trix, the vibrator. I'd fallen asleep with it there, and when the bathroom situation happened, it was the furthest thing from my mind.

That was what he saw before he rushed out of the room.

"Fuck my life."

***

"What the hell were you thinking, Callie?" Evelyn shouted at me. "You need to put the Rabbit away immediately after use. Immediately!"

"Will you keep your voice down?"

We were at the park at lunchtime the following Monday. I'd called her in crisis mode to tell her about everything, and she met me there. Since it was Aaron's first day back at work, I was with Delilah on my own and figured she could play while I had an emergency summit with Evelyn.

"I'm so embarrassed. Everything I'm doing is wrong," I said, shaking my head. "I'm trying, but every step I take, it's wrong. Everything feels like one disaster after another."

"Don't be dramatic. It hasn't even been an entire week yet. You're just nervous or being, well, you."

I shot her a look. "What is that supposed to mean?"

"Sweetie, what is this really about?"

She knew. I didn't want to admit it to myself, but Evelyn saw right through me.

My emotions—fear, sadness, and humiliation—attacked me like a firing squad, so many at once I couldn't separate them all. Tears stung my eyes, a completely out-of-character response, but justified. "I haven't felt such a…in so long… and…"

"Okay. Okay," she said, grabbing hold of my hand. "I get it. You caught feelings. So, let me ask you this. What is it that you want? And believe me, I realize that's probably an uncomfortable question for you."

"Again, Ev. What is that supposed to mean?"

"It means, you never think about what *you* want. You never

think about what you deserve. As long as I've known you, you've never thought you were good enough."

The tears I was holding at bay threatened to spill over, and my nose began to run as I tried to explain. "What do you think I'm doing with school? And wanting to be a teacher? That's me. That's all me."

"That's a career. I'm talking about *you*. What do you want for you?"

She was right. I hated to admit it, but she was. My life had become a series of steps, one in front of the other, without looking around me to see what life had to offer. It was work and school and that was it. It had always been that way. Between raising my little sisters and focusing on making a better life, there wasn't much time to consider what I wanted. It was survival mode. Now, as the road narrowed toward my goal, and I could see my degree at the end of the tunnel, I wasn't sure if it was going to be enough anymore.

Guilt began to overwhelm me, but I had to tell her what I was thinking.

"Him," I whispered, quickly wiping away at the tears that had fallen. "I want him."

I was afraid to look at her, to see her reaction, but I forced myself to. She tucked a lock of her blond hair behind her ear, pressing her signature tinted red lips together. "What do you want to do about it?"

I shrugged, digging through my purse, looking for a tissue to wipe my running nose. "What can I do? It is what it is and that means nothing can come out of it."

"I don't know," she mumbled. "He's single. You're single."

"He's my boss. I'm his employee. We live together. Most of all." I paused, pointing to Delilah. "And she's the most important thing, regardless of how I feel."

I found a tissue and dabbed my eyes, before blowing my nose. "Callie," called Delilah, interrupting. She ran toward us, waving her hands and looking worried about something.

"What's wrong, honey?" I asked when she stopped in front of me.

"Why are you crying?" she asked, concerned.

"Oh, I'm not crying."

"Yes, you are, I saw you. Are you sad?"

I looked at her sweet face, eyebrows crinkled in worry. I did whatever any good caregiver would do and lied.

"No. I promise I'm not sad. I did have a couple of tears, but that's because Evelyn stepped on my toe with her high heel. It hurt."

"Did she say sorry?" Delilah asked.

"She sure did," I said, looking at Evelyn and giving her a wink.

"I have a happy face ice pack at home for when I get hurt. Daddy got it for me. You can borrow it for your toe if you want to."

She skipped over to the slide before I could answer her, but the sweetness of her comments made me smile.

Evelyn nudged my shoulder. "Come on. Let me buy you some frozen yogurt."

And because she was the *best* best friend, and that was what best friends did, she ran across the street and returned with a massive fro-yo sundae.

* * *

Aaron was still not home by the time I put Delilah to bed, and I couldn't help but think it was because he was still avoiding me. Uncertain what to do next, I decided to go up to the balcony, without visiting the hot tub, to clear my head.

A calm came over me once I stepped into the chilly night air. The city stretched out in front of me was illuminated. Everything from the restaurants to the streetlights glowed. Sounds of people enjoying their evening lifted to my ears, their laughter reminding me that there was a world surrounding me that was living. I moved toward the edge of the balcony, stopping to rest my hands on the tall wrought iron railing.

It was still strange to have my nights free. When I worked at Venom, I would be getting ready for work, and here I was done for the day. My off nights weeks ago were spent studying and trying to play catch-up. Now, things were gradually changing. I wondered if anything else was going to change.

The door from the stairs to the balcony opened, startling me, until Aaron stepped outside. He glanced around, not immediately seeing me.

"Aaron?" I called.

His head snapped up and looked in my direction. "Hi."

He looked confused, almost surprised to see me. "Are you okay?" I asked.

"Yeah. I..."

He moved toward me, but stopped, making sure to keep his distance. His eyes looked tired, but that didn't take away from the vibrant blue that came from them as they fixated on me. I could tell he was struggling, trying to find the words to fill the silence between us, but couldn't. It was like the other night in the bathroom. The slow dance between us kept us far enough away from doing something we both knew was so wrong, but close enough to get a glimpse of what we wanted.

"Are you okay?" I repeated.

His eyes moved to mine, and he shook his head with a slow hesitation, so subtle I wasn't sure if he was answering my question or not.

With tentative steps, he closed the distance between us.

All I could do was wait. I waited and watched his chest rise and fall with each rapid breath. I waited as his hand reached to mine, brushing the tips of his fingers against mine. And when his head moved closer and closer to me, I waited because I was so scared that if I didn't, the spell would break.

He inched closer and leaned his forehead against mine, letting out a deep sigh. "I can't," he whispered.

He squeezed my hand before dropping it and retreating to his own space. He waited only long enough for me to sadly nod, and then he walked back to the door. There was no looking back as he disappeared behind the door and down the stairs.

I stood there alone while the sounds of the living lingered around me.

No more waiting.

Chapter Ten

AARON—

I was in so much trouble.

Once I got to my room and closed the door, I stood with my back pressed against the middle before lifting my head and banging it into the door.

When I walked onto the roof, I didn't see her at first. It was her soft voice whispering my name that brought my attention to her. I turned in her direction and everything... stopped. It was clichéd as shit, but my entire being was drawn to her.

As my heart pounded, so did my dick, and with her body so connected to mine, I knew she could feel how turned on she made me. Just the light touch of her fingers against mine lit me up.

It still wasn't enough. The simplest touch drew her in close to where I wanted her to be, but it was still too far away. *She* was still too far away.

I needed more.

Maybe it was a breakthrough of my conscience telling me how wrong it all was.

Maybe it was fear. Her touch electrified my body and awoke a part of me that had been dead for so long that it scared me.

Maybe it was self-doubt, wondering if I was good enough for her.

Maybe it was guilt because I was her boss, in a position of power.

Maybe it was all of these things that snuck into my brain at the most inappropriate time, but whatever reason it was, I knew I had to stop it.

So I did.

I told her I couldn't because I *couldn't*.

I couldn't risk my daughter's heart. I couldn't risk allowing Callie in just to have her leave. She was young. I was a single dad with so much baggage. We were destined for failure, and I wouldn't take that kind of risk with Delilah involved. And that was what this was all about. It was always what it was all about.

And like the awful bastard I was, I left her standing on the roof with no explanation. I still leaned against the door, listening to see what she would do. I wouldn't have blamed her for walking out on us because she had to be so damn confused.

After several minutes, I heard the door to the stairs to the roof shut followed by another close of her bedroom door. A wave of relief came over me.

She had stayed. For now.

* * *

I awoke the next morning to the closing of the front door. I sat up, startled, immediately worried that Callie had in fact decided to leave, but once I looked at the clock, I realized that it was her scheduled time for class. With a deep sigh, I let my head fall back onto my pillow, feeling emotionally and physically drained.

"Daddy," Delilah shouted from outside my door. "I see the sun."

"Come in."

The door swung open hard, banging itself into the opposite wall. She realized what she had done, and her hand flew in front of her mouth.

She turned toward me, anticipating being scolded. "Sorry, Daddy." She looked so adorable with her bedhead and Minnie Mouse pajamas.

"It's okay, baby girl," I said. "You want to come lay with Daddy for a few minutes? We can watch *Dora*." I patted the pillow next to me.

"No. Can I go wake up Callie? She said we can go to the pet store today."

"Callie's at school this morning. Now, why don't you come sit with me?"

"No, Daddy," she whined. "I'm going to go wait for Callie to come home."

"She won't be home for a while, sweetie. We can do something."

She folded her arms across her chest and continued to pout. "Callie is funnier," she whispered.

I raised my eyebrows at her curiously. She was what this was all about, and it occurred to me that it was only fair to ask her how she felt about things.

"So, have you been having fun with Callie? You like her living with us?" I asked.

"Oh yes," she responded enthusiastically. "She likes to play Barbie and color and she painted my toes and she made me Play-Doh and she smells pretty."

I smiled while my heart ached. Even with my mom being a constant, Grandma fit into the grandma role. She couldn't fill the mom role. Callie was the first woman Delilah had known to live in this house, and even if she understood her place as the nanny, it wasn't going to take much for her attachment to grow.

She'd missed out on so much not having Lexie around, and now that Callie was here, I was messing that up, too.

"I'm glad you're having fun," I said.

"Daddy?"

"Yes, sweetie."

"Can Callie live here with us forever?" she asked.

I paused before answering. "I don't know what will happen in the future, baby girl."

"I hope she does because I think I love her," she said before skipping out of the room.

My heart.

Attachment? Already attached.

I busied myself with Delilah while Callie was gone, but tension riddled my body. While Delilah played on the iPad in the kitchen, I decided to get in a quick workout, which I hoped would release some stress. For times like this, when I couldn't get to the gym, I had a small setup in the laundry room. This way, with Delilah in the kitchen, I could keep an eye on her while I worked out.

I entered the laundry room and retrieved a workout mat that I opened and spread onto the concrete floor. After I removed my T-shirt and tossed it onto the washer, I cranked the music on my phone again before I laid out on the mat and started doing some ab crunches. I did my regular rotation of exercises from abs to weights, but with a higher intensity than I usually did.

As sweat covered my chest and dripped from my brows, I realized I was pushing myself harder than I should, but I couldn't help it. The burn in my muscles, the strain of my body, was a welcomed pain different than the one I had been carrying around in my heart since last night. I pumped and pumped, thrusting my body to the edge until my concentration was broken by a tap on my shoulder.

I spun around, and Callie was standing there. "Hey. Sorry I didn't hear you," I said.

"Hi. I'm sorry. I didn't mean to disturb you," she spoke at the same time I did.

"Just wanted to let you know I was back." She turned to leave, but I couldn't let her leave without saying something about the night before. I owed her that much.

"Callie," I said, breathless.

"Your brother's here. Quite the charmer, isn't he?" she said with a snort. No doubt he was being his usual man-hungry self the moment he met her. "He's in the living room with Delilah."

She started to walk away again, but I grabbed her arm. "Callie, please hear me out."

Her eyes moved down my arm to where my hand was holding hers. "Yes?"

I dropped my grip. "There's no excuse for what I did last night. I never should have…" I trailed off while I tried to think of the right word.

"What?" she asked.

"I never should have," I said, pausing again. Sweat rolled down the side of my face, and my breathing was all off. I was sure it was from the workout and nothing else, at least that's what I told myself.

"I don't know what came over me, but it was wrong," I said.

She nodded and looked at the ground. "It's okay."

"No, it's not okay," I said in a raised voice. "You work for me and you live here with us. I didn't mean to walk away and leave you standing there, either. I feel horrible about the whole thing. In fact, I'd understand if you didn't want to work here anymore."

Her eyes shot up and met mine straight on. While trying to decipher what she was thinking behind those green eyes, she pressed her lips together tightly. It was almost as if she wanted to tell me something, but was holding back, frightened at what her words meant.

"I don't want to leave," she whispered. "Not unless you want me to."

"No. I don't want you to leave, but I need you to understand that whatever happened, it was wrong. I'm your boss. Your job is taking care of my daughter and whatever this is"—I paused, wanting to make certain I was clear—"or was, is in the past now."

She nodded her head, but I could tell there was still something she was holding back.

"Is there something else you wanted to talk about?" I asked.

She took a deep breath, and to my surprise, after everything I said, she reached out and grazed her fingers along the side of my hand. "I knew all that. I mean, I know and I agree it should be in the past. It's just that I wish…," she struggled to say.

I went to grip her fingers, wanting to reassure her, but remembered what I'd just said. I pulled away from her touch, not because I wanted to but because I *had* to.

"What do you wish?" I asked.

Her lips parted as she pointedly stared at my naked chest covered in sweat. "I wish," she repeated.

We were interrupted by Abel's voice. "Come on, Aaron. Delilah said that she isn't allowed to have the cookie I brought her until after she eats lunch and that you're starving her."

I didn't know who moved first, but without words, we stepped back from each other knowing it was done.

It didn't matter what we wanted, either of us. We nailed down what we were to each other: boss and employee.

I wouldn't mess up again.

This time when she turned to walk away, I didn't stop her. Just as she began to exit the laundry room, my brother stopped her.

"Want a cookie, Callie? I brought plenty for all of us," Abel said.

"Thanks, but I'm not really hungry." She turned to me. "You're leaving in an hour?"

"Yeah. I'm going to shower and then head out," I said.

"Okay. I'll be in my room studying until then."

Abel and I were quiet as she left, but I knew he was thinking something by the way he was staring at me. "What?" I asked.

He raised his eyebrows. "Did I interrupt something here?"

"I was working out. I didn't know you were coming. Just surprised to see you."

I knew what he meant, but I was trying to ignore it. Abel wouldn't give up easily, though. Stubborn asshole.

"It looked like you and Callie were holding hands right before I walked in," he said.

Shit.

He must've been watching us before I pulled away from her.

"Nope. We definitely weren't," I responded.

"No judgment if something was going on."

I gave him a dirty look and rolled my eyes. "She's my nanny, asshole."

"Yeah, you've said that before, but I'm still not buying it, especially after meeting her. Damn, man."

I wasn't going to have this conversation with him again. "I'm not blind. Of course I think she's attractive. I've told you that before. I hired her not for her looks, but for her ability to take care of my daughter."

"That's cool," he said nonchalantly. "Then I assume it isn't a big deal if I ask her out."

Yes, it was a big deal. It was a big fucking deal, but again, I couldn't let him know that. I couldn't even let myself know that. If I protested in any way, he would see right through it, I knew he would. Plus, I had to stand my ground with Callie and show her I meant it when I told her there couldn't be anything between us, even if I wanted there to be.

"Why would I care who she went out with?" I responded before grabbing my shirt. "I mean, it's a little close for comfort, so be careful, but go for it."

We went into the kitchen where I made a green protein smoothie. I had to force every bit of it down because the thought of Callie and Abel going out together made me sick.

"Thanks for the cookies," I said to Abel when we were finished. "Delilah should call you Uncle Sugar considering you show up with it every time you're here."

"Huh?" He said, running his hands across his beard. "Uncle Sugar has a nice ring to it."

"Daddy?" Delilah asked.

"Yes, sweetheart."

"Can I go ask Callie if it is time for the pet store yet?"

"Why don't you wait a few more minutes until she's ready, okay?"

"That's all right," Callie said, breezing into the room. "I'm ready now. Why don't you go get your shoes on and we'll go see the puppies?"

Delilah ran off to get her shoes and the three of us stood in the kitchen.

"So, Callie when are your nights off?" Abel asked.

"I'm off on Friday and Sunday nights," she responded. "Why?"

"I was wondering if you'd like to have dinner with me Friday night."

Her eyes opened wide, surprise written across her face. "Well, I don't know…," Callie said.

She looked at me, waiting for me to say something.

I shrugged my shoulders. "Fine by me. You're free to go out with whoever you want," I said.

Her face fell, and I instantly felt like an asshole. It was the first time I saw genuine hurt in her eyes. I'd basically offered her up to my brother and implied I didn't give a shit.

She smiled brightly. "Thanks. I'd love to, Abel."

Fuck.

Chapter Eleven

CALLIE—

So, what does the brother look like?" Evelyn asked.

I was in the kitchen, making Delilah's lunch, after taking her to the pet store. A quick phone call to Evelyn was needed to fill her in on my impending date with Abel.

"I dunno. He's okay looking. Tall, dark hair, beard, and dimples."

"Oh yeah," she snorted. "Totally sounds like he's just okay."

I smeared some peanut butter on a slice of toasted whole wheat bread. "Well, you know what I mean."

"Yeah. He isn't the one you're interested in. I get it, but hell. Good looks run in that family, huh?"

"I suppose," I said.

"So what's the problem?"

I drizzled some honey on another piece of bread before putting the two slices together. I was quiet because I assumed the problem was a given. It was like she said. I was going out with the brother of my boss—the brother who I wasn't the least bit interested in of the boss who I was most definitely interested in.

In my head, it sounded even more ridiculous than I'd considered.

"Is it wrong of me?" I asked. "I feel like I'm using Abel."

"Oh please. Everyone uses everyone."

I sliced the sandwich in half and placed some banana slices on a plate. "That's a good attitude," I said sarcastically.

"It's true. I'm sorry if it's not what you want to hear but it's true. Abel is probably using you in some way. Maybe he wants to get back at his brother about something. Maybe he has some twisted fantasy about banging a nanny. Maybe they have some sibling rivalry. Who knows?"

As she talked, I had arranged the banana slices into a happy face design. Here I was, talking about things I shouldn't have been talking about, let alone even contemplate, while trying to secure my place for Nanny of the Year. If only banana slices and trying to keep my distance from Aaron were categories in the pageant.

"Delilah," I called. "Lunch."

"Talk to you later?" Evelyn asked.

"Yeah," I said. "I'll need your advice on what to wear for the date night part of the competition."

* * *

Mother Nature had opened her warm arms that afternoon, granting Chicago with one of the first warm days of spring. It made me antsy, and with all the other thoughts spinning around my head, I knew I needed to get out of the house. Delilah had asked me a few times if we could go ride the Ferris wheel at Navy Pier, and with the weather as it was, it seemed like the perfect idea after our trip to the pet store.

We had a wonderful time at Navy Pier through the late afternoon and into the evening. Besides riding the Ferris wheel, we went to the Children's Museum and had hot dogs and cotton candy.

"I like your shoes, Callie," Delilah said as we sat on a bench watching the Ferris wheel go round while we ate our cotton candy.

"Thank you." I looked down at my raggedy Toms and smiled.

"I wish I had a pair like that," she said with a mouth full of pink cotton candy.

"You have lots of pretty shoes, Delilah. In fact, I think you have more shoes than I do."

"Yeah, but not like yours. I want ones like yours. Can I?"

I looked at her with her big eyes and hair wild from the Ferris wheel. "You'll have to ask Daddy, okay?"

"He'll say yes. I want pink, like yours."

"You know, they come in all different colors. You could get whatever color you wanted," I explained.

"No!" She stood up and stomped her feet. "I want them like you. JUST LIKE YOU!"

"Okay, there is no need to yell. I told you that you'll need to ask your Daddy and then we'll see."

"He'll say yes," she said under her breath with her arms folded.

"I hope so. For now, I think it's time to go home."

She stomped her foot again, and before I could say anything, the tears started to fall. "But I don't want to go yet," she said through sniffles and tears.

"Sorry, kiddo. Let's go."

This only seemed to enrage her because she threw the rest of her cotton candy on the ground and proceeded to jump on it while screaming about new shoes.

I was ill prepared for such an outburst because I'd never seen her have such a meltdown. After trying to reason, bribe, and threaten, I realized there was little you could do to calm a four-year-old having a tantrum.

The best part of the evening, probably the entire day, was when Delilah got herself so worked up that she threw up all over herself and me right before we walked in the house.

Once inside, I got both Delilah and myself cleaned up and threw our clothes in the wash. By that time, Delilah had calmed down and was tired and clingy. I put her to bed, but she begged me to stay with her, claiming that her stomach was still hurting her.

Close to ten o'clock, I heard the front door open downstairs, signaling Aaron's return home from work. I slowly began to get up to make my exit, but once again Delilah woke up and started crying.

"Callie, please don't go," she whimpered.

"I'm still here, but you need to go to sleep," I whispered. "It's so late and you have to be all rested if we want to go to the zoo tomorrow, right?"

"But I don't feel good," she whined.

"Hey, baby girl," Aaron said from the doorway. "What's wrong?"

I stood and began picking up my things, making sure that I didn't look him in the eye. "We went to Navy Pier, and she ate something that didn't agree with her."

He walked in and sat on the edge of Delilah's bed.

"You okay?" he asked.

"I threw up, Daddy."

"You did?"

"Yeah and I got it on my shirt and Callie and in her hair."

Aaron looked at me. "You okay?" he asked.

"I'm fine," I said. I turned my attention to Delilah. "Feel better, sweetie. I'll see you in the morning."

"No, Callie," Delilah said, reaching her hand out to me. "Please stay with me."

Before I could respond, Aaron took over. "It's all right. I'll stay with you. Do you want to sleep in my bed?"

"No, Daddy," she pouted. "I want Callie."

I watched Aaron's face fall into a frown, and a twinge of pain hit my heart. While I was sure he knew Delilah wasn't showing preference to hurt his feelings, it did exactly that.

I set my things down by the door and walked back to her. "Listen, I know you want me to stay with you, but I need to go sleep in my own bed. Plus, Daddy's bed is nice and so big, right?" I leaned over and whispered in her ear. "He misses you when he's gone."

She nodded and reached for Aaron's hand. "Okay. Daddy, can I sleep with you?"

He brushed his hand across her hair. "Of course."

"Good night, Delilah," I said. "Sleep well."

I was out of her room and almost to mine when Aaron called for me. "Callie?" He stood in the hallway, a few steps from Delilah's room.

"Yes?"

"Callie, I..." He trailed off as he struggled for what to say. I was tired and didn't want to stay to watch him battle with his words or thoughts anymore today. Turning around, I took the last few steps to my room.

"Good night, Aaron," I said without looking back.

Then I closed the door.

* * *

My head pounded from the lack of sleep I got. My morning shower did little to alleviate it, but I managed to pull myself together enough to make it downstairs before Delilah was awake.

I smelled him, soap and his aftershave, before I even entered the kitchen. It was so sexy, a mixture of sandalwood and just...*man*.

Him.

I peeked in, and he was facing the sink, bringing a coffee cup to his mouth. In an attempt to further drive me crazy, he was wearing fitted navy-blue pants and a crisp, white collared shirt.

"Morning," I said, walking into the kitchen.

He glanced over his shoulder and gave me a curt nod. "Morning."

I moved next to him, opening up the cabinet to get my own coffee cup. "How's she feeling?"

"Better," he said, taking a sip from his cup before setting it in the sink. "She slept good."

"Good."

"I gotta run, but I'll be home in plenty of time for your"—he paused to roll his eyes—"date."

His eyes narrowed at me as he waited for me to respond. I wasn't going to give him the satisfaction.

I smiled. "I appreciate it. Have a good day."

He shook his head and started to leave. "You, too. Let me know if she still isn't feeling okay."

"Of course. Anything else?" I asked.

My tone was as sweet as honey, but judging by his glare, he wasn't tempted.

He briskly walked out. "No," he said, in a voice so quiet I almost didn't hear it.

Delilah and I decided to have a quiet day at home to make sure she was recuperated from the previous night. I started to get ready for my date after I gave Delilah dinner. She sat on the toilet next to me, watching me curl my hair into loose waves and apply makeup. It occurred to me that aside from her grandma, she may never have seen a woman do this before.

At her begging, I brushed just the tiniest bit of blush onto her cheeks. She was so excited she kept checking herself out in the mirror, doing little twists and turns to look at herself at all different angles.

When I heard Aaron get home, I sent Delilah down to greet him and give him the cookies I helped her make for him. I used the time she wasn't around me to get dressed. The short black dress I put on had been sitting in my closet for over a year before it made its way to Aaron's house. I almost gave it to Evelyn when I left, but I'm glad I didn't.

No bra was needed, or in this case could even be worn. It was much tighter than I'd normally wear, hugging every single inch of my body and in all the right places. The only thing holding the plunging neckline and low back up were two tiny, delicate straps. I added some heels, my highest pair of open-toed, black patent leather ones.

"Callie? Are you coming down now? I want Daddy to see you," Delilah called.

"Yes. I'm coming right now," I shouted back.

I grabbed my purse and gave myself one final look in the mirror before heading downstairs. As I reached the top stair, both Delilah and Aaron were waiting at the bottom of the stairs, and the entire situation was more awkward than a junior high dance.

Aaron stood there, mouth hanging open and seemingly unable to speak. Of course, my mind jumped to the worst-case scenario.

I look like a stuffed sausage in this outfit, right? I knew it.

"Wow," Delilah exclaimed. "Callie's pretty."

"Yes, she is," Aaron said, continuing to stare.

Relief washed over me when I realized that he didn't think I was a fat ass trying to shove myself into a too tight dress.

"Thanks," I said, descending the stairs.

Once I reached the bottom, Aaron's blanket stare was replaced with something that looked like anger. I waited for him to say something and justify his reaction, but the doorbell rang, breaking the tension.

"And she smells nice, too," I heard Delilah say as I headed down the hallway.

I didn't hear Aaron respond to her. Instead, I smoothed my hands down the front of my dress and tossed my hair over my shoulder as I reached the door. Before opening it, I took in a deep breath.

"Hi," I said, pushing the screen door open. "Come in."

Abel grinned, stopping to look me over from toe to head in a very overt way. I didn't know whether to be flattered or creeped out. After stepping inside, he took me in a hug, resting his hand a little too close to the top of my ass to make me comfortable.

"You look amazing," he whispered.

"Thanks," I said. "You, too."

He did. A navy-blue blazer was over the plaid shirt and dark denim jeans he was wearing. His hair was coiffed into a perfect pompadour and appeared to have more product in it than mine.

My head turned to see Aaron and Delilah watching us from down the hall.

"Bye, Callie." She waved. "Bye Uncle Abel."

"See ya, squirt…Aaron."

I leaned over to grab my coat that rested on a hook by the door. Abel took it from me, holding it open to put on me.

Nice touch. He definitely has moves.

"Callie, a moment before you leave please?" Aaron asked sharply.

"I don't really want to keep Abel waiting," I said.

"The kitchen," he said through clenched teeth, "now."

Heat and anxiety rose over me at his indignation. His tone and the way he commanded me, in front of Delilah no less, wasn't cool.

"Yes, sir," I said sarcastically. I turned to Abel. "Give me one second."

He nodded and stood behind as my heels tapped loudly against the marble floor of the hallway. I followed Aaron as he pounded into the kitchen, stepping to the other end.

"Do you mind telling me what you're doing wearing that?" he asked.

"First of all, don't talk to me like that in front of Delilah," I said.

"Well…it's just…okay," he stammered. "Sorry."

"Second, what do you mean about what I'm wearing?" I asked.

"What do I mean?" he asked, raising his voice. "Do you go out on all your dates looking like that?"

I placed my hands on my hips. "What are you talking about? What *exactly* do I look like?"

He ran his hands through his hair in frustration, pulling at the ends. "You look like you're a walking invitation for sex."

The wind whooshed out of me. Yes, I wanted him to get a little jealous, but now he was implying some not-so-nice things. "Are you saying I'm dressed like a slut? Is that what you're saying?"

"No, of course not. You look…nice. It's just you don't even know Abel and you're giving him quite a preview."

"Ohhhh," I said. "That's what's bothering you. Not what I'm wearing, but what I might do when I'm not here."

He bit down on the side of his lip, not willing to either confirm nor deny what I'd accused him of.

"I was under the impression that I was free to do what I wanted when I was off for the night. If that isn't the case, please say so."

"Of course, you're free to do what you want, but—"

"What do you care?" I snapped. "You made things very clear to me yesterday. Did I miss something?"

"No, you didn't miss anything, but I'd like to remind you that there is a very impressionable little girl in this house who seems to worship you. You might want to consider that when you dress and act like this around her."

Rage and tears filled my eyes. "I'll remember that. Anything else?"

"I know my brother. I'd be cautious. He goes through women like gum."

"Good. Maybe I'll finally get lucky for once."

With that, I turned on my heels and exited the kitchen. I stopped in the living room to tell Delilah good night before I continued down the hall.

I opened the front door and waited for Abel to step out to follow him. Just before I did, I glanced at the other end of the hallway. Aaron was standing there, glaring at me.

"Have fun," he shouted.

"I plan on it. Don't wait up," I yelled as I slammed the door shut.

"Damn," Abel said.

"Sorry about that. I shouldn't—"

He took my hand. "No worries," he said with a wink before walking us to his car parked in front of the house. "Let's just have a good night."

He stopped to open the passenger-side door for me, and once I was seated, he closed it. I glanced around his car, taking in how incredibly clean it was, except for the faint smell of cigarette smoke.

Once he was in the driver's seat, he started the car and turned to me. "So, I have two questions before we start out our evening. Crimson 23. Have you ever been there before?"

I nodded. "Yeah. A few times."

"You okay with going there? I think they have the best mojitos in Chicago."

"That sounds great."

"And I have one more question."

"Then there's technically three questions."

"Technically," he said, leaning over in his seat, bringing his face close to mine, and placing his hand on my knee. His face inched toward mine, slowly and calculatedly. My senses were completely overcome; the scent of his cologne, the ache in my stomach, and the vision of another man were clouding my mind.

My heart beat frantically as I came to a realization of the situation crashing down around me. I couldn't do this.

"Abel…I…"

He placed his index finger on my lips to silence me. "Shhhh," he whispered. "Please let me ask you this one question." He dipped his head down, his hot breath close to my ear.

"Callie?" he asked.

"Yes."

"Exactly how long have you been fucking my brother?"

* * *

We were sitting at Crimson 23, and after a mojito each and a plate of appetizers, I spilled my guts out all over the table. To say the night turned out the opposite than the way I'd anticipated would be an understatement.

"I still don't understand," I said. "How did you know something was going on between Aaron and me? I mean, like I told you, we aren't sleeping together, and he's made it very clear to me he isn't interested."

He sighed and leaned back in his chair, resting his hands behind his head. "Callie, I know my brother better than he knows himself, and I have never, *ever* seen him react like he did with you today."

I snorted. "React like what? A PMSing jackass?"

"No, reacting like an out of his mind with jealousy man who saw the woman who he's claimed as his own go out with another guy. And not just any man, but his brother for Christ's sake. He was so fucking incensed I'm surprised he didn't spew venom all over his pristine, marble foyer."

"How do you know this stuff?"

He picked up his glass, downing the rest of his drink. "Guy code. Those looks he was giving you and me are reserved only for extreme circumstances. Circumstances like when another guy invades your territory."

Guy code? Venom? Territory? Where did they learn this stuff? Is it a secret class they take? Perhaps there were refresher books I could find. Mental note: Check when you get home and look for books: How to Be an Asshole to Women in Ten Easy Steps, Finding Your Inner Caveman, *and* Dickheadness for Dummies.

"You know," I said. "For as much as guys claim they don't understand women, you guys are as equally screwed up. Plus, we create and carry life, so that makes us all around better."

He shook his head and then signaled to our server. "It's all a game. You know that as well as I do."

"Oh, I know. I worked behind the bar at Venom for three years. Huh. Now that you mentioned venom, I get the pun in the name. I saw mating rituals that made the primates look civilized."

"And Aaron used to be part of it," he said, with a wink. "But no shit. You worked there? I don't think I ever saw you. Man, I've met a few girls who worked there. Did you have to wear those ruffled pink things under your skirt and those hooker boots?"

"Yes, I did. By the way, I have a sense of humor so I'm not easily offended, but you might want to get a filter for that mouth of yours."

"Yeah, I know. I lost my filter around the time I lost my virginity."

"And when was that?"

"Ahh...Stephanie McCallister...," he said, drifting into his own thoughts. "I thought she was the hottest little thing, and while I didn't want to know where she learned it, she'd suck my dick with the enthusiasm of a fat kid at an ice cream eating contest."

"How sweet," I remarked sarcastically. "How old were you?"

"Fourteen."

"What? Fourteen."

He shrugged. "What can I say? Even then I was irresistible."

"I'm sure you were. Both of you, Aaron and yourself, must have been quite a handful for your parents."

He waved over our server for a second time. "Nah. We were good kids. Aaron more so than me, but I was still manageable. We are very different, though. I would chase skirts and Aaron would read about how they were made."

"I don't buy that for a second."

"What?"

"You mean to tell me Aaron never entertained a ridiculous number of women? I'm not stupid. He's very attractive, successful, and really the whole package. It doesn't take a brain surgeon to figure out he had more tail than a dog in heat at the dog park."

He took in a deep breath, crinkling his brows together as his chose his words. "The thing you have to know about Aaron is that who he was ten years ago isn't the same Aaron you see now."

"How do you mean?"

"He had it all, or at least I thought he did. He was smart, never a shortage of women, and he was on his way to a stellar career. He met Lexie and everything changed."

I looked down and twisted the white linen napkin in my lap. Aaron lived a lifetime before I even set foot inside his house. It was something I couldn't even begin to comprehend.

"Look, Callie, it's not for me to tell you all about Lexie and Aaron. What I can tell you is Aaron is the oldest thirty-one-year-old you'll ever meet. He's had virtually no life since Lexie took off because he has had to compensate for her not being around for Delilah."

His daughter and her happiness was and should've been his only concern. It wasn't screwing the nanny. He had no room for that. I wasn't sure what was happening between us except it was this connection I'd never had with anyone, ever. Even if he did feel the same way, why would he? His life didn't need the chaos. His life didn't need me.

"Don't look like that. He may have brushed you off so far, but I'm really feeling it for you two. There is something there. Besides, you're superhot. A man would have to have a malfunctioned dick with an OUT OF ORDER sign on it to pass you up."

I laughed, not only at him, but also the absurdity of the entire situation. "You're quite charming in a very sexually defective kind of way."

"Thank you," he said proudly. "And you're a spitfire. Man is Aaron going to have his hands full with you."

"I try to keep myself much more dignified in the workplace and around Aaron."

"Yeah. Me, too. Well, except for the Aaron part. But I have to keep all my inappropriateness in check as a teacher."

My lip curled in curious disgust. "You are not a teacher."

"I certainly am," he said sternly. "Just waiting for the right position to open up."

He paused and snorted to himself. I wasn't even going to

ask him why, and our perky server with the pleather skirt and bad boob job came bouncing over.

"Another round for you guys?"

"Sure thing, gorgeous," Abel said, giving her a wink.

I rolled my eyes for the thousandth time because really there was no end to Abel's quest. He knew he wasn't going to get between my legs, so he figured he'd move along to the next ones available.

"Do you, like, work at the Merc?" Abel's new friend asked.

"No. I'm a bartender."

Her eyes widened. "That's *so* cool."

He wrapped his arm around her waist. "What time do you get out of here?"

"Two. Will *you* still be here?" she asked, eyes darting to me.

"I'll see what I can do," he said.

I decided to save him the trouble. I stood up, and leaned down to kiss him on the cheek. "Thank you, Abel. Best date I've had in a long time," I said, grabbing my coat.

Chapter Twelve

AARON—

I stared at the bottle of Johnnie Walker Blue Label on the table in front of me for God knows how long before I decided to pour myself Scotch number three. The ice cubes at the bottom of the glass were slowly melting, condensation running down the side.

I took a long swig, the slow burn of alcohol coating my throat and trying to cover up my overwhelming anger for what had happened earlier in the evening.

"Fucking idiot," I muttered.

I figured that after I'd tucked Delilah in for the night, the next step would be drowning my sorrows with a few Scotches. It wasn't working.

I had no one to blame but myself. No one to blame but my stupid, play-by-the-rules self. Look at where playing safe got me. I was sitting here, alone and half in the bag, while the girl I wanted was out with my brother.

The girl I wanted. It sounded so trivial and barbaric. Like I should pound my chest and drag her back here from wherever she was because *I* wanted her. But this deep, primal attraction I had for her exceeded anything I'd ever felt before.

And it all happened so damn fast tonight.

I knew I was in trouble the moment I saw her. I'd never seen another woman look as beautiful and as sexy as she did in that moment. She was wearing a tight-fitting, short black dress that dipped down to a V right between her breasts.

When she got close enough, I noticed how amazing she smelled. It was sweet and hot all rolled into one, and judging by the way she was dressed, that was exactly the message that she was trying to send. It fucking killed me to know that all she had done, her dress, the shoes...all of it...wasn't for me, but for another guy. It wasn't just another guy, either. It was my brother.

While I always knew when she was near, tonight was different. The want and desire I had for her was amplified where the only thing I could do besides fuck her was to be mad at her. I focused on all the things that drove me wild with desire for her and threw it right back in her face. I accused and spewed ugliness at her, doing everything short of calling her a whore.

I'd stepped so far over the line with her again after I'd told her the day before that I wouldn't. I led her in every which direction, telling her one thing one moment and changing my mind the next. I kept doing it over and over again.

Overthinking, overplanning, over and over. That was all I ever did.

Why didn't I realize up until Callie walked out the door that no matter what I said or did, I couldn't shut down my feel-

ings for her? I could try to rationalize how it was inappropriate
to date an employee who lived in my house. I could even try to
accept the fact that it was totally irresponsible for me as a father to bring someone into my daughter's life who wouldn't be
anything less than a permanent figure.

Logic could be found in any explanation I had for not following my feelings, but I wanted to follow my heart.

My stupid fucking heart.

I gave up the right to lead with my heart when I became a
father. I hadn't chosen this life. It chose me.

Delilah.

It was always about her. No matter what my heart wanted,
or how I longed for Callie, it still always came back to that little girl.

What was happening to me, to Callie and me, was something out of our control and it didn't happen every day. It was
a deep, chemical, cosmic reaction that demanded I be near
her. Could I live with myself knowing a once-in-a-lifetime was
looking me right in the face and I walked away?

Here I was thinking of once-in-a-lifetimes, and hell, we
barely knew each other.

I didn't know her middle name or what her favorite color
was, but I knew what her face looked like when she laughed
deeply. I wasn't sure if she had any siblings or if she liked
the Cubs or the Sox, but I knew she had a tiny, little heart
tattoo on her hip I dreamed endlessly of tracing my tongue
around.

All of this became very clear to me as the evening went on
and the Scotch settled.

I looked down and noticed my glass was empty once again. As I began to refill it for the fourth time, my eyes focused on the clock: 1:09 a.m.

Shit.

Please don't do something that I'll regret pushing you into, Calliope.

I sat and wallowed a while as I drank my Scotch. Once my glass was empty and I was numb enough, I decided I'd had enough for the night. The fact it was getting later and later only fueled my foul mood. I had to accept the fact that maybe it was too late. That I had pushed her away for good.

The thought made my stomach churn.

After returning the bottle of Scotch to the liquor cabinet, I walked to the kitchen and set my glass in the sink. As I came out of the kitchen, I heard the front door. Relief washed over me that she was home, but anxiety was close behind. I had no idea if my words caused too much damage, and if they would be the final thing to make her leave.

From down the hall, I watched her quietly shut the door and remove her shoes. As she leaned over to pick up her shoes, her hair hung across her face, blocking me from seeing her expression. She tiptoed toward me, but with the lights out, it took her a few steps before she saw me.

She really was beautiful.

The contrast of her auburn hair and green eyes. Her dress that hugged every inch, every curve, of her body. Her cheekbones, her lips…She continued down the hall until she reached me. After pausing for a brief moment, she stepped aside to avoid me.

"Can we talk for a second?" I asked. "I need to apologize."

She stopped again, but didn't want to look at me. "Yes, you do."

"What I said was beyond wrong. I don't know what came over me."

Of course, I knew what came over me. I was going mad from being so close to this girl, wanting her so bad, that I was acting irrational.

"You know," she said, turning to face me. "This is the second time you've told me you don't know what came over you. The funny thing is I *know* what came over you, but I want to hear you say it."

She caught me off guard because I thought she really didn't know. There was no way for her to understand what was going on in my brain. While I suspected the attraction was mutual, the constant battle I had in my heart versus my mind was something I couldn't comprehend her sharing.

"I'm not sure what you want me to say," I said. "All I can say is I'm sorry."

She stepped closer to me, dropping her shoes to the floor with an echo. "Okay. You're sorry, but you still didn't answer me. I want you to say it. Tell me what came over you."

Her proximity made me edgy, pushing me into a different direction than where I'd said I'd go. I moved back, and she followed, relentless for an answer.

"I don't know what you want," I said.

I stepped back again, and again, she followed. She put her hands on my chest, physically pushing as she continued to coax the truth out of me. I wanted to tell her, to be honest, but

I knew once the words were out there, it was done. There'd be no hope.

She looked up at me and held my gaze before pushing up on her tiptoes. There wasn't going to be any backing down on her part, especially after the way she was working so fucking hard to get my eyes to hers. It was like she knew the truth was hidden behind them, and if she got close enough, she'd see everything.

Her perfume surrounded me along with the hint of whatever cocktails she'd had with Abel.

Her hands pressed against me harder. "Aaron?"

One small dip of my head and the space between us would close. She was so close.

"How was your date?" I said, almost spitting out the last word.

I didn't know why I asked. Maybe I wanted confirmation she wasn't into Abel. Maybe I wanted her to say she was into him because it would make things easier.

"You didn't want me to go out with Abel tonight, did you?" she asked.

I shook my head. It was obvious and admitting to it was one less thing I had to lie about. "No, I didn't. Now you know what was bothering me."

"Why didn't you want me going out with him?"

"Because he's my brother, and you're my employee. It seemed like—"

Her eyes dug into me, strong and constant. She still wasn't backing down. "You aren't telling me the truth. Tell me the truth, Aaron."

Her hands and words continued to push me. I wanted nothing more than to dig my hands into her hair, kiss her lips, and bring her to my bed. I wanted to lay her out, strip off her clothes, and fucking devour every inch of her body. I wanted to know what her skin tasted like and how she felt when I fucked her from behind. I wanted her, just her.

"You told me the other night you couldn't," she said. "I think you should've said shouldn't."

I shrugged because I wasn't sure it mattered. "Maybe."

"Is what we shouldn't do the reason you didn't want me to go out with Abel?"

Her hands moved from pushing on my chest to gripping the white fabric of my shirt. She was losing her patience and rightfully so. I hated it when people did that to me—keeping things hidden because they thought it might hurt. It only hurt when the truth was encased in lies.

I unclenched her hands from my shirt and placed her arms at her side. "Yes. That's the reason I didn't want you to go out with Abel."

She folded her arms across her chest, waiting for more.

"Fine. I'll say it. There's obviously something here between us, and we're both fighting it like crazy. But I can't fight it anymore," I said. I paused, taking in a deep breath. "It can't happen, Callie."

Her face softened, or maybe it fell. I couldn't tell.

"I mean, there are too many reasons and too many implications," I said. "I'm your boss for Christ's sake. You live here, with me and my daughter. So, I don't know whether it's a case of shouldn't or couldn't. It's both. I can't."

She bent to pick up her shoes and walked toward the stairs. After ascending three steps, she turned. "That's all I needed to hear."

I didn't know what I expected, but it wasn't the hurt sketched across her face or the cold tone of her voice. It was deserving. I knew that, but as I watched her leave me, I wasn't sure if I could keep my word. The screaming inside my brain to follow her, to make her understand, crushed my insides.

She put up a good fight. I'd give her that.

I wished she would've fought a little longer.

My resolve, along with my bluff, was crumbling. I knew what was right, and I knew what I wanted. I was *almost* certain she felt the same.

Even though I laid it all out for her only moments before, if she came to me now, only moments later and told me it was okay, that she wanted me the same, I'd break.

Chapter Thirteen

CALLIE—

I wanted to say something more, but he made himself clear. He could be the respected business owner, the protective father, and the righteous boss, but taking a chance on us was something he wouldn't do. In a strange way, I was glad. He vocalized all the things I couldn't, my emotions fighting against logic, the battle of want versus right.

What was right was that we'd stay away from each other. It didn't matter how he made me feel alive and connected or how I knew I'd never felt this before. I couldn't, *we* couldn't, let it overtake us. There were too many reasons not to.

I flopped facedown on top of my bed, feeling both exhausted and antsy at the same time. After rolling over to my side, I remembered I left my phone in my coat downstairs. *Shit.* I needed to text Evelyn and have her talk me down from the ledge, a ledge that included me quitting my job, moving back in, and dusting off my Venom pink bloomers.

I waited a half hour before I peeked down the hallway and

saw Aaron's bedroom door was closed. Light illuminated from the gap under his door made it a safe assumption he was in there, and I wouldn't be running into him.

With gentle steps, I hurried down the hallway and stairs until my bare feet hit the marble floor. I moved fast down the darkened hallway until I reached my coat. Before I even retrieved my phone, I heard it ringing from the front pocket. The *Friends* theme song alerted me that it was Evelyn calling.

"Hey," I said, answering.

"Finally!" she said. "I've called you like five times."

"Sorry. I forgot my phone."

I started walking back down the hallway as Evelyn shouted expletives. Just as I entered the kitchen, she paused to take a breath.

"I'm assuming you want to know how the date went?" I whispered, retrieving a glass from the cabinet.

"Obviously. And why are you whispering?"

"Everyone's sleeping, and I came downstairs to get my phone."

I turned on the faucet, filling up my glass before continuing. "The date was probably one of the best I ever had, and I have no intentions of going out with him again."

"Uh. Okay," she said. "What does that mean?"

"It means neither of us are interested because he knows full well I am only into his brother."

I took a sip of water as I leaned against the cool granite counter. Evelyn's silence meant she was processing, and any moment she would explode into either another round of cussing or a barrage of questions.

"Holy shit," she gasped. "How the fuck did he know that? Did you tell him? Oh, shit. Did Aaron tell him? What did he say? Abel not Aaron, I mean. So, was the whole date thing a setup?"

"I'll give you the condensed version now, but will fill you in completely tomorrow," I said, pausing to take another drink. "The date itself and what we discussed really doesn't matter. Aaron and I talked when I got home and things are much clearer to me now."

"Are you serious? What did he say?"

"That it didn't matter if we felt anything for each other, but that it wasn't going to happen."

"Wait. He said he felt something for you?"

"Yes. No. I don't know," I said, pushing down the lump that had formed in my throat. "Again, it doesn't matter. It can't happen. I needed him to be firm with what's at stake, and that it's bigger than us. I wish it was different. I know whatever this is doesn't happen often, and it has never happened to me."

"Oh, sweetie. I'm so sorry."

"Don't be. I'm…tired. I'll call you tomorrow, okay?"

"Okay. Love you."

"Love you, too."

I ended the call and set my phone down next to my water glass. My entire body shook from all the emotions I was processing. All I wanted to do was run home (the home I shared with Evelyn), climb into my bed, and forget about ever meeting Aaron.

"Callie?"

Startled, I spun around to see Aaron standing in the entryway of the kitchen. I placed my hand on my chest as I tried to catch my breath.

"Speak of the devil," I said. "You scared me."

"The devil, huh?" he asked, dragging his fingers through his dark hair.

There was no smile, no hint of joking. I didn't know what he was doing by coming to me again. There was no room left in me to try and figure him out.

"Did you need something?" I asked.

He shrugged. "I heard you down here and—"

"Wait," I said, stopping him. "Did you hear me on the phone?"

His large shoulders lifted as he took in a deep breath. He didn't need to say a word. He absolutely did hear. There are times when you'd think to yourself, *Wow. Things can't get much worse than this.* Then like magic, it does. This was one of the moments.

I turned back toward the sink, and after a moment, I heard him move, stepping cautiously toward me. I couldn't face him.

"I didn't mean to listen," he said. "But I need to know."

"What?"

"If what you said was true."

He came up behind me, but I still couldn't look at him. I knew if I did I would lose what little control I was holding on to.

His movements got closer.

Closer.

Closer. So close.

My body adhered to the warmth coming off of him, willing

me into submission. I knew in my mind I couldn't do that, but my body, my body was screaming something different to me.

"Calliope," he whispered into the back of my neck. "Tell me. Please."

His hands circled my waist, and I lost all resolve when he pulled me into him. His lips grazed my ear. "Tell me," he repeated.

I was almost light-headed, our bodies melting into each other, his warm mouth breathing softly on my neck. "What do you want me to tell you?"

His grip around my waist tightened, and he spun me around, our faces just inches apart. His eyes lingered over my face, settling on my mouth. He dragged his tongue over his bottom lip, the energy between us enough to make me tremble.

Before I even knew what he was doing, he shifted me away from the sink and picked me up from the waist, lifting me onto the countertop. With his eyes still fixed to mine, he placed his hands on my bare knees, spreading apart my legs.

He stepped into me while lazily dragging his hands from my knees to my hips. His movements continued up my side, increasing pressure while passing my breast and letting a thumb graze over the swell underneath it.

He still hadn't answered my question when his hands reached my neck, and he intertwined his fingers behind it.

He leaned forward. "Tell me it's okay for me to kiss you. I need you to say this is okay," he begged.

I shut my eyes tightly, knowing the only way I could refuse him would be if I didn't have to see him. "I can't. You said—"

"Look at me," he demanded.

I should've shouted at him that enough was enough, and we couldn't keep doing this dance. I should've reminded him about Delilah and how she was the most important thing in all of this. I should've told him we both knew it was wrong. I should've told him that despite the pull, the unstoppable force chipping away at our resolve, we could never be right together because the twenty-four-year-old nanny wouldn't be enough for a man like him. I couldn't ever be enough for him.

I should've said all these things.

I should've pushed past him and run out of the kitchen.

But I didn't do or say any of those things.

Instead, I did the one thing I knew I shouldn't. I opened my eyes, met his, and willed myself to stay strong.

He reached his other hand up to the side of my face, cautiously and painfully slow. "I know you feel it, too. I see it in the way you look at me, the way your entire body responds when I move close. I just heard you say the words on the phone. I'm telling you I feel it, too. I've fought it, but..." He trailed off.

I tilted my head, resting my cheek into his touch. Everything about him surrounded me, and I fought against the voice inside of me, the screaming voice that shouted this was wrong.

But there was another voice that told me that this was maybe a once-in-a-lifetime thing, that if I walked away I'd never feel this kind of intense pull to another man again. Yeah. That voice was so much louder.

"Are you sure?" I whispered. "Only if you're sure."

His expression looked almost pained, and I knew he was battling the same voices in his own mind. "I'm not sure, but I can't walk away anymore."

He was leaving it in my hands. It was all me. I knew what I *should* do, but…

I grabbed his shirt in two fists and pulled him toward me, our lips almost touching. "It's okay."

Our lips connected in a fiery passion and my body lit up *everywhere*. The answer was right there. This was what I wanted.

And it was what he wanted, too.

It was in the way he kissed me. The way his hands forced me closer to him. The sounds he made, mumbled against my lips. My entire body tingled and pulsed.

My legs wrapped around his waist, begging him to keep going and to assure him I was as sure as he was. My hands, my fingers…my entire being wanted him without any barriers. There had already been too many barriers between us, and I wanted nothing to come between us and this moment.

Except something could and I had to ask him about it. I pushed him away gently. "Delilah. What if…?"

"Don't worry," he interrupted breathlessly. "The gate is up at the top of the stairs. She won't come down."

Our lips were back on each other's in a half second, and the kisses took on a ferocious tempo, the softness of our lips mixed with the subtle bites of urgency. His tongue slid into my mouth effortlessly, and when my tongue met his, our excitement was lifted to an entirely different level. He tasted of mint and alcohol and of *him*, and I wanted to drink him in.

His hands moved to my hips where he gripped the sides of

my dress roughly and pulled me further into him. His lips left my mouth and traveled to the crook of my neck. Kissing, sucking, and running his tongue along my skin.

"Please don't stop. Please," I pleaded.

His nose ran along the side of my jaw until he reached my ear. "I'm not stopping. I won't," he whispered.

"Promise?"

His hot breath mixed with words returned to my ear. "I'm never fucking stopping again. I want you more than I've ever wanted anyone in my life."

"Me, too."

"Feel that?" He swiveled and jerked his hips into me, his erection rubbing against me. "That's how much I want you."

Instinctively, I ground myself into him harder, wanting him to feel how much I wanted *him*. As if he didn't trust what he was feeling, he pushed my skirt up further and his hand dipped between my legs.

"Jesus," he hissed.

His mouth was back on mine before I could even register his movement, kissing me deeply.

I wanted, I *needed*, more of him. Sliding my hands around his waist and under his shirt, my fingers brushed along his smooth, warm skin. I gripped the bottom of his shirt just as he broke our kiss and leaned his forehead against mine.

"Your hands on me, they feel so good," he whispered.

I gripped his shirt at the hem, causing him to pause as I lifted it over his head. The shirt was tossed to the floor, and I took in the perfection of his bare chest, running my fingers over his hard muscles.

"I want to feel you *everywhere*," I said.

He worked his mouth down my neck until he reached just below my collarbone, burning a path down my chest to in between my breasts. His fingers slipped under the small straps of my dress and eased them down with a deliberate, determined resolve, until my breasts spilled out from the top.

The tip of his tongue met the top of my erect nipple, swirling around and around until he bit down, subtly evoking the most intense mixture of pleasure and pain I'd ever felt. His hand rubbed and caressed the other breast until he switched. I could barely take how good it felt. His hands went to my waist, and while still focusing on my breasts, he starting pushing the rest of my dress up.

He stopped and brought his attention to my eyes. "I want you."

His tone was almost pleading, but it was his eyes that told me it was all desire. It was the words I'd waited to hear.

"Then take me."

I made quick work unbuttoning the top of his pants, dragging the tips of my fingers across the skin of his lower stomach. The heat between us grew stronger, his mouth getting closer to mine again.

A low, primal moan echoed from deep within his chest right before his arms reached around and he lifted me up. My legs wrapped his waist as he walked toward the stairs.

"My bed?" he asked.

"Yes."

I rested my head on his shoulder until we were in his room, and he placed me on the bed. In a fervent rush, his lips were back on mine as we both wildly removed each other's remaining clothes. I unzipped his pants and pushed them down as he slid the rest of my dress down. I watched as his eyes moved from my shoes, up my leg, and stopped at my black panties. His brows furrowed, and I could see the question written all over his face.

"I didn't do anything with him. He's not the one I want. *You* are the only one I want," I said, placing my hands on both sides of his face.

His hands cradled my face, his thumbs running softly across my cheeks. As he leaned in to kiss me, his erection pushed against me. Our tongues swirled together as I reached down and slid my hand under his boxers to take his cock in my hand, gripping from base to tip in a twisting, strong hold that had him growling into my mouth. I continued pumping him, feeling his pre-arousal at the tip and working it all the way up and down his thick shaft.

"I want you. All of you," I begged.

He leaned back and grabbed the modest strings of my panties and practically ripped them, pulling them down my legs.

I worked his boxers off, while he leaned his head against mine. "It's been a long time for me. I don't have a condom or anything."

"It's okay. I'm on the pill and have always been careful."

He nodded his head, the back of his hand brushing my cheek. "You're so fucking beautiful."

With one careful movement, he slowly eased himself into me, stopping just before he was completely in. I gripped the side of his face, begging him silently to look at me. His eyes met mine, and that was all the reassurance he needed.

He continued to push himself inside, inch by inch, until he filled me completely. My breath halted, and it took a moment for me to get used to the overwhelming sensation.

He slid himself in and out, in…and out…unhurriedly, each of our bodies welcoming the other. His hand reached down behind my left knee and lifted my leg up just far enough for him to place his hand under the bottom of my heel. The altered movement drove him deeper inside me, causing me to whimper.

"You like that?" he asked.

I nodded my head because at that moment, I was completely incapable of words.

My other leg wrapped around his waist as his tempo accelerated, our damp bodies rocking together in perfect unison. He burrowed his face in the crook of my neck to stifle his loud moans, and although I wanted to fucking scream out how good he felt, I knew we had to be conscious of our voices.

He nibbled and sucked all around my collarbone like he wanted to taste every inch of me. Such a subtle gesture, but one that pushed me that much closer to coming completely undone.

"Fuck, Calliope, you feel so good," he said through ragged breath. "And seeing my dick slide in and out of you is the hottest thing I've ever seen."

"You," I panted, "are going to make me come. Please tell me you're close."

"Are you kidding me? I was ready the minute we walked in here."

I laced my fingers through his hair and roughly brought him back to my mouth. I kissed him deeply as he moved to drive himself into me harder and faster.

"Yes," I said, gasping. "Just like that."

He kept fucking me with the same steady, hard pump, but he swiveled his hips slightly, creating an entirely new sensation.

"Oh God, yes…," I cried into his shoulder.

The moment the words left my lips, my orgasm took over my body, and I bit into his shoulder to keep from screaming. I contracted around him, encouraging him to follow suit.

His body shook against mine before he cried out in the same wave of pleasure that I'd just experienced. The warmth of him came inside me until his head rolled back in ecstasy.

The rocking of his body slowed until he lazily rested his head on my shoulder. We stayed like that, our rapidly beating hearts pressed against our naked chests, for several minutes. As soon as our breathing returned to normal, he slowly pulled his body away from mine.

"Wow," he whispered as he tucked a strand of my hair behind my ear.

"Yeah, wow."

"I'm sorry," he said trailing off, worry etched across his face.

I took his face in my hands. "What is it?" I asked.

His brows furrowed. "I'm sorry I didn't last longer. It's been so long, and you're just so beautiful, and I've been wanting you so badly, and…"

"Shh," I said, tapping a finger over his lip. "It was amazing. Actually, it was beyond amazing."

"Yeah?"

"Absolutely."

I tucked myself into his side as his arm wrapped around me, his fingers dragging lazily across my skin. We were quiet for a while as we came down from our high. My mind went in so many different directions—what did this mean? Would it happen again? Would it happen often? How long should I stay in his bed? Did he regret it?

There were so many questions, but I pushed them all away. For the moment, I was going to lay in his arms and not think.

"Shower?" he asked, breaking the silence.

"Absolutely."

He took me by the hand and walked us to his bathroom. I watched him as he turned the water on the shower, testing the temperature with his hand, before turning toward me with a devilish smile.

If I could've high-fived myself, I would've. Better yet, if there was an award for the best receiver of the fuck of their life, I'd be winning it.

"Hey, you," Aaron said, stepping into the shower. "Get that sexy ass in here before it gets cold."

I thought we were about to get down in the shower all over again since we were making out like crazy, and he was hard all over again. But when he shut off the water and stepped out, I thought maybe he was a once-a-night trick pony.

He wrapped a towel around me, and while I dried off my hair and body, he got me one of his T-shirts to put on. It was so sweet and unbelievably hot. Once ready, we climbed back into his bed.

He leaned into me, kissing me softly on the lips. It was playful at first, but the kisses grew more intense as our bodies began to grind into each other. When he pulled away just slightly, I was ready to grab him by the shirt and beg for more.

His hands crept under my shirt and circled my waist. "Hi," he said.

"Hi. Something I can help you with?"

"Perhaps. You see, I've been waiting entirely too long to do something, and now that you're lying here in my bed, I don't think it's fair of you not to let me do it." He cocked his eyebrows up.

"And what would that be?" I asked.

His fingertips, along with his right hand, delicately traveled down my side, stopped at my waist. He urged my body to the side slightly before turning his attention to my left hip.

"This," he said, rubbing his thumb over my little heart tattoo. "I've wanted my tongue all over this since that first night in the hot tub."

Without waiting for a response from me, he lowered his head and used the tip of his tongue to trace his way around the heart. I watched him lick, suck, and nibble his way around the entire tattoo, and when he was finished, I wasn't sure what was hotter—the feel of his tongue on my skin or the fact he thought to do so in the first place.

He looked up at me. "Tired?" he asked.

"Depends on why you're asking," I said, winking.

He rolled me onto my back before he followed, looking down at me. "I could be asking for several reasons."

"Is that so?"

"Mmm-hmm," he said as the corners of his mouth turned up into a smile.

"Definitely not tired even though it's been a roller coaster of a day," I said, running my hands through his hair. I twirled my fingers across the smooth, curled edges.

"Do you like roller coasters?"

"Sometimes," I said, turning my head to look at him. "It depends on the ride and how you feel when it's over."

He nodded, but concern was etched across his face. "How did you feel about this last one?" he asked hesitantly.

"It was the best I ever had. I can't wait to ride it again. Over and over again."

Chapter Fourteen

AARON—

*K*nock.

Knock knock.

Callie was snuggled next to me, warm and comfortable, when a light knocking began to rouse me from a deep sleep. Before I could register where the knocking was coming from, a little voice on the other side of the bedroom door told me.

"Daddy! Daddy! I see sun!"

My head popped up off the bed at the sound of Delilah's voice. I quickly glanced at Callie who had the same half-sleepy, but frantic look I was probably sporting.

We heard her tiny hands fumbling with the doorknob. "I'm knocking before coming in like you told me to do," she said.

"Shit," Callie mouthed to me.

There was no time to think.

She jumped from the bed and threw herself under it; the last glimpse of her legs hidden a split second before Delilah came walking in.

Delilah ran into the room. "Daddy, what's wrong with your face?" she asked.

I cleared my throat. "What do you mean, sweetie? Do I have something on my face?"

"No, but you have your scared face. It's the same one you had when I was hiding from you in the store, and you couldn't find me."

"Well…I…," I stuttered. "I'm not scared. I was surprised when you came in. I was asleep, and you surprised me."

"I surprised you? Wow."

The bedsprings squeaked as Delilah climbed up the side of the bed next to me and stood up on it.

"Sweetie, sit down. I don't want you standing on the bed."

She giggled, and the bed began to move up and down, the squeaking increasing. "Five little monkeys jumping on the bed…"

The bedsprings were bouncing up and down, and all I could think of was a half-naked Callie getting squished underneath it.

"Delilah," I shouted.

"One fell off and broke his head," she sang while she continued to bounce.

The jumping and singing continued. "Momma called the doctor, and the doctor said, 'No more monkeys jumping on the bed!'" She ended the song with a big jump and thump to the mattress, her laughter filling the room.

"I can't believe this is happening," I said under my breath.

"Why don't you go downstairs and watch *Dora*?" I said to her.

"The gate is up so I can't go downstairs."

I sighed. "Come on," I said, getting up from the bed. "I'll unlock it."

I hurried down the hallway, with Delilah following, and unlocked the gate. "Just give me a minute, okay?" I said.

"Okay," she said, hopping down the stairs.

"Shit. Shit. Shit," I whispered, running back down the hall and into my bedroom.

I knelt down next to the bed and popped my head underneath. "Are you okay? Did the jumping hurt you?" I asked.

"No, I'm fine. It's my heart I'm worried about. Ugh. Thank God you were wearing pajama bottoms." She wiggled out from under the bed. When she was free, I held out my hand to help her up.

"Your heart?" I asked.

She cleared the bed frame, and I extended my other hand, helping her to stand up. "She scared the shit out of me," she said, holding her chest.

"I'm sorry. We should have or I…," I stammered before she cut me off.

"I'm the one who should apologize. I dozed off and thought I'd be awake in time to sneak back to my room, but I didn't."

We stood silent for several moments, our hands still held together. The dust had settled around us, and my thoughts were transported to the reality of the situation.

It was all out in the open. No more tiptoeing around each other or wondering. The heaviness I'd been carrying around was lifted and with it an even more prominent awareness came to me.

Last night was the best sex of my life.

Although no words were said, I couldn't help but think, hope rather, she was thinking the same thing I was. We'd shared an incredible night together, and I had zero regrets.

And I wanted to do it again.

Repeatedly...

And often.

I smiled, recalling moments of the night before. Her body had responded to mine so instinctually, so confidently. Every touch and move I made, she matched me, pleasing me right along with my desire to fulfill her. It was like she knew me. It was like I knew her. Last night only made it much more real.

I was thinking of all the clichés. That it was fate. That it was magical. That it was all the bullshit I didn't believe in. But were there really any accidents?

"What?" Callie asked, breaking up my thoughts.

She moved from one foot to the other nervously, avoiding looking in my direction.

I tapped her chin, insisting she look at me. "I was thinking..."

"Yeah?"

"I was trying to find the right word," I said, bringing my hand up to her face. I brushed my hand across her cheek as I sensed the apprehension coming off her. "But nothing quite fits for how amazing this all feels."

A slow smile erased her concern and was replaced by a giggle and shake of her head. She patted my chest and backed away. "I'm going to go get dressed."

"Wait," I said, pulling her back to me.

I let go of her hand, and starting at her collarbone, I lightly dragged my index finger down the open skin along the V-neck of her T-shirt. I stopped above her left breast before drawing circles around her heart.

I lifted my eyes to her. "So, what was this about your heart?"

She took in a sharp breath, and I saw her body react. Her nipples hardened between the thin cotton of my T-shirt, and she squirmed as I continued to circle her heart. She wasn't the only one responding. My hardening dick did as well.

"My heart?" she replied. "It was just Delilah walking in jolted me and my heart was beating so fast."

"You know, Callie, the average heart beats over one hundred thousand times each day," I said, continuing to swirl my finger around and around. "When you're anxious or excited, the rhythm can increase," I continued.

My circling finger left her heart but continued a downward path to her breast. My hand grazed it lightly before palming it completely while my thumb ran across the nipple.

She playfully slapped my hand. "Knock that shit off."

"Why?"

"Because you're driving me crazy."

"Hmm. I can hardly see how I'm doing that. I'm simply explaining the *massive* organ in you, which *pulses* and carries blood to every area of that hot-ass body of yours."

"Is that so?" she asked. "Do you have a massive organ?"

I nodded. "I do. I'm sure you can recall."

She narrowed her eyes at me. "Wow. I remember nothing massive about your body last night."

I wrapped my free arm around her waist and pulled her into me. With one swivel of my hips, I knew she could feel my erection against her thigh. Instantly and automatically, she rubbed against me as a soft moan left her lips.

"Do you want to rethink that?" I asked.

Her faced flushed, a stunning color of pink. "I think it's coming back to me now."

"Last night," I whispered. "It was beyond amazing."

She reached up on her tiptoes and wrapped her arms around my neck. "For me, too."

I lowered my head, bringing her lips closer to mine.

"Daddyyyyy! I need youuuuuu!"

So close.

I planted a quick peck on her lips. "I guess we should get used to that, huh?"

"What do you mean?" she asked.

I walked over to my dresser and opened the top drawer. "Well, I mean Delilah. We have to get used to the interruption," I said, taking a T-shirt out.

I pulled the shirt over my head and down my chest, looking in the mirror for a second to run a hand through my hair. When I glanced back at Callie, her eyes were looking me up and down. She was blushing again, twirling a piece of her hair as she checked me out.

It was so fucking sexy.

"Are you done staring?" I asked with a chuckle.

"I wasn't."

"Save it. Yes, you were."

"I better go change. I'll see you downstairs," she said

quickly before running toward the door, pulling the back of her T-shirt down to cover her ass.

"Hey?"

She stopped and turned. "Yeah?"

"Don't you dare cover that fine ass of yours. Move your hands."

She casually released her grip on the bottom of her T-shirt, letting her arms fall to her side.

"Good. Now, I'm going to stand here and watch you walk out of *my* bedroom."

That's right, gorgeous.

She opened the door, peeking to make sure Delilah hadn't made her way back upstairs. Just before she stepped out, she looked over her shoulder back at me.

"Hot tub tonight?" she asked.

Fuck. Yes.

I decided to go with a more dignified response. "Absolutely."

Once I heard her bedroom door close, I left my room to join Delilah.

"What's up, sweetie?" I asked, leaning over the back of the couch to kiss the top of her head.

"I'm hungry," she whined. "And you were taking so long."

"I'm sorry. Do you want cereal?"

"I want Callie to make me breakfast," she said, folding her arms in front of her.

"She's still getting ready," I said, brushing my hand over her curls. "I'll get it for you. Cheerios or Life cereal?"

She swatted my hand away and mumbled. Like father, like

daughter. I wasn't always a morning person, but as I let her be and headed into the kitchen, I knew I hadn't faced a morning feeling so exhilarated in a long time.

I grabbed the coffee grounds and added them to the coffeemaker, thinking about meeting Callie in the hot tub later. There were so many things I wanted to do with her there. I'd had fantasy after fantasy about it, after the first night we shared there, and there was never a time when the fantasy ended that I believed it could really happen. I never thought she'd want me the way I wanted her.

"Fine," Delilah said, entering the kitchen. "Cheerios."

"You got it," I replied, gathering a bowl.

I got her all settled, sitting with her as she ate while showing me some of the new stickers in her sticker book. Callie had taken her to this sticker store, which had hundreds of varieties to choose from. This was something I'd never thought of doing, but Callie did. The way she was with Delilah, the bond that was growing between them, made things make sense in a way I couldn't have comprehended even a day ago.

"Morning," she said, breezing into the kitchen. "Daddy got you all set, Delilah?"

"Mmm-hmm," she said.

Callie walked past me, leaving the scent of her shampoo and body lotion in the air. I'd soaked in her smell last night, honey and orange, but fresh from her shower it was overwhelming me.

She walked to the cabinet where the coffee mugs were and stepped up on her toes to reach one down. She was still pushing a few aside to get to hers when Delilah got up and ran out of the kitchen. Perfect timing and a perfect opportunity was all I needed to reach over and grab her tight ass.

She spun around, almost dropping her coffee mug. "Stop it," she hissed and gave me a slap on the arm.

"Ow," I replied, laughing and rubbing my arm. "She ran out to go watch TV."

"I could've dropped my mug. This," she said, holding her Tinker Bell mug out to me, "is my favorite. Evelyn brought it back for me from Disney World."

"What would you rather? My hand on your ass or that mug?"

She leaned against the counter. "Let me think," she said, tapping her chin. She set her mug down and wrapped her arms around my waist. "To be honest, I'd rather shatter the mug into a million pieces and eat it off Wedgwood than never have your hands on my body again."

I had to remind myself there was a little girl in the room next to us, otherwise I would've picked Callie up and fucked her in my kitchen for driving me so completely crazy.

The doorbell rang, and with a knowing wink, I left the kitchen to get the door. Delilah skipped behind me, and when I opened the door, I knew I was in trouble.

"What are you doing here?" I asked.

Chapter Fifteen

CALLIE—

"What are you doing here?" I heard Aaron say.

"Good morning to you, too."

Abel? Why was he here?

Was he coming by to evaluate the situation between Aaron and me? Did he regret everything we talked about and was planning to come clean to his brother? Or maybe something to do with their parents? Were they okay? Stupidity and guilt sucker punched me, and I realized what an asshole I was. Everything wasn't always about me.

"Abel needs to see you." Aaron said, walking back into the kitchen.

Never mind. It's all about me.

"What's up?"

He shrugged his shoulders. "Don't know."

I picked up my coffee mug and walked into the living room where Abel was tickling Delilah on the floor, and she screamed with laughter.

"Stop," she shouted through her giggles.

"Say it. Say it, and I'll stop tickling," Abel said.

"Uncle Abel is the best uncle…ever and is more funnier than Daddy." As soon as she managed to get all the words out, he released her.

"I gotta go potty," Delilah said, running out the room.

I shook my head at him. "If she had peed on the carpet, I'd have made you clean it up."

"No way," Abel replied, standing up. "You're the nanny. You clean up all the bodily fluids."

"What do you want?"

"You left this lipstick on the table last night," he said, handing me a shiny plastic tube.

I opened the top and twisted to see the color. "Thanks, but this isn't mine."

"Is isn't? Are you sure?"

I flipped it over to look at the name on the bottom. "Oh, I'm sure," I said, putting the top back on and handing it back to him. "Floozy Fuchsia isn't really my color."

"Huh," he said, tucking it into his pocket. "My new friend must've left it after our drink."

"The server?"

"No, she was my friend later," he said winking at me.

"Jesus, Abel."

"So," he said, rocking back and forth on his heels. "How are things?"

"Fine. Everything's fine."

"Fine as in fine. Or fine as in lots of other words besides fine."

"Just knock it off and say whatever it is you're thinking."

"Well. Since you asked…"

Raised voices in the other room put a stop to our conversation, and I couldn't have been more pleased. Abel and I walked to the kitchen and stopped in the doorway to take in what was happening.

"I said no, Delilah," Aaron said firmly.

"But I want to go to Uncle Abel's and Nana-Papa's. They're more funnier than you."

Abel lived in the same building as their parents, and if Delilah was going to see one of them, she got to see all of them.

Aaron sighed. "Delilah," he warned.

"Callieeeeee," Delilah whined. "Daddy's being mean."

I'd made it a rule that when Delilah tried to get me to side with her in disagreements between her and Aaron, I wouldn't say a word. I raised my eyebrows at Aaron, letting him know I wasn't touching the topic with a ten-foot pole.

"What's the big deal?" Abel asked.

"The last time I let you spend the day with my daughter she had nightmares for a week."

Abel rolled his eyes. "That's only because she begged me to take her to Rainforest Cafe, and she got all freaked out over the talking gorilla."

"Please, Daddy," Delilah begged.

"Yeah, please, Daddy?" Abel said.

"All right," Aaron said.

"Yes!" Delilah said.

"In fact," Abel said, reaching into his pocket for his phone. "Mom asked if she could spend the night there."

"No, she didn't," Aaron said.

"Yes, she did. Call her if you want," he said, holding his phone out to him. "She knows how hard you've been working and thought you might want a night to yourself to do… who…whatever."

Aaron looked at me, and I shrugged. There was no way Abel could've been any more transparent. He might as well have been encased in plastic wrap.

Aaron stepped close to Abel and whispered in his ear. I couldn't hear what they were saying, but saw Abel nodding his head.

"Can I please have a sleepover, Daddy? Please," Delilah asked.

"Yes."

Aaron looked at me out of the corner of his eye and winked.

"I'll go get a bag ready for Delilah," I said.

"Don't worry about it," Aaron said. "My parents have two of everything of hers there. Clothes, toothbrush…you name it."

"Come on, squirt," Abel said, leaning down and throwing her over his shoulder.

"Bye, Callie," she said waving at me.

"Bye. I'll see you tomorrow."

"I'll walk you out," Aaron said, following them down the hallway.

And with that, the deal was sealed, and I could barely wrap my brain around what Delilah gone for the night meant.

Aaron and I.

Alone.

My mind ran wild. Places, situations, and positions all filtered through my consciousness and I considered how many of those we could get to in one night.

"An entire day and night to ourselves," he said, coming back down the hallway. "What should we do with all that time?"

I knew what I wanted to do, but there were things I *had* to do. As I silently contemplated, Aaron approached me, brushing his hand against my lower back.

"Is it that…hard…to figure out, Calliope," he whispered in my ear. "I could help you if you want."

My knees went weak as his lips brushed against my earlobe. "I, um, school and finals this…um, this week," I mumbled.

"Then that is what you're doing today," he said, placing a kiss on my neck. "I will busy myself with things, and you study. That's the most important."

I began to pout, but a mischievous smile from him stopped me. He was right.

"See you later?" I asked.

"I'll pick you up at nine right in this same spot," he said with a wink before walking around me toward the stairs.

"Huh?"

"I'm taking you out tonight. I'll pick you up at nine."

"We are? Where are we going?"

"Surprise," he said over his shoulder.

"Tease."

While I had a productive day (there was only so much I could get done knowing that Aaron was downstairs and I could be having sex instead of studying), I was eager to start getting ready for the evening.

I remembered working all those Saturday nights at Venom, and while it was the biggest money night of the week for me, I couldn't help but think it sucked that I was on that side of the bar. Week after week, couples came in on their Saturday date nights and ordered their cocktails. They would snuggle into one of the many love seats strategically placed around the perimeter of the enormous space. I would catch them making out in the hallways or in one of the offices. And while there were many one-night hookups that occurred there, I developed a keen eye for detecting the lovers from the one-night standers. Now it was my turn, a night out with a lover, and I was ready. I'd waited and I was ready.

As I dressed for our evening out, I settled on a formfitting sweater dress, which hit right above the knee and boots, I applied simple makeup, and let my hair lay natural down my back. While the night before my intent was to make Aaron seethe with jealousy about how I looked, tonight my intention was to make him happy.

I walked downstairs promptly at nine, and there he was. All smiles and waiting for me at the other end in the hallway.

He was dressed in charcoal twill pants and a V-neck sweater. As he greeted me with a hug, his incredible scent embraced me as well, all Ivory soap, aftershave, and him.

"You look incredible," he said.

His large, muscular arms held me tight for a moment before he leaned down and firmly pressed his lips to mine. Our bodies relaxed into each other, the comfort we were developing helping to pave the way. The tip of his tongue taunted my bottom lip while his hands began to roam across my back and settled on my ass.

Feeling restless and eager, I parted my lips to allow my tongue to slide into his mouth. The moment our tongues met, I groaned against his mouth, his hands sliding up the back of my dress.

All too soon, he pulled away. "Keep that up, and we'll never get out of here."

"Is that so wrong?" I pouted.

His hands returned to my waist while still keeping me close. "It's not wrong at all, but let's go have a cocktail, relax, and then I'll bring you back here. And tonight, we won't have to worry about being quiet."

One more quick kiss and I surrendered. The man wanted to take me out for drinks, and although I was eager to get naked, it was endearing that he would attempt to treat me like a lady with a date before bringing me home and nailing me.

And take me for drinks, he did. He took me to Wild Honey, Chicago's newest, private nightclub. It also happened to be one of *his* nightclubs. We bypassed the line, which was waiting along the side of the building, and were ushered right in.

Dimly lit and intimate, Wild Honey was nothing like Venom. No loud music and drunken frat boys. It was couples and small groups gathered around U-shaped leather upholstery. Etched glass ran the width behind the bar with the crystal drinking glasses reflecting off the candlelight.

People stood straighter, smiled, and greeted us with the upmost respect. Basically, there was a lot of kissing ass to the Boss

Man. It was a complete pleasure, one which I wasn't prepared for. He *was* the boss and everyone there knew it.

It was so damn sexy.

"Mr. Matthews," said a stunning leggy blond approaching us. "What a pleasure."

He smiled and took her hand. "Nice to see you again, Monica. And it's Aaron, remember? How are things here?"

"Very well," she said. "I think you'll be pleased when you see the numbers at our meeting next week."

"I'm sure I will."

I stood next to him, awkwardly looking around the room, realizing he couldn't introduce me. He knew he couldn't say, "Oh! This is Callie. She's my daughter's nanny and I'm banging her on the side." The connotation left so much room for interpretation that I wasn't even bothered by it.

What I was bothered by was the way Monica was throwing glances and subtle innuendo at Aaron. She was probably used to getting any guy she wanted. She was that gorgeous. Aaron continued to grin as they chatted, their conversation now only noise to me.

It wasn't insecurity. Maybe it was a little, but it was more curiosity. He worked around sophisticated, smart women every day. *He* was smart and sophisticated. I wondered what he saw in me.

"Callie?" he asked, brushing his fingers against mine. "Did you hear me?"

Monica was gone, and Aaron was looking at me confused. "I'm sorry, what?"

He smiled, a different smirk than the one he was only

moments ago giving Monica. "Ready? Are you okay?"

His eyes shifted across my face as his smile disappeared, and I knew I had to get myself in check.

"Ready and better than okay," I said.

Once we were nestled in a private corner and ordered our drinks, we settled into conversation. It was oddly comfortable considering the dynamics between us. Whether it was the dirty martini I sipped or the realization that this thing between Aaron and me had finally come to fruition, I felt something I hadn't in a long time.

Happy.

"You know," I said, taking a sip from my cocktail and placing it back down. "It blows my mind that this is yours."

He leaned against the back of the booth, his hands resting behind his head. "I like blowing your mind, Calliope," he said.

I knew we were only one drink in, but I didn't want to waste any more time. Such a short window was available to us, and I wanted, I needed, it to be only us.

If I wanted to get him out of there soon, I was going to have to pull out the big guns. Fortunately for me, I'd witnessed more mating rituals working as a bartender than a *National Geographic* photographer.

"I don't think I mentioned it," I said, placing my hand on his knee. "But you look really hot tonight."

He raised his eyebrows. "Why thank you. I'm glad you approve."

"I more than approve."

He leaned forward, and when I thought he was going to kiss

me, he tilted his head and placed the kiss on my neck, right below my ear.

"And I more than approve of what you're wearing or *not* wearing," he whispered in my ear.

Still wanting to play it cool and not let him know how turned on I was, I rubbed my hand over his leg before dragging my fingers across his pants and resting it on them.

"Speaking of *not* wearing," I said. "I may or may not be wearing underwear."

His eyes immediately widened, and he drew in a sharp breath. "I fucking knew it."

"You did, did you? How do you figure that out?"

"Earlier. When my hands were all over your ass, I thought either she's wearing a very tiny thong or nothing. I decided to go with the tiny thong theory."

"Why?"

"Because if I let myself believe I was taking you out wearing nothing under that dress, we never would have left."

And it's time to go in for the kill.

"Well, now that you know," I said, inching my hand up his thigh, "how do you *feel*?"

"How do I feel?" he repeated in a low voice.

"Mmm-hmm."

He stood up, surprising me with his abruptness. "I feel like I need to get you out of here, immediately, and go home so we can fuck our brains out."

He grabbed my hand and took off toward the front of the bar, stopping only briefly to say good-bye to his employees. We got our coats from coat check and rushed to the door. When we got outside, there was no line for the valet, and his car was quickly retrieved. We hurried in, and when Aaron pounded the gas pedal, his tires squealed as he peeled out.

His hand rested on my leg as we drove home, which wasn't far from Wild Honey. While neither of us would condone driving recklessly, I was pleased we were getting there fast.

The car had barely stopped and been put into park before we both jumped out and raced to the front door. My need for him was so overwhelming I couldn't stand not having his lips on mine another moment longer. I snaked my hands into his hair and grabbed a fistful; I yanked him forward. Our lips met, and that same intense energy I still was not used to lit my insides afire.

He broke our kiss long enough for us to step inside, but instead of walking farther in, he pushed me against the wall. He unzipped his coat and shrugged out of it, letting it fall to the floor. My coat, which I was holding, was taken from me and tossed to the ground alongside his.

Without a word, he ran his hands down my arms and stopped at my wrists. In one fluid movement, he grabbed both of them and raised them above my head as he stepped in close. He gathered both wrists in one hand and used his free hand to trace his fingers down the seam of my dress.

Both impatience and desire overpowered me, and I leaned forward to kiss him. Our mouths became perfectly in sync, our tongues meeting together with such aggression I wondered if it was the same for him. Was he feeling this? His taste, his hand curling under the bottom of my skirt, his moans…it *all* turned me on.

His lips left mine and attacked my neck, while the hand under my dress was working its way up my thigh. When one of his fingers grazed over where I was aching for him, he groaned into the area of my neck he was sucking on.

His head lifted and he whispered in my ear, "You're too fucking ready for me not to get you off right this second."

He slid his hand between my thighs and applied gentle pressure as he rocked his hand back and forth. I leaned my head back against the wall and started moving my hips along with him.

"Yes," I moaned as I tried to push myself further into his hands. Any which way I tried to move was hampered by the fact he was still holding me in place by my wrists and his other hand between my legs.

"No one is here. No one can hear you," he said while increasing his pressure and tempo. "I want you to come for me. I want to hear how good I make you feel."

My quiet whimpers were exchanged for louder noises because hell if I didn't want him to keep going and know how good he made me feel.

"That's it. Let me hear you," he said.

My impending release grew. "Yes. Just like that," I said.

"I love hearing your voice so close to coming. It's so fucking sexy."

I moaned louder and louder until I knew I was about to orgasm. "Faster, please. Faster and harder," I pleaded.

He obeyed, and the slight increase in motion was the perfect adjustment to send me over the edge. I cried out as my orgasm overtook me.

Both our movements slowed as I started to descend from Mt. Orgasm. His grip on my wrists loosened, and as I was freed, my arms fell limply to my sides.

"Mmm, thank you," I said.

My hands wrapped around his neck, and I rested my head against his chest, listening to his heart beat rapidly. We held silent and still together until he withdrew his hand from between my legs.

As I lifted my head, my arms moved from his neck to around his waist where I felt the hardness of his erection.

"Looks like you have a major situation with that massive organ of yours, huh?" I questioned.

He shrugged his shoulders. "Not too major. It'll calm down in a minute."

I slid my hands around the top of his pants, stopping short of the top button. "Or I can help it calm down. Why don't you let me take care of you now?"

"I'd love nothing more," he said, brushing a piece of hair away from face. "But I wanted this to be all about you. The sexiest thing for me is knowing that I'm pleasing you."

"You mean, you don't want me to—"

He laughed. "Of course I do, but there's time for that after we finish up one last order of business."

"And what would that be?" I asked.

"Hot tub."

The way the corners of his mouth turned up in a mischievous grin and how he had to readjust his package told me everything I needed to know.

He didn't want a hand (or blow, if asked—I was an equal

opportunity worker) job in the hallway. He wanted to get me in the hot tub, so he could fuck me there.

"Meet you there in ten minutes," I said.

After going to our respective bedrooms. I contemplated whether the bikini was even necessary, but I couldn't help but remember how he'd looked at me in it before. Plus, it was all about the show, giving him something to wonder about and eventually unwrap all on his own.

I exited my room and walked down the hall, noticing that the door to the balcony was ajar. He was already there, waiting for me. As I climbed the stairs, my assurance grew with every step. He could've had anyone he wanted with him tonight. He wanted *me*.

When I opened the door I saw him situated comfortably in the hot tub. The cold wind hit me hard, and I made a quick sprint toward him.

"We need to get you a robe," he said, extending his arm and helping me in.

I sat down opposite him and settled my body into the hot, steaming water. "I don't need a robe."

He ran his hands through his hair, brushing it away from his face with his wet fingers. "You're going to freeze your ass off running back and forth."

"It'll get warm out soon, and then I won't need it anyway."

"It's always breezy up here," he explained. He leaned down and grabbed hold of my foot, bringing it upright to him. He sat back, and as if there was any doubt that this man wasn't the living version of every woman's dream, he began massaging my foot.

"Besides," he continued, "when you get out of the water and the lake breeze hits you, a chill will run right through you."

I gave him a wink and a smile. "I think a chill is already running through me. If it isn't a chill, something is sure making me tingle all over."

I lifted my foot from his grip and stood up. His expression was confused until I stepped forward and straddled his legs, planting myself on his lap.

I took his arms and guided them around my body. "Put your hands on me."

His eyebrows raised, and a small grin began to emerge. He tried to hide it, but as I adjusted myself closer into him, there was no hiding his excitement, both in his facial expression and the hardness grazing my leg.

I pressed myself into him as his hands slid down my back and settled on my ass. His wet skin glistened against the moonlight, his face damp from the rising steam.

I wanted him to want me as bad as I wanted him. I wanted it to be agonizing, the need so deep it was almost painful. I wanted to bring him there, as close as I could, and pull away just enough to make him beg.

He lifted his head toward mine, bringing his mouth close, but I backed away. The way he looked up at me, his face so serious and honest, made me question if there was something more to this. It could've been the desperate need for closeness that I'd been missing for so long or the way his touch felt so different than anyone else before. So much chaos in my mind, but one thing screamed louder than the rest. I just needed to hear him say it.

"Whatever you want," I whispered. "I want to be whatever you want."

His finger ran down the side of my face, stopping at corner of my mouth. "You already are," he said, brushing his thumb across my lip.

His mouth crashed into mine, a groan of yearning echoing from deep in his throat. I bit down on his bottom lip and held until I released and slid my tongue into his mouth.

He moved.

I followed.

As his lips slipped away from mine, he grasped a handful of my hair and yanked my head back. In that position, he had free rein to run his tongue down the center of my chest, stopping to nibble between my breasts.

"So good," he grunted. "I've waited too long to fuck you like this."

The steam continued to rise around us, carrying away all our inhibitions, everything we'd held back up until the moment vanished into the air.

I was scared because I didn't know how long these moments would last. I didn't know if tomorrow would be the day when he said it was all a mistake. So I'd wait.

Our hands had found each other, and with our fingers intertwined, a warmth radiated across my body. It was fear and exhilaration, and it was so foreign to me that I didn't recognize it at first.

I held on tighter, gripping his skin and pulling at his hair. My mouth, my kisses following his.

We, our molded bodies, our unspoken wants, couldn't separate.

Just like he wanted.

And how I needed it to be.

His arms wrapped around me tightly, and my head rested against his shoulder—the foreign feeling came to fruition.

And with that realization, I watched my wet hair drip droplets across his chest, telling him in the only way I knew how what I'd just concluded.

I was falling in love with him.

Chapter Sixteen

AARON—

I'd been awake for a half hour, maybe more or maybe less; I didn't know for certain since the actual time was irrelevant. All I was focused on was her. Callie was in my bed, her head lying just below my heart, and her hair spread across my stomach and chest. The closeness of her, the warmth of her body on mine, and her arms wrapped around my waist was something I didn't know I'd been missing. It was the closest I felt to another person in, literally, years.

A lock of her hair lay haphazardly across her face, and while I was sure it wasn't bothering her, the need for me to touch her was so overwhelming, enough for me to tuck the loose strand behind her ear. She stirred slightly, and a soft sigh fell from her lips. I thought she was starting to wake, but after a few moments, her breathing became deep and peaceful once again.

What a crazy few days.

I laid it all out for her and devoured her in the only way I knew how. I tasted her skin and connected us, both of us reaching new heights with each pass of our tongues. I sought her out, and I discovered. It was one of the single, most intense nights of my life.

The night enveloped us, locking us away in our own world where there were no questions, no judgments, no reservations. It was just us. I sank my teeth into the pleasure of it all and relished in every moment we shared. Even now, the visions were so fresh in my mind. The way she shivered when my tongue touched her neck, the swirl she made with her hips as she rode me, her cries of orgasm, all of it better than any fantasy I'd ever imagined.

There was no greater turn-on than seeing her come for me. Nothing more arousing than to watch her get her release, knowing it was me who brought her there.

And that *fucking* white bikini.

Although I'd thought it before, she'd never looked hotter than when she was hovering over me, her skin glistening from the tub water and eagerness in her eyes. The pull between us wasn't merely superficial, there was something visceral about it. I couldn't explain it.

Something changed. This time was different. Maybe it had been so long since I *felt*.

So long since I felt the touch of intent.

Or the breath of want.

I couldn't get close enough. Even when we were fucking, I craved something that was just out of my reach. My body clung to hers because, in some basic form, I knew she was helping to mend the part of me that had become broken and dormant.

With each touch, she placed her healing hands on me and

gave my heart a little hope. I didn't know if it could be repaired or if I was capable of being the man I once was, but the more time I spent with her, the closer I got—I started to believe in everything I lost.

Or never had.

I was deep in my thoughts when I felt her move against my stomach and look up at me. Her eyes still looked tired, and she was obviously not getting enough sleep lately. I softly ran my thumb over her cheek, grazing over the darkness under her eyes.

"You should sleep longer. You look like you still need it," I said.

She smiled sleepily at me. "I'm good. In fact, I've slept better the last two nights than I have in ages."

"Is that so?"

"Mm-hmm."

"I wonder why that is."

She shrugged. "I have no idea especially considering I've been sharing the bed the last two nights with someone who snores."

I gasped. "I do not snore."

"Want to make a bet?"

"No, that's fine. I may snore, but you talk in your sleep."

Her cheeks flushed, and she knew I wasn't lying. "Well, I...," she stuttered. Her eyes looked away from me. "Did I say anything inappropriate?"

"Not at all." I laughed.

There was no need to embarrass her by telling her she repeatedly said my name in her sleep followed by a series of words and phrases so naughty they might've been illegal.

She lightly dragged her fingertips over my stomach while she stared at me with a small smile. Her eyelids lowered and followed the movements her fingers were making. Circling and swirling across my abdomen, from hip to hip. The touch was so simple, so chaste, but it turned me on hard. *Really* hard.

Her fingers tugged at the top of my boxer briefs, and while I wished she would yank them down and get to the main event, I loved watching her take her time.

She slid herself further down and eased one side of my boxer briefs down. "Mmm," she hummed softly.

I looked down at her, and her finger was tracing a small circle around the tattoo between my pelvic bone and hip.

"I didn't say anything inappropriate," she said. Her head cocked to the side as she glanced at me. "But maybe I should *do* something inappropriate."

She leaned down further, gripped both sides of my boxers, and pulled them down, my raging erection ready and willing.

The cool tip of her tongue connected with my warm skin, making me groan from the sensation. She swirled round and round my inked words as if she was soaking up each one and trying to make them her own.

Her tongue glided away from my tattoo, and she continued to lick and kiss her way across my stomach. When she reached my dick, she looked up at me, gazing at me through her eyelashes and tousled hair. She lifted her head briefly while she was still looking at me before she dipped her head down and ran her tongue along the tip of my cock.

"Calliope," I hissed.

"Tell me," she paused. She wrapped her hand around me and slid down from the tip to base. "Tell me what you like, what you want."

"Everything. Everything you do I want."

With that, her mouth took in the top of my cock, her tongue swirling around the tip as she started moving her hand up and down me. Her lips and fingers met and together they created the most spectacular suction action my dick had ever known. She rotated her hand up and down while simultaneously sucking me, her teeth grazing over my length ever so, so gently.

"So good," I said.

Her face was partially hidden behind a veil of her hair. I reached down and brushed her hair away because my cock in her mouth was something I wanted to watch.

I left my hand on the side of her face, and she continued to suck and pump me off. The building of my release intensified, and I hoped I could hold out a little longer, but Callie and my cock had other ideas.

She used her free hand to grip my balls lightly, and all at once, I felt my orgasm surge forth.

Her mouth. Her hands. Her tongue. Her smell.

Her.

I came undone.

"Callie. I'm going to come."

I smoothed my thumb and finger over her cheek, warning her that she was about to get all of me if she didn't back off.

She moaned with her lips still around me, and the added sensation, both on my cock and in my ears, proved to be too much. I came in her mouth without her ever moving an inch.

My head fell back against the pillows, my hand leaving her face, while I continued to orgasm. When I was done, I glanced at her, her head propped up on her hands, and I knew I'd be hard again for her soon.

"Thank you," I said breathless.

She pushed herself up and crawled up the side of me until she was tucked under my arm. "My pleasure."

I wrapped my arms around her and held her close, kissing the top of her head.

She snuggled in closer, emitting a soft sigh. "So nice."

"Mmmm. I wish we could stay like this all day."

"Me, too," she said, propping her head up on my chest. "But you have a little girl you need to pick up. I'm sure she has run your parents ragged by now."

"I know they love having her there, but I swear every time I pick her up my dad has grown three new gray hairs."

She giggled and settled her head down on my chest. Her arms wrapped around my waist and she squeezed me for a moment before placing a soft kiss on my chest. She threw back the covers of the bed before starting to get out.

"Where do you think you're going?" I asked as I grabbed her and pulled her back to me.

She fell back against the bed, and I looked down at her, so beautiful and real. I leaned down to kiss her, but she caught me and threw her hand over my mouth.

"No," she shouted.

"What? Why?"

"Morning breath," she said, covering her mouth.

I rolled my eyes. "You sucked my dick first thing in the morning, and you're worried about your breath?"

"And my mouth…just…you."

"Will you relax? I'm not much into the kiss-after-jizz thing, either. I don't want to make out. Just a little kiss, okay?"

She looked apprehensive, but eventually she dropped her hand and puckered her lips.

So fucking cute.

I lowered my head and gave her a quick peck. "See, that's all I wanted. Was that so bad?"

She shook her head, but I noticed her body stiffened and sensed something was askew.

"Hey, what's up?" I asked.

She shook her head again, but this time she looked down at the bed and started fumbling with the stitching on the blanket.

I reached over and took her face in both of my hands. "Tell me."

Her eyes rose to meet mine, and for the first time ever, they looked different. Gone was the confidence, the playfulness, and in its place was distance.

Panic rose up through my chest with the realization she might be reconsidering what we had going. The past few days—hell the past few weeks—had been overwhelming, and I never stopped to ask how she felt about it all.

"Tell me," I pleaded.

She took a deep breath. "This is all so…" She trailed off.

My heart sank. "Look, I know this all happened fast, and we haven't really had time to talk it all out. I'm sorry if you thought I was pushing or if it's all too much."

"No, no," she said, shaking her head. "It's not that."

"Then what?"

Her stunning green eyes tore right into me. "What I was going to say was, this is all so new to me and..."

"I totally get that. I feel..."

"Will you let me finish?" she said, raising her voice. "This is all so new to me, and sometimes I wonder what the hell I'm doing here. You can have anyone, and you're choosing me. I look at you and lose part of my head because I don't know where this is going, and I don't want it to stop."

When she seemed finished, I held still until I saw the hint of a smile.

She moved closer and placed her forehead against mine. "It's all so surprisingly wonderful," she whispered.

And with that...

I came undone all over again but in a totally different way.

I didn't know how to respond to her because I was afraid if I said anything, I would tell her in that moment I realized I was falling in love with her.

Instead I held her while our foreheads still touched. We got lost in simple silence and just being for a while. Unspoken words were said with subtle kisses on necks and hands. Such simple gestures, which were able to convey what we couldn't say or didn't want to. And for now, that was enough. It was more than enough.

I didn't know how long we stayed like that, but when I looked at the clock on my nightstand, I noticed it was no longer morning, but afternoon. While I would have stayed like that all day, I knew I had to get Delilah off my parents' hands.

"Will you come with me?" I asked her, breaking the silence.

"Where?"

"Well, into my shower first," I said, grinning. "But then to my parents' to pick up Delilah."

"I'd love to, to the first, of course, but no way I'm going to your parents."

"Why?"

"Why?" she shrieked. "How the hell do you think that would look if you and I came waltzing in together?"

I shrugged my shoulders. "I don't think it would look like anything more than the nanny and me coming to pick up my daughter."

"You don't think it would look a little odd?"

"No."

"Well, what did you do in the past? Did nannies or babysitters or other randoms go with you there?"

"Okay, first off, you aren't someone random. Furthermore, I never had a nanny or babysitter around to take to my parents."

"Oh."

"Come on," I said, tugging on her arm. "Let's go take that shower."

She followed me into the bathroom, and I went to the shower and turned the hot water on. When I turned back around, she was standing behind me pulling her tank top off over her head. She tossed it to the floor and went for her panties; she started to ease them down but looked up at me just short of showing her goods.

"Like staring much?" she asked.

"Very much so."

Once in the shower, it was so hard to keep my hands to myself, so I didn't.

She didn't seem to mind.

Once we finished up our shower and dressed, she went to her room to blow-dry her hair. I went downstairs, made some coffee and toasted some bagels. By the time she came down, I had two mugs ready to go with coffee—hers in her Tinker Bell mug—and a baggie filled with the bagels that I figured we could eat on the way to my parents'. She mumbled something about me being too much when she saw what I had ready for us and walked down the hallway for her coat.

It was a short drive to my parents' who lived in a high-rise near Navy Pier. We were quiet, drinking our coffee, eating our bagels, and probably a little distracted by our own thoughts.

Once I parked, we exited together and walked around the building to the front entrance. At one point, I grabbed for her hand with mine, which she swatted away.

"Knock it off. They could be watching," she said.

"I assure you they aren't, and even if they were, they wouldn't know it's us from how high up they are."

"As long as they don't figure out you're banging the nanny, then everything will be fine."

"Do you have to be so crude? You make it sound so dirty...so...*wrong*." I barely got the words out before I busted out laughing and she kicked my shin.

It was funny, in the context that it was, but she was thinking exactly what I was. How were my parents—hell, the world—

going to react to us? There was going to be a lot of opinions, and before it came out, we'd have to figure out how to handle it. Together.

We took the elevator up to the forty-ninth floor, and I snuck one final kiss before the doors opened. After walking down the red-carpeted hallway, we reached my parents' condo, but before I even opened the door, I heard Abel's voice bellyaching about something.

"MAAAA," Abel shouted.

"What?" Mom replied.

"This orange juice?"

"Yeah?"

"It's got too much pulp in it," he whined.

We stepped inside, and as I closed the door, I heard Mom's footsteps coming down the hallway. "What do you want me to do about it, Abel?"

"Can you strain it like you did the last time?"

"No, because your father likes that kind of orange juice."

"But I don't, and why do you buy the kind that only Dad likes?" he continued to complain.

"Because he lives here, and you don't, sweetheart."

"Don't you want me to…" Abel walked into the hallway carrying a Minute Maid carton where we were standing. A broad smile stretched across his face. "Well…well…well… look who's here."

Callie flashed him the look of death, and before I could harm him physically, Mom's head poked around the corner.

"Hello there, darling," my mom said. She approached us and gave me a warm hug while Abel started drinking from the orange juice carton, obviously no longer concerned about the pulp factor.

"Mom, this is Callie. She's the nanny I hired for Delilah."

"Of course," Mom said, taking Callie's hand in her own. "I'm Leslie Matthews. Delilah talks of nothing but you. Have you settled into Aaron's well?"

Abel started choking, and orange juice spewed out of his mouth everywhere. I made a mental note to have a little talk with him later and threaten him with any means possible to keep his comments and actions to himself.

"I have. Thank you. It's so nice to meet you," Callie responded. "You have a beautiful home."

"Thank you. Come on in."

She followed Mom toward the living room, but Abel grabbed her, mumbling about having to talk to her for a second.

I looked at Callie as he pulled her away.

She looked at me.

Mom looking at the both of us.

Shit.

Chapter Seventeen

Callie—

I was walking down the hallway to greet Mr. Matthews when Abel jumped in front of me and grabbed my arm, pulling me into the kitchen.

"Well, well, well," Abel said, leaning up against the counter.

I rolled my eyes at him. "What?"

"Remember what I told you? That I knew Aaron better than anyone else."

"Yeah."

He stepped away from the counter he was leaning against. He crossed the kitchen and stepped in close to me. "I was right, wasn't I?" he whispered. "I saw it and called it from the very beginning. And judging by how you both looked when you walked in here, I know exactly what's going on."

"You're being creepy," I said. "Besides it's really none of your business."

He stepped back. "Listen, if you want my advice. Tread carefully. He's all or nothing. He's obviously all in now, and I want it to work out for you both, but you need to be smart about it."

"I'd ask you what you meant by that, but I don't think I asked for any advice."

He opened the refrigerator and stuck his head in. "You want my help," he mumbled.

"Whatever," I replied.

He emerged from the refrigerator with an apple and took a large bite of it. "Es oh mo hal," he responded with a full mouth.

"You think you can stop eating that for a second, and for the sake of trying to be polite, swallow before you start to talk?"

He swallowed what was in his mouth and then snorted. "That's what she said," he chuckled.

I walked over and punched him on the arm. "Will you get serious?" I hissed. "Jesus. It's a wonder you can function as an adult at all."

He smiled. "That's debatable."

"That's great. Can we get back on topic?"

"Right. I realize this," he said, waving his arm around, "isn't conventional, but if it's going to work, you're going to need to tread carefully before things get too serious. I've seen Aaron really unhappy for a really long time. I think you could change that. Win-win for the both of you."

"It isn't like that. We're just having fun," I said.

"Good. Have fun. And if you need any advice on how to keep having fun, let me know. You have my number from the other night, right?"

Aaron poked his head in the kitchen. "Everything okay?" he asked.

"Yeah," I said. "Your brother needed girl advice."

"Ahh. Well, we should probably go get Delilah and be on our way," he said. "As long as Abel is done with you."

"Done," he said, winking at me.

I followed Aaron down the carpeted hallway and small set of stairs to the living room. As soon as Delilah saw Aaron, she ran into her father's arms. "Daddy!"

Cinderella was playing on the television, the room scattered with Barbies and accessories.

"Hi there," said the man I assumed to be Aaron's father. He was tall, like Aaron and Abel, but with gray hair and a round midsection. He stood from the sofa and extended his hand. "I'm Daniel Matthews," he said warmly.

I shook his hand. "Callie. Nice to meet you."

"Yes, this is my Callie!" Delilah said. "Papa, she lives with me now."

Mr. Matthews let out a deep laugh. "I know, darling." He directed his attention back to me. "I trust my son is making you comfortable."

Abel snorted loudly from the kitchen before he segued into a coughing fit.

I felt my cheeks heat up. "Oh yes, very comfortable. Thank you for asking," I said.

"Delilah, go clean up your things. We have to get going," Aaron said.

"But Papa said we were going to go to the park," Delilah pouted.

"Maybe we'll go to the park later, baby doll," Aaron responded. "But for now, I want you to pick up your Barbies so we can go home."

"I can take her to the park and drop her off later, Aaron," Mr. Matthews said.

"I appreciate it, Dad, but she's been here since yesterday. We have some things to take care of today."

Mr. Matthews nodded his head, but Delilah, in all her four-year-old glory, was not having any of it.

"I don't want to go home," she shouted while pounding her feet. "I want to go to the park."

"Delilah, I'm not going to ask you again," Aaron said in a tone that told her, and everyone else in the room, he was losing his patience. "Now, pick up your things, or we won't go to the park at all."

Delilah burst into tears and ran to me. Looking up at me with big, fat tears streaming down her face, she grabbed my hand. "Callie, tell Daddy he's being mean."

"I think you need to do what your dad said," I responded.

"But…but," she tried to say through her hysterical sobbing. "I don't want toooooo."

"Delilah Leslie Matthews! That's enough!" His voice was loud enough to make me shudder. Although there were times when he raised his voice to her, I'd never heard him shout at her so loudly.

Before anyone could say anything else, Aaron picked her up, kicking and screaming, and carried her out of the room. Abel and Mrs. Matthews heard the commotion and entered the living room from the other side, looking at us for answers. Mrs.

Matthews was stunning. She was petite, with short blond hair that was cut close around her face. Her face was nearly flawless, even with minimal makeup on, but it was her eyes that made me pause for a second. They were the exact same shade of blue Aaron and Delilah shared.

"She's just having a tantrum. She doesn't want to leave," I explained.

"Oh dear, poor thing," Mrs. Matthews said, concerned. "Maybe I should go check on them?"

Mr. Matthews shook his head. "She'll be fine. Just let Aaron handle it."

"Man, she's got a set of pipes," Abel said. "Then again, her mother has a big fucking mouth."

"Abel…," Mr. Matthews warned.

He shrugged his shoulders, but continued. "Well, she did, or I'm sure still does. It's not something likely to disappear, or cured even if she found some magical antifungal to help."

The room grew quiet, and I was suddenly feeling very uncomfortable and very out of place. I wanted to look at the others and study their expressions, but I decided that avoiding everyone else's eyes was my best bet. I stood there biting my bottom lip, feeling myself begin to perspire and silently praying for Aaron to come back in the room. Everything stayed quiet for what seemed like hours until Aaron and Delilah walked back in, hand in hand. Aaron looked stressed and tired, and Delilah, her skin blotchy from crying, was sniffling.

"Go ahead," Aaron said, nudging Delilah forward.

"Sorry," she said softly.

Aaron nodded his head. "All right, now go clean up."

She obeyed her father and returned to her Barbie belongings to pack them away while Aaron gathered the rest of her things. I was relieved when we left because while his family was extremely cordial, it was a painful experience.

Reality gave me a big slap in the face. The last few days had been a fairy tale, but what was happening now was real life. As we quietly drove home, I had a few minutes to consider what it all meant. What I concluded was...

How was I going to do this, balance sleeping with Aaron, being the nanny, and perhaps anything he expected of me in between?

Was I going to step into a girlfriend role I wasn't sure I could measure up to? His age, situation, and maturity was no match for the insecure undergrad twenty-four-year-old me.

Was I going to be expected to then step further into this ready-made family and take on a mom role? Was I ready for that?

I didn't have a clue about any of it, and I was too scared to even question Aaron about it.

Once home, Aaron sat down to watch a ball game on television and Delilah went to her room to play. Feeling overrun by emotion, I texted Evelyn.

Callie: Where are you?

Evelyn: The apartment. Why?

Callie: I'm coming over. Be there soon.

Evelyn: Are you okay?

Callie: I'll tell you everything when I get there.

I threw my phone into my purse, and walked into the living room. "Hey, I'm going to head out for a while."

"Yeah?" Aaron said. "What's up?"

"Nothing."

He laughed. "I mean, where are you going?"

"Just to Evelyn's place for a while."

"Will you be back in time for dinner? I thought maybe we'd go out."

"I don't know."

His eyes narrowed at me, carefully taking in my face. "Is something wrong?"

I shifted uncomfortably. "No. I didn't know I needed to tell you everything I did, and everywhere I was going."

I immediately regretted what I'd said. Before I could even apologize, he shook his head and returned his attention to the television.

"Of course. It's your day off, Callie," he said. "You're free to do whatever you want."

A cold chill ran through me as his flippant words hit me. I felt like such a jerk.

"Aaron—"

"See you later," he said, cutting me off and not looking at me.

I quietly left the room, and then the house, with my jackass tail between my legs.

* * *

"Holy shit! You fucked him?" Evelyn shouted.

I was sitting on the couch in my old apartment with Evelyn, a bottle of wine opened in the middle of the afternoon for the occasion. "Can you be any louder? I don't think the neighbors heard you."

"Tell me everything," Evelyn said, settling back with her wineglass.

Okay, so I didn't tell her *everything*, but I did divulge pertinent information that any good girlfriend would share with her best friend. Of course, this included how the whole sexcounter occurred, size of penis, how well he knew how to work said penis, if he visited the little lady and how his technique was, how long he lasted, and how long it took him before he could go for another round. When I'd finished recounting, we sat quiet for several moments, taking sips from our wine and waiting for one or the other to say something.

"Shit, sweetie," said Evelyn. "That's a tall order for a girl that doesn't get laid regularly. How's your little lady feeling?"

I was sure my skin was blushing, even after everything I'd told her, because my lady parts had never been happier. "I thought the G-spot was an urban myth. Turns out I was wrong."

She raised her hand, and I slapped her palm. "That's my girl."

"Seriously, though, what am I going to do?" I asked. "Am I already in over my head?"

"Who knows and really, Cal, who cares? He's obviously into you."

"But what do you think about what Abel said? That it's all or nothing with him," I asked.

She took a sip from her glass. "Aaron doesn't need to know that Abel is coaching you from the side. Plus, he's only doing that because he wants what's best for Aaron."

"But am I being deceitful?"

"I don't think so. Besides, what are you supposed to say? You can't throw Abel under the bus and tell Aaron what he said."

"I guess," I replied, shrugging my shoulders. "Who knows if it'll even make a difference. He was acting so cold when I left."

"He's acting like a dude. I swear, they always talk about how girls get so clingy once the sex starts, but I think it's the opposite. They turn all caveman and shit, like they peed on you or something to mark their territory."

"Ew," I said. "Really?"

"I don't mean actually pee on you. No, that's gross. Although, people have a fetish for anything. Maybe your handsome new lover has a few you'll find out about."

"If he wants to pee on me, I'm out of there."

She rolled her eyes. "In any case, you were bitchy to him, and now he's probably processing everything like you are."

She had good points. I just needed to wrap my brain around the whole thing. I needed to sort through all the emotions I was having, some of which I wasn't ready to share with Evelyn. What I'd thought was simply an intense physical attraction now seemed like much more, especially after the previous night. There was a shift, a very surprising one. It was overwhelming, so palpable, I had to believe he felt it, too.

"Check in with Abel and see if he went crying to him about the whole thing," she said.

"Really? I don't know."

"What?" she asked before taking a sip from her wineglass. "Abel told you it was cool for him to be your go-to. You get an objective male point of view with the added benefit of Abel knowing how Aaron is."

She had a point. I wasn't sure if it was the correct one, but I didn't think it would hurt.

I retrieved my phone from my purse in the kitchen and scrolled through my contacts to call Abel.

It took three rings before a rough-sounding Abel answered. "Hey."

"It's Callie. Are you sleeping?"

"Ah," he said clearing his throat. "No. I…hold on."

Muffled sounds of female laughter and something that sounded oddly like the slapping of skin filtered through my phone, damaging some major hearing artery.

"Okay. I'm back," he said with a chuckle. "What's up?"

"Are you seriously talking to me when you have a woman lying next to you?"

"Nah. I was just sending her on her way."

"How do you do that? I just saw you drinking orange juice out of carton while spraying apple remnants all over the kitchen an hour ago."

I sighed loudly, shaking my head. The guy was attractive, of course, but Abel's ability to keep his bed on a steady rotation of women was something to behold.

"Well, now that you're alone, I need some advice," I said.

"Lay it on me."

I explained the whole situation, my uneasiness, and Aaron's reaction.

"So what exactly are you asking me?" Abel questioned.

"Did I mess this whole thing up already? What am I going to walk back in to when I get home?"

"Oh, Jesus. Aaron is such a sensitive, feeeelingggggg asshole. You didn't mess up. He's pouting, and he'll be fine. Trust me."

"There's nothing wrong with being sensitive, Abel. You could probably learn a thing or two. And why should I trust you?"

"Because I know Aaron and he's a man. I'm also a man and I can tell you getting laid by a hot lady, who also is smart and stuff, is something we don't want to fuck up."

Words of wisdom. Abel Matthews style.

I spent the rest of the afternoon and into the evening with Evelyn, drinking wine and eating Chinese takeout. I was in a pleasant state of drunkenness when I left the apartment after midnight, leaving my car behind and taking a cab back home. Lucky for me, I wasn't technically back on the clock until seven a.m., and I'd need time to sleep off the wine and the day's events. As I entered the dark house, a wave of panic came over me, wondering what would happen when I saw Aaron. As luck would have it, the house was quiet and he was nowhere to be found.

I tiptoed up the stairs and to my room, quietly closing the

door behind me. Feeling exhausted, I slipped off my clothes and put on my most comfy pajamas. I crawled into bed, pulling the covers over me tight, and waited for sleep to come. It didn't take long before I was in a deep dream state, but woke startled when a touch grazed my face. I sat up, momentarily frightened, before I realized Aaron was standing next to my bed.

"What's going on?" I asked, confused.

He sat down next to me, returning his hand to my face and caressing my cheek lightly. Even in almost darkness, I could see that the stressed lines of his face, his visible distress from earlier, were gone. In its place were soft, pleading eyes. His hand moved from my face to my hair, smoothing it down and carefully tucking a stray piece behind my ear. The space between his eyebrows creased subtly, alerting me to the fact there was something he deeply wanted to say but didn't know how. Not that it mattered anyway.

He didn't have to say a word.

But I did.

"I'm sorry," I whispered.

He picked up my hand and brought it to his lips, kissing it softly before bringing it to his bare chest. I traced my fingers across the hard, solid lines of muscles and watched as his skin erupted into goose bumps. My eyes roamed his exquisite body, the only thing covering him was a pair of dark, cotton, boxer briefs. I continued my path up his chest until I reached his neck, intertwining my fingers behind it to pull him to me. Wanting to feel him closer, I leaned my forehead against his while his eyes grew lazy, closing slightly, as his breathing accelerated.

His hands moved to cradle my face, lifting it gently to his. "Sorry," he said, opening his eyes. He brought his lips to mine and kissed me gingerly.

I didn't ask questions. I didn't care.

In that moment, the only thing I needed was him.

I needed his eyes to tell me I wasn't imagining what I was feeling.

I needed his lips to ease the conflict between my body and mind. I needed his hands…his fingers…to touch me, to erase my doubt.

I needed his body to remind me that nothing else mattered.

It was him and me.

He gripped the back of my hair as his lips languidly moved against mine. Our bodies molded together as our lips parted and our tongues met. I whimpered faintly as I tasted him, the mixture of whiskey and peppermint. I leaned back against my pillows as Aaron followed and anchored himself above me. His leg moved up between my open legs as he lowered himself on top of me. A soft moan echoed from deep in his throat, causing me to press my body into his to be even more connected.

The dimness of the room proved to be the perfect setting for this exchange, shrouding both expression and emotion in darkness. Wanting his skin on mine, I sat up, breaking our contact, and lifted my shirt over my head, tossing it to the floor.

Confusion and greed replaced sex tonight. There were no more words exchanged so maybe it was me needing the space. I didn't know why, but I was scared.

No.

I wasn't just scared. I was petrified.

The only thing that made it better was clinging to him tighter until we both drifted off to sleep, his body spooned up behind me.

* * *

"DADDY!"

Aaron and I shot up from bed and looked at each other with half-asleep, confused faces. Knowing she was awake and was going to barge into his empty room any minute, Aaron hurried off the bed, grabbed his boxers and rushed into my bathroom. Before shutting the door, he said. "She's going to wonder where I am. Tell her I had to run out."

He closed the door, and I jumped from the bed to gather my pajamas. Once I had them on, I opened my door and saw Delilah standing outside Aaron's bedroom.

"Hey, sweetie. Your dad had to run out. He'll be right back," I said.

She skipped down the hallway to me. "Where did he go?" she asked.

Where did he go? Where did he go?

"He's not at work yet, right?" she questioned with a sad expression. "He promised, if I was a good girl the rest of the night, you'd take me to the park today since we didn't go yesterday because he was mean."

I rubbed my temples from the blinding headache that formed. It was going to be a three-hitter day: aspirin, water, and caffeine.

Caffeine. Good call.

"No, he didn't go to work yet. He went to Starbucks to get coffee," I explained.

"Is he getting me a hot chocolate?"

"I'm sure he is."

"With whipped cream?"

"Of course," I replied. "So why don't you go to your room and get dressed, and by the time you're ready, he should be almost home, okay?"

"Okay," she answered and ran from the room.

"And close your door when you get dressed, okay?"

"Okay," she shouted before I heard the slam of her bedroom door.

One door closed…the other opened. My bathroom door flew open, and Aaron rushed out looking tired and disheveled.

"Thanks," he said, approaching me.

His hand reached out and rubbed my arm. "No problem."

"I better go get dressed before she catches me."

"Sure."

"Sorry for a…crashing here…last night. I was just…you know…"

"Don't worry about it."

It was all so awkward and uncomfortable, and I couldn't wait for it to be over. The conversation was the most we'd talked to each other in twenty-four hours, and after the intense exchange the night before, I was much more comfortable leaving everything where we left it last night…in the dark.

He started to exit the room, but right before leaving, he turned around, his expression concerned.

"Callie?"

"Yes?"

"A double-shot vanilla latte, right?" he asked.

A slow smile took some of the worry out of his expression, and I was both relieved and smitten. It may not be much, but the simple act of him remembering my drink of choice was something.

"Yes," I replied with a smile of my own. "Thank you."

While he was gone, I started breakfast, letting Delilah help me make funny shapes with pancake batter. She was already sitting down, eating her pancake she proudly said was a spider, when Aaron walked back in.

He looked more awake and at ease as he handed Delilah her hot chocolate and me my latte.

"You feeling okay?" he asked, looking me over.

I rubbed my temples. "Too much wine with Evelyn last night, but I'm fine."

"Here," he said, reaching into the cabinet above the stove. He took out an aspirin bottle and, after opening it, shook out two pills and handed them to me.

He filled a glass next to the sink with water and extended it to me. "Take those and see how you feel. Do you want to go lie down for a while?"

I shook my head. "No, I'll be fine once this and the coffee kick in. By the way, I'm sorry about this. Showing up to work with a visible hangover is probably something my boss frowns upon."

He smoothed his hands over his white cotton shirt before shoving his hands into the pockets of his jeans. "Well, I think your boss has a bit of a crush on you, so he might let it slide," he said with a wink.

My stomach did a flip-flop, and I was reminded for the moment, at least in this house, he was mine.

He looked over my head to Delilah, who was occupied with her pancakes, and motioned me to the other end of the kitchen.

His hand brushed up my back as I joined him. "I feel, like, I should say something…explain…about last night," he said uncomfortably.

I shook my head. "No, you really don't have to."

I wanted to say more, but my brain made the words stop before I could let them out. I was navigating new territory, one in which I wanted to be everything he wanted me to be, but still be true to myself. I had no idea how I was going to do that. I'd been on my own for a long time and worked really hard to build a life for myself. I wasn't going to sacrifice that for anyone.

It was what my brain said. It was what I knew to be true, but things with him were too good to risk a truth with.

He leaned down, bringing his mouth close to my ear. "I missed you," he whispered. "I felt like a jerk for being such an asshole to you, and I thought I messed up."

"You didn't…mess up."

He pulled away to look me in the eye once again before whispering back in my ear. "I couldn't stop thinking about you when you were gone all day."

I pressed my lips together and processed what he said. I tried to think of an appropriate response, something between jumping on top of him, begging him to do it again, and running around the room screaming because I was so freaked out.

"I understand," was all I could manage.

"I don't know how we work this or what the rules and shit are, but I care about you and am having a good time."

"I am, too. I think we just need to take it one step—"

"Is it time to go yet, Callie?" Delilah interrupted.

"At a time," I finished.

He nodded his head at me. "We're cool, then?"

I looked into his beautiful blue eyes and saw all I needed to know. "Yeah, we're perfect."

Chapter Eighteen

AARON—

"Can we wake her up yet, Daddy?"

"Shh," I said, rushing down the hallway. "Not yet."

She was about to knock on Callie's door, waking her early even after I told her to wait until at least eight a.m.

"Why?" she shouted.

I reached and took her hand, leading her toward the stairs. "First off, don't shout."

She crossed her arms and pouted, but when I raised my eyebrows, she knew I was waiting for an apology. After mumbling an "I'm sorry" under her breath I pointed downstairs. I followed her and when we got to the bottom, I took her hand.

"Second," I said. "I told Callie to sleep in today. She's been so busy with taking care of you and finishing school a few weeks ago that I thought she needed extra sleep." It was the last Saturday in May and Callie had finished up her finals, planned and thrown Delilah's fifth birthday party, and had barely had a break since. Plus, with her nightly visits to me, she could've used the added rest.

She brushed a curl out of her face, her eyes still sleepy. "Okay. But when she wakes up then we can tell her the surprise?"

"Yes, but not—"

"What surprise?" Callie asked from the top of the stairs. Even with her hair in a messy bun on top of her head and no makeup, she still gave me an eyeful. Her short T-shirt that exposed a sliver of her midsection, and lounge pants that were sexier on her than anything else she wore just made me want her more. I recalled the night before, the way I peeled off her clothes, piece by piece, kissing and tasting my way across her body. I needed to have her; she had almost become my obsession, and I didn't see that ending anytime soon.

"Well?" she asked, crossing her arms.

It was the same pout-arm cross as Delilah had just done. Two women under my roof, and I had to answer to them both.

"We have a surprise!" Delilah said, jumping up and down. "Can I tell her, Daddy?"

I narrowed my eyes at Callie, watching as a smile overtook her morning crankiness. "How about we give her a hint and see if she can figure out?"

"Okay!"

I knelt down and whispered in her ear. When I stood again, I nodded at her to tell Callie.

"Pancake beans!" she shouted. "It's a hint, Callie!"

"Pancake beans?" Callie asked confused.

Delilah and I nodded. Technically, it wasn't exactly what I said, but it made for a more interesting reveal.

"Delilah? Do you want to go eat a banana? We aren't going to eat breakfast for at least an hour."

"Yes, please. I can do it," she said, running down the hallway.

Callie descended the stairs, shaking her head at me. "What are you up to?"

"Just...nothing." I winked and pulled her into me as soon as she stepped off the bottom stair.

She buried her face in the base of my neck, inhaling softly. "I don't like surprises," she mumbled against my skin.

"Sorry she woke you," I said, rubbing my hand across her back. "You looked so exhausted last night."

"She didn't wake me. I'm on automatic once the clock hits seven a.m."

She lifted her head and looked up at me. Her hands wrapped around my waist, her fingertips dipping below the hem of my shirt. As soon as her touch met my skin, a heat came over me. I closed the gap between us, pressing my lips to her as she softly sighed.

As we pulled away, she ran her tongue over her lips, like she was saving a bit for later.

"Pancake beans, huh?" she asked.

"Nothing fancy. I'm taking my girls out for the day."

"I'll go get ready," she said.

And just because I couldn't help myself, I slapped her perfect ass as she started walking away.

And then left coffee in her Tinker Bell mug on the vanity of her bathroom so it was ready for her when she got out of the shower.

* * *

"So, I get the pancake part of the hint now obviously," Callie said, slicing into her blueberry pancakes. Wildberry Cafe was my favorite brunch spot, and it was the perfect first stop for the day. It was always ridiculously busy, especially on the weekends, so by the time we got our food, we were all starving.

"Was the beans coffee?" she asked, tapping her coffee cup.

"Nope," Delilah said, her mouth full of pancakes and lips smeared with chocolate. "It's the Bean."

Callie brought a napkin to Delilah's face, wiping away the mess. When she was done, she placed the napkin in Delilah's lap and whispered something in her ear. Delilah nodded and went back to her pancakes. There was nothing on the surface of the interaction, but something inside me hurt. Callie had more maternal instinct than I ever saw in Lexie, but it was her genuine affection toward Delilah that made me see past the "nanny" label. It wasn't just a job to her. It was who she was.

"What are you staring at?" Callie asked.

I shook my head out of my thoughts. "I wasn't staring. I was just—"

"Staring," she said. Instead of probing further, she saved me any explanation. "This is so good. Thank you for taking us. I've never been."

"How could you live in Chicago and have never been to Wildberry?"

She shrugged, dragging her fork across the syrup that had gathered in the corner of her plate. "Well, before," she said, motioning between us. "If I wasn't still sleeping through breakfast or recovering from work the night before, then I was in class. I didn't get out for brunch much."

It was a subtle reminder of her life before she was with us. "You weren't always so busy, right?"

"Always," she said, without missing a beat. "When my dad died, I had to step up with my little sisters and help my mom. Then, I had to take care of myself on top of that."

I didn't know any of this, but really, I didn't know much about Callie.

"Your daddy's in heaven?" Delilah asked.

Callie closed her mouth and mumbled something to herself. "Sorry," she said to me. "I shouldn't have brought it up."

I reached across the table and put my hand on hers, a gesture neither of us was used to in public. "You can answer her. She gets it a little."

She held my gaze for a moment, a mixture of sadness and fear hidden behind her green eyes. Just as soon as my grip on her tightened, she pulled her hand away and shifted to Delilah.

"My daddy got hurt in a bad car accident and went to heaven. I was fourteen years old then, and I still miss him a lot. But"—she brushed her hand across Delilah's curls—"you don't need to worry about that. You have one of the best daddies ever, and he's not going anywhere."

"I'm five now since my birthday, and I still don't have a mommy," Delilah said matter-of-factly. "Like how you don't have a daddy."

"And I think we're both pretty amazing," she said. "All families are different, right?"

Callie looked at me, and I winked. She handled it perfectly. She'd never mentioned her dad before. In fact, she never mentioned much about her family at all. She knew a lot about my family already, about my history, but there were these large chunks of her life I was missing. I was going to have to make it a priority to get in there and find out more.

"You're staring again," Callie said annoyed. "Do I have something on my face?"

She wiped at her face with her napkin, but I yanked it out of her hand. "Sorry. I didn't mean to stare. I just wanted to say I'm sorry about your dad."

She took in a deep breath and blew it out in a long, staggered exhale. A pain that profound never lessened. I could see it all over her face.

"Thank you," she said. "It was a long time ago, but…thank you."

The remainder of brunch was quiet, the noise of the restaurant and Delilah's chatter filling in the gaps between us. Once finished, we moved on with the rest of our day. First, the Art Institute of Chicago and then a visit to Cloud Gate.

"Can you believe I never knew it was named Cloud Gate?" Callie said. The lake breeze blew her hair around her face as the sun warmed her cheeks to subtle pink. My eyes drifted between her and Delilah, who was running and twirling beneath the sculpture.

"No. I can't believe it," I said, laughing.

"I thought it was just the Bean, you know? I mean, that's what everyone calls it. I thought—" She paused and pointed her finger at me. "Bean. Pancake beans."

"Now you got it."

She was smiling into her reflection off the stainless steel panels of the Bean. I stepped behind her and wrapped my arms around her waist. She instantly struggled to get away, but I held her tight.

"Aaron." She squirmed. "Delilah."

I wanted to say "Who cares?" but I knew she did. We both did, but for a moment, I wanted to pretend we were just us. I pulled my cell phone from my pocket and held it up to our reflection.

"Look up there, Calliope," I said.

She backed herself in to me, tilted her head up, and matched her smile to mine as I snapped the picture. We were just another couple among hundreds there doing the same, but we were different. We only had moments, and we had to take those moments when we could. I glanced over at Delilah who was making silly faces at the Bean.

"Now, look at me," I said.

She dipped her head back, and I kissed her only briefly, but long enough for me to snap another picture. "There," I said. "I wanted documentation of kissing you at the gate to the clouds."

Her head shook as she spun around. "So full of schmoopy, you are. Delilah," she called. "Come here!"

She ran over, slipping her hand into Callie's. "What?"

Callie brushed Delilah's hair back and straightened her shirt. "Take a picture with your Daddy."

Callie started to step away, but I grabbed her hand and tugged her back. "Let's take one all together."

"Aaron." She sighed.

"Come on. It's just a picture," I said.

I didn't want to push, especially over something simple, things like photos. So I waited to gauge her reaction.

"Yes!" Delilah said. "Come on, Callie."

She smiled. "You, I can say no to," she said, pressing her finger into my chest. "You, I can't, Delilah."

The three of us squeezed together, grinned into the Bean, and I snapped another picture. Another moment saved.

"Now what?" Callie asked. "Home?"

"Nope," I said. "I thought we'd head over to Lurie Garden, walk around a bit, and then Sophie is coming to pick up Delilah for the rest of the day."

"Who's Sophie?" she asked.

"She's the other lady that watches me sometimes. Can we go get a pretzel when she gets here?" Delilah said.

Callie raised her eyebrows and smirked. "Two ladies not enough for you?" she asked.

"Actually," I said, "anything more than one is one too many for me, which is why Sophie is coming for her."

She began to fidget again, shoving her hands into her pocket and avoiding eye contact. "And what does that mean?" she asked.

"A few more surprises."

"I hate surprises, Aaron."

* * *

Once Sophie picked up Delilah, after we went to Lurie Garden, we took a stroll down Michigan Avenue to Water Tower Place. It was a beautiful day, one of those rare early summer/late spring days in Chicago where it was warm enough to go sans jacket, but cool enough to not get overheated. With her done with classes for the semester, and the first time we'd been alone in ages, I'd never seen Callie so relaxed and completely mindful of her surroundings.

I trailed behind her, an opportunity to stare at her ass and take in her excitement. She was viewing the city like a tourist, and it made me wonder so many things.

"I remember you saying in your interview you hadn't always lived here," I said. "When did you move to Chicago?"

"Ah, six years ago," she answered without turning around.

"For school?"

"Uh-huh."

"Where did you grow up, then?" I asked.

"California. Central coast. Do you think we can take one of those architectural tours of the city sometime?"

She was deflecting. Maybe. Or maybe she really was just enjoying the day and didn't want to talk about her past. Either way, I wasn't going to push it. There would be plenty of time to hear, to know, all I needed to.

We crossed Michigan Avenue and were a few blocks down

before turning to head down Rush Street. Distracted, I almost bumped into her when she abruptly stopped in front of a bar.

Her head tilted up to the sign, RETROCADE—AN OLD SCHOOL ARCADE BAR. "Are you kidding me?" she asked. She stepped up to the tinted windows and leaned in, cupping her hands over the glass to try to see inside.

"What?" I questioned.

"This is seriously awesome," she said with her face still pressed up against the glass. "I haven't been to an arcade in like, well, since I was kid."

It certainly wasn't a stop I'd planned for the day, but it couldn't hurt to make a detour. Spontaneity and unexpectedness was something I wasn't used to in a relationship, especially when I was with Lexie.

"Want to take a look?" I asked.

Her head spun around, and she nodded. "Do you mind?"

"Like I can say no to you," I said, opening the door for her.

I followed her inside, taking a moment for my eyes to adjust to the dimness in contrast to the sunny outside. It was crowded for late afternoon, the bar area filled with twentysomethings drinking draft beer and watching a NASCAR race. Callie stepped farther inside, turning around to take in her surroundings. Her face lit up from excitement and the glow of the games and neon signs.

She grabbed my hand and dragged me through a maze of games before stopping at a row of old-school ones. "They have so many," she said.

She looked back and forth between them all, and I didn't know if she was deciding on what to play or waiting to see if I was game.

If she only knew.

"Are you waiting for me to impress you with my above-average arcade game skills?" I asked. I looked over my shoulder to see if anyone was looking, and when I saw no one was, I grabbed her ass, giving it a playful squeeze. "Or we can just get out of here and get a hotel room for the rest of the afternoon."

I pressed my lips to the side of her neck and waited for her to agree that a place alone to do whatever we wanted was a better option than a large arcade with sticky floors.

She snorted and turned. "I wouldn't underestimate my Ms. Pac-Man playing abilities, Matthews. I would annihilate you."

Always keeping me on my toes.

I had to bite down on my lower lip to keep from smiling. "Is that a dare?"

She shrugged. "Call it whatever you want, but if you're game, you're going to need a whole lot of quarters, so I can wipe that grin right off your face."

This was a side of her I hadn't seen much of outside the bedroom. Of course, there were times she was dominant there, but outside? Not so much. It was both a turn-on and, well, a massive turn-on.

"Keep smiling, pretty boy," she said. "I'm going to wreck you."

I leaned up against the machine and folded my arms. "You're pretty confident, huh?"

"Yes. And you're not. I can tell you, I'm *very* confident."

"Okay. How about a friendly bet, then?"

"Name it."

I ran through a list of possible wagers, most of them deviant in a sexual nature. It must have been written all over my face because she called me right out on it.

"And before you even go there, no. The answer is no," she said.

"You don't even know what I was going to say."

"Yes, I do. You were either going to propose breaking the World Record for the amount of blow jobs in twenty-four hours or, well, butt sex, of course."

I let out an incredulous gasp in an attempt to fake my way out of her spot-on prediction. In my defense, I hadn't thought about the twenty-four-hour blow job.

"That is ridiculous," I said. "Despite what you think, I am able to think of other things involving you that don't include sex. Frankly, I'm offended, Calliope."

"See," she said, pointing at me. "I know you're lying because you only call me Calliope when you're trying to butter me up or get in my pants. And for the record, I'm an exit-only girl, so you can just get any kind of bum fun out your mind."

She had me again. Shit.

"In an attempt to save what little is left of my dignity, I'm going to get quarters and then we'll get down to business. Want a beer?"

"Yes, please," she said, smiling. She hopped up on the stool next to Ms. Pac-Man to await my return…

And have me embarrass her.

But it was Callie who embarrassed me. Badly and by over

one hundred thousand points. In fact, if there was a term for utter obliteration with a side of eating crow, it would be referred to as me.

"Well done," I pouted while draining my beer.

"Thank you," she said, wrapping her arms around my waist. "And now I know what to bet on."

"You can't make a bet after you've already won," I said. "Besides, isn't my humiliation enough for you?"

"Aww. Poor baby," she said, playfully tapping my cheek and giving me a quick kiss. "Actually, I think the win for me can be mutually...beneficial...for the both of us."

My internal antennae became alerted. "What did you have in mind?"

She took my hand and led me out of the bar, the sky slowly losing the sun to night. We walked, with our hands to ourselves, a few blocks until we reached Red, a small, romantic Italian restaurant hot spot. She paused in front of the door and jerked her head toward the entrance.

I looked down at the front of my jeans. "Not really dressed for a nice dinner. Plus, you had me waiting so long while you played, I ate a slice of pizza because I got hungry."

Her laugh came out loud. "I had no idea," she said. "And I don't want to go in for dinner. Just want to pick up something that's a favorite of mine from here."

Intrigued, I followed her inside and up to the crowded wait stand.

"Can we get one slice of tiramisu to go, please?" Callie asked the hostess. She side-eyed me and winked. "And one spoon. If that's okay with you, Aaron?"

My plan was to take her to dinner and a movie, but the arcade messed up my plans. Retrospect? It was the best thing that could've happened. We were able to step outside the box, and because of that, we both were able to see a different side of each other.

"There's nothing wrong with a little sugar from time to time, Calliope."

Chapter Nineteen

CALLIE—

The early morning sun had begun to peek through the curtains and reminded me it was time to return to my room. It was my morning ritual, and although it was day after day, I never minded. I'd look to my right, and there, lying next to me, would be the most beautiful man I'd ever known.

One day. One night. They all rolled into the next with a delicious blend of passion, delight, and excitement.

One week into the next. The month turning into the following. It'd been almost four months since I moved in and became the nanny. It was the most exhilarating four months of my life.

I leaned over and gave him a kiss on the cheek before sneaking out of bed and his room. Tiptoeing down the hallway to not wake Delilah, I entered my room and closed the door quietly. I crawled into my bed, and while it usually didn't take me long to fall back asleep, I struggled for an hour to find sleep. When I finally realized at six a.m. it wasn't going to happen, I decided to shower and get ready for the day. I rose from the bed and headed to the bathroom, turning the shower water on to get it nice and hot. Steam began surrounding me, and once I stripped naked, I stepped under the heated water.

The warmth poured over me, washing away the night and relaxing my stiff body. It wasn't as if I wasn't comfortable sleeping in Aaron's bed, I was, but it was the constant turning over of thoughts in my mind that kept me from a peaceful night's sleep.

I couldn't remember a time when I felt so many different areas of my life coming together so perfectly. I was about to be in the home stretch with school, starting my last year in the fall. Plus, with the money I was making working for Aaron and not having to pay rent, I was able to start making a dent in my student loans, which was a huge relief. I adored Delilah and was lucky I was getting paid to spend time with such an amazing little girl. It didn't escape me how attached she'd become to me, but considering she'd never had a permanent female figure around, besides her grandmother Leslie, I embraced it.

And then there was Aaron.

There was no way I could articulate what had transpired between us during the last several months. What started off as purely physical attraction had turned into something much more. We trapped the words we wanted to say deep inside, allowing physical touch to convey our emotions and desires. With every kiss, every caress, I let him into my heart more and more, and although I didn't know for certain, I sensed he was feeling the same thing. Something happened to us. We didn't need to identify it and dress it up in fancy words or discussions; it was just there. I didn't need to ask him because I knew in his actions, his touch, that he felt it, too.

Every day, I felt it more and more. I was completely in love with him. He was filling a part of my heart that, until I met him, had been left untouched and ignored.

I'd been so lost in my thoughts, I hadn't noticed how long I'd been in the shower. I stepped out, dried off my body, and wrapped a towel around my head. When I opened the bathroom door I almost screamed when I saw I had a visitor sitting on my bed.

"Hi there," Aaron said with a sexy smile.

"Shit," I responded, holding my heart. "You scared the hell out of me."

"I'm sorry." He stood up from the bed, freshly showered as well.

I took the towel off my head and wrapped it around my body. "What are you doing in here?"

He stepped in close to me, putting his arms around my waist. "Why did you cover yourself? Didn't we talk about this before?"

"I asked you a question first."

"I couldn't sleep after you left, so I got up and showered. Thought I'd get a head start at work and stopped to say goodbye."

"What about…," I started to say.

His head dipped down and he placed a kiss on my neck. "Delilah's still asleep." His grip on me tightened as his nose ran across the skin below my ear. "Now, I want you to answer me," he whispered. "Why did you cover yourself?"

"I…mmm…you smell nice," I said, taking in his scent, Ivory soap and mint and…just Aaron.

"As do you," he responded, nibbling on my neck. "Are you avoiding answering my question, Calliope?"

I hated anyone else calling me Calliope, but him…he did this thing where my name rolled off his tongue like liquid. He knew it drove me crazy, and at that moment, I was happy for the fact that I wasn't wearing any underwear, since I would have to change them immediately.

"I…um…was just…feeling…oh God, that feels good… um…a little…exposed," I struggled to respond.

"Exposed, huh?" he said, pulling away from my neck to look at me. "I happen to like you exposed."

His hands ran from my waist down, settling on my ass and palming it firmly. He began slowly rocking our bodies while shifting his stance, moving back slightly before pushing his leg between my legs, separating them. I felt him hard, against my upper thigh, through the thin fabric of his khaki pants, and I had to bite down on my lower lip to stifle a whimper. I never, ever stopped wanting him.

"What are you doing?" I asked.

His hand gripped the front of my towel and playfully tugged at it. "Trying to expose you, of course."

He brought his mouth to mine, and our lips connected and worked together naturally. Not wanting to get too worked up, I started to pull back just as he trailed his tongue along my bottom lip.

"Look at you putting on all the moves," I giggled as his mouth returned to my neck.

He smiled against my neck before his tongue darted out to flick and suck on my earlobe. "Think I'll get lucky?"

"We can't...Delilah..."

"Is sleeping for at least another half hour and your door is locked."

I lowered my hand to the top of his pants, unbuttoning with one hand as I placed the other over his, which was tugging at the top of my towel. I observed his massive bulge and worked quickly until the button and zipper were undone; I loosened the pants and slipped my hand down the inside of his boxers, my fingers meeting his immense erection. My hand moved down his smooth length, and my fingertips stopped to circle the tip. His eyes closed as he pushed himself into my hand further; a low groan fell from his lips.

"Are you sure the door is locked?" I asked.

He nodded.

I used my free hand to push his pants down over his hips, and he lowered them the rest of the way himself. I momentarily removed my grip on him and took a couple of steps back where he could have a full view of me. As I lifted my hands to unwrap my towel, his eyes followed, watching as I removed what covered me and let it drop to the floor.

"Perfect," he said, closing the distance between us.

Heat warmed my cheeks, not from embarrassment, but from delight. It wasn't only from his words alone, or the way he looked so deeply into my eyes, but from his entire self. There was such conviction in his voice and in his actions that

I had no choice but to believe him. He *made* me feel beautiful and that alone allowed me to adore him more than any man I'd ever known.

With my eyes still on his, I sunk to my knees in front of him and took him in my mouth. He groaned deeply and began moving his hips back and forth, as I aggressively, yet gingerly, licked and sucked him. I wanted him to feel good...to feel pleasure...from no one else but me. His hands intertwined in my hair and helped to guide me to the rhythm of his choice, and I followed his cue, wanting to give him all that he desired. I wanted to...I would...give him anything he wanted.

He came in my mouth, powerfully and warm. Once his movements halted, I finished him off, leaving him fully satiated. So much so, that when I sent him out the front door twenty minutes later, he was grinning like a virgin after his first lay.

Once Delilah got up, we had breakfast together, and she watched cartoons while I cleaned up a bit. It was a hot August day, so I dragged the little, turtle-shaped kiddie pool out and brought it onto the balcony. After I had filled it with water, I let the Chicago sun heat it up, and after a bit, brought Delilah out to play in the pool. She splashed around while I lay on a long lawn chair, soaking up the sun and relaxing. The new semester was starting in a couple weeks, and splitting my time between Delilah, school, my friends, and Aaron was going to be difficult once again.

I was lost in thoughts and sunshine when my cell phone began ringing on the small table next to me. I picked it up and saw DUMBASS on the caller ID, alerting that it was Abel calling. I briefly thought about answering it, but I never liked to talk to him when Delilah was close by so I let it go to voice mail. Little ears pick up the smallest things, and the last thing I needed was for her to blurt out something to Aaron she had heard when I was on the phone with Abel.

It didn't strike me as unusual, at the time, that Abel was calling me since we talked off and on. He was still my go-to guy for all purposes related to Aaron. He talked me through a few freak-out moments, keeping me calm and explaining the best way to handle the situation.

It wasn't malicious in intent, nor were we trying to hurt Aaron. It was very much the opposite. Abel understood him, his past and his struggles, in a very private way. I wasn't at a place to know those things he kept hidden from me. Logically, I knew it was wrong, but the peace of mind it gave me canceled out the wrong I felt.

Soon after, I got Delilah out of the pool, and once we changed, we headed down the street to Manny's for Italian ice. Even though it was a hot day, the wind off the lake gave a brief reprieve from the heat, so once I got an Italian ice for myself and for Delilah, we sat outside. She busied herself with a color book while I took the time to text Abel back instead of calling.

Me: What's up?

Abel: Hey. Need to give you a heads-up. Mom and Dad know about you and Aaron. I guess someone they know saw you guys out playing video games or something and asked

about his new girlfriend. I dunno how they know it was you, but
they do.

Shit. Okay. So we were hesitant to tell them because of the
negative connotation associated with a nanny and boss relationship. It never came across well, even if both parties were single.

Me: Does Aaron know this yet?

Abel: Yeah. Dad told me they talked. Are you freaking out?

Not exactly.
But I wasn't exactly not, either.

Me: I don't know, but thanks for telling me.

I didn't know if I should reach out to Aaron now or wait for
him to come to me. I quickly realized then that I would have
to admit to Abel telling me first and I wasn't sure how well that
would go over.

Land mines were all over at this point, and one misstep
would blow everything up in my face. Things were already
complicated. I fought every day to find the balance between
being Aaron's girlfriend, his lover, and the nanny, but still try
to not intrude since I'm not *actually* part of the family...even
though it sometimes felt like I was. When we were alone,
things were near perfect with us. It was outside of the bedroom, away from when we were just *us* that my anxiety crept
in about being enough for him.

I'd wait for him to come to me.

We finished our Italian ice and I occupied myself the best I could back home with getting Delilah set up with a viewing of *Finding Nemo*, all the while waiting for a phone call. I looked at the time compulsively, telling myself that I would hear from him soon, but as the sky began to darken and still no call, my nerves began to take a front seat to being rational.

I got Delilah to bed and proceeded to aimlessly walk around the house, unable to stay still for more than a moment or two. There were some dirty dishes left over from the day, so in order to continue to keep my mind busy, I slipped on my yellow kitchen gloves and got to washing. I could have loaded them in the dishwasher, but I needed to do something, anything, besides pacing.

"Callie?"

I spun around, and there he was, worry written across his face.

"Are you okay?" I asked.

"I'm fine," he said, tossing his keys on the counter. He stared at them, avoiding looking at me. "How are you?"

"All right," I said softly.

"You don't have to pretend not to know. Abel told me he talked to you," he said.

"I wasn't going to pretend, or I don't know, maybe I was, but I wanted you to discuss it when you were ready."

He waved his hand around. "It doesn't matter. My parents know. They have concerns, but I'm sure once they see us together, they'll get over it."

I shrugged my shoulders, unable to find words, but eventually nodding.

"Callie," he began, taking a deep breath in. "We've been living in this…fucking fantasy world for too long. The tiptoeing around and pretending we'd be invisible. I should have stopped all this sneaking around, all the lying to my family and daughter, a long time ago. It would've never been as salacious as it's been perceived, or reason for concern on their part, if we were honest from the start."

He walked toward me, watching me intently. "Of course, the right thing to do is for us to quit giving a shit what other people think, and be together, completely together, in and out of this house."

I stared at him. "What?"

He walked closer, a slow, steady smile coming across his face with each step he took. Once he reached me, he took one of my hands in his and pulled me close to him. Desperate to feel him close, I wrapped my arms around his waist and laid my head on his chest.

"Did you think I was going to let this ruin us? That I'd give a shit what my parents, or anyone for that matter, thought about us?" he whispered.

"I don't know what I thought."

His hand was smoothing my hair before his fingertips drifted downward and stopped under my chin. He gently lifted my chin from his chest so I could look at him. Once I did, he took my face in both his hands. "Don't you know how crazy I am about you? Shit. I can't even see straight at times because I'm so crazy about you."

I nodded. "Me, too," I sniffled. "But if you want out or if this is too much for you. If I'm not—"

"You still don't get it do you?" He leaned his forehead against mine. "I'm falling in love with you."

My heart skipped a beat. Literally. "You are?"

"It's okay if you don't feel the same way." He lifted his head to look me in the eyes. "I just needed to tell you. I don't care if you don't feel the same way or are not ready to say it, too."

His hands were still cupping my face, his thumbs rubbing against my cheeks.

"No, it…isn't that," I said.

"What is it then?"

I put my hands on his, which still caressed my face. "I feel the same," I said.

"You do?" he responded, his eyes opening large and a smile forming.

"Oh God. I've wanted to tell you, too, for so long, but I didn't want to fuck up what was happening, and you're just so amazing, and I want to be with you. I *know* I've never felt this way about someone, and you're just so incredible; you make me feel so good and you're so…everything…for me and thank you for feeling the same way," I blurted out.

He wrapped his arms around me and pulled me to him. We hugged as my hands gripped his shirt to bring him as close to me as possible.

"Oh, shit," I said, looking at his shirt when I pulled away. "I got you all wrinkled."

"No," he said. "It's perfect. Everything is perfect."

Our lips met; he kissed me gently, slowly, and for the first time, I knew everything I felt behind that kiss was real.

I didn't have doubt or wonder any longer. He was mine.

I was his.

We pulled away, reluctantly, but our faces stayed close, our foreheads touching. He wiped and kissed away the remainder of my tears as I allowed my mind and my heart to soak up the moment.

He was all that I needed, and I was going to be everything he wanted.

Chapter Twenty

AARON—

That night I took her by the hand and walked her upstairs to my bedroom. Closing and locking the door behind us, I took in her face, full of the same want for me I'd come to recognize, but there was something more there now. I'd seen the burning desire in her eyes, the light flush of her cheeks before, but her expression meant something new to me. I never fully identified it in her before, but now it was crystal clear.

I took her face in my hands and brought it close to mine. "It's you and me. No more secrets, no more hiding, just us."

I kissed her softly, so very slowly. Her scent and breath was all mine now, and at that moment, I couldn't tear myself away. I'd been void of all things connected with loving another person until the moment I met her and resurrected feelings I'd buried long ago.

Her hands moved across my face, her fingertips burning a path across my skin as we continued to kiss. I gripped her around the waist while my mouth parted to ease my tongue in and find hers. Her body relaxed beneath my grip, and she whimpered against my mouth as our kisses deepened.

Walls were crumbling down, and from behind them, a flood of powerful emotions came crashing down over us. I wanted to hold her closer and tighter as we sunk deeper and deeper. The sexual desire we always had was being mixed and connected with the feelings we had professed, pushing everything we were experiencing into such perfection I wanted to fucking drown in it. Our bodies, our kisses, couldn't get me close enough to all I wanted her to know.

She broke our kiss only long enough to whisper, "Make love to me."

I bent down and lifted her up as she wrapped her legs around my waist. She brought her lips to the crook of my neck, running her nose and mouth along my skin as I walked her to the bed. I laid her down in the middle of the bed, and she watched as I stood, removing my shirt and tossing it to the floor. After I crawled across the bed and between her legs, I anchored myself above her, staring into her pleading eyes.

I lowered myself down as a chill ran through me. I teased her lips, grazing mine against them lazily. "So beautiful," I murmured.

She lifted her head off the bed, bringing our lips together, and connecting us once again. My fingers moved rapidly down the buttons of her shirt, and once completed, she hurried her arms free, removing the shirt completely. Her arms wrapped around me, and the heat of our skin pressed together made my already prominent erection throb.

Any time before, I would've torn her remaining clothes off and ravaged her until we both were exhausted, but tonight was different. I wanted to take her slowly, loving on every inch of her body because now, well, I fucking could. I could revel with every touch, every kiss, and have no fear of my true feelings for her being known. It was all different now. I wanted her to know.

My head dipped down, my lips tracing the delicate lines of her collarbone and down the center of her chest. I slipped my fingers under the straps of her bra and eased them down her arms, her breasts spilling from the cups. My tongue dragged across the warm skin of her breast until I reached the peak of her nipple, which I took into my mouth. As I lightly dragged my teeth over the sensitive area, her hands tugged at the top of my pants.

"I want you so bad," she pleaded.

I trailed a path of kisses from her breast back up to the side of her neck where I stopped to taste and suck at her skin there. Bringing a hand between our bodies, I fumbled with the button of her jeans before releasing it and pushing the zipper down.

"And you will have me…all of me. I want to taste you…feel you…everywhere first," I whispered in her ear.

And that is what I did.

I lingered over her upper body, heated kisses across her skin, her hands gripping and fingertips digging into my back as I did. The remaining articles of clothing separating us were removed, piece by piece, until our naked bodies were grinding together, begging for more. I pushed myself up, my hard dick positioned up against her.

When I couldn't hold out any longer, I slid my cock into her, slowly as her warmth enveloped me. I held still, reaching to intertwine our hands, before I started moving inside her.

Her eyes were closed as I brought myself deeper with each thrust. I leaned my head against her forehead. "Look at me," I said.

Our leisurely lovemaking changed when her green, lust-filled eyes met mine. The longer she held my stare, the more I couldn't control how hard I fucked her.

Our bodies damp from excitement and movement continued to work in unison until I was orgasming into her with an intense rush. She cried out into my neck as her own release ripped through her. She pulsed around my cock, urging me to continue to come harder and harder until we were both completely satiated. I drifted off to sleep with her head lying in the middle of my chest.

When I woke the following morning, she was gone, just like she always was. I wasn't under any impression that everything that happened the day before meant things would instantly change between us. We couldn't wake up in the same bed, at least not yet, because I hadn't decided how to explain this all to Delilah. She'd grown so attached to Callie, even asking me on several occasions when she could start calling Callie "Mommy." She understood, as much as a five-year-old could, that Callie was there to help Daddy watch over her when he was gone, and while Callie loved her, that didn't mean she would be her Mommy.

Things were different now. In a matter of hours, everything had changed.

I began to see a future with Callie, a future that included her being with us in a permanent way, which didn't involve her being my employee. In this short amount of time, I wasn't sure what all that meant, but I knew, from everything that happened the day before, I was willing to put almost everything I had been fearing on the line, to have her stay in my life. I'd been petrified of people finding out what we were doing, the whole "the boss banging the nanny," cliché. I worried people would think I was a shitty father or what my family would think and how it would affect my career, but once it was out there, in black and white for the world to see, it all became glaringly obvious. I wasn't afraid of people finding out and all the implications associated with that. I was afraid of Callie not feeling the same way about me.

As I left my room to go downstairs, I was more committed to my decision than ever. I wanted every part of the secret we had been keeping to be public.

I stopped at Delilah's room and peeked in to see if she was awake yet. "Hey baby doll," I said. "Whatcha up to?"

She was kneeling in front of her dollhouse, the contents scattered all around her. "Daddy, I'm NOT a baby!"

"I know. I know. You're not a baby. It's just what I like to call you."

"I don't want you to call me that," she pouted.

"All right. I'll try and remember, okay? What are you doing? Rearranging?"

"Uh-huh," she said, concentrating on the kitchen part of her dollhouse. "The mama is making muffins."

"You want to come downstairs with me while I have breakfast? I have to leave for work soon."

"No, I'm busy."

I laughed knowing this wouldn't be the last time she would be telling her old man she was too busy for him. "Okay, I'll see you when I get home this afternoon. I love you, bab… Delilah."

"Love you, too, Daddy."

I walked away smiling and headed downstairs, the smell of something baking filling the downstairs. I followed the scent to the kitchen and found Callie wiping down the counters, unaware I'd walked in. Slowly and quietly, I snuck up behind her and wrapped my arms around her waist.

"Shiii…shoot!" she gasped. "You scared me. Why are you always doing that?"

"Sorry. You scare too easily," I said, nuzzling her neck. "Something smells good."

She leaned into me slightly, her body relaxing from my touch. "I made blueberry…" She trailed off.

I ran my nose up her neck, placing a soft kiss behind her ear. "I'm sorry. What was that?"

"I made…Mmmm…God, I can't think when you're doing that."

"Doing what?" I asked, smiling against her skin.

"Muffins. Blueberry muffins," she said as her breathing halted.

"That wasn't what I was referring to when I said something smelled good."

She snorted loudly, an adorable noise she made whenever

she thought I was bullshitting her. She swatted at my hands, wrapped and untangled herself from my grip.

"Oh, come on," I moaned. "It's true. You do smell nice. Always with the orange and honey body wash from the shower."

She turned around to face me, rolling her eyes at me once she did. "You think you're so smooth."

I took the sight of her in and watched as she turned and bent down to retrieve something from the oven. Wearing simple white cotton pants and a light-colored T-shirt was anything but ordinary on her. The pants were snug in the perfect place to accentuate her killer ass and her T-shirt was just tight enough to emphasize her breasts, which were sans bra at the moment. Her hair was piled up in one of those ponytail, bun thingies exposing her long neck and delicate ears. I continued watching her as her back was turned to me and she removed the muffins from the pan, placing them on a plate next to the stove. Once she was finished, she picked up the plate and turned to face me.

"What?" she asked.

"What? What?"

"What are you staring at?"

"I wasn't staring...," I stuttered. I quickly realized I was coming across rude, glaring without telling her why. If we were going to give us a real chance at a relationship, I'd have to learn to not be embarrassed to express these things to her. It was new territory for me as well, Lexie never being one for any type of affection, whether physical or verbal, but with Callie, she was open to it.

"Quit gawking before I punch you," she snapped.

I snatched a muffin from the plate before she yanked it away from me quickly. She placed it on the counter, grabbing a paper towel and shoving it at me.

Yes, she's so very open.

I smiled at her slight temper as I started picking the blueberries out of my muffin. "Sorry I was staring. You just…you're so beautiful."

She snorted. Again.

"I'm serious," I insisted.

Her eyes casted downward. "Look, you don't have to go all…gooey…because of last night."

"I'm not being gooey," I said. "Well, maybe a little, but is that so wrong?"

She was quiet for a moment, continuing to look at the floor, until she lifted her eyes to me slowly, a cautious smile emerging. "I'm learning. Thank you."

"Me, too," I responded, grabbing her hand. "There are going to be a lot of things to get used to, to figure out together."

"Daddy. I can't find my My Little Pony," Delilah screamed from upstairs.

"Like that," I said, pointing upstairs. "She's going to be something we're going to have to figure out together."

"We? Together?"

"Yeah, together," I responded.

"What are we going to tell her?" she asked.

I sighed. "Honestly? I don't think we'll tell her anything today. I need to wrap my brain around how to explain to her first. She's already placing you in the 'mommy' role. She's upstairs right now playing make-believe and having the mommy make blueberry muffins, like you."

"I think you're right."

I did my best to ignore the sting in my heart when she mentioned the possibility of us not being together. I wasn't an idiot. There was always a possibility of things not working out. No one knew that better than me, but it was too soon to think about it.

"Daddy!"

I brought my hand from hers to her face and settled my palm against her cheek. Her eyes flutter closed, her face content against my touch. I brought my face closer to hers, but just before I kissed her, I heard the tiny steps of my daughter pounding her way to the kitchen.

Callie's eyes opened, hearing the same thing I did. "She's coming."

We stepped away from each other, our private moment over.

"Daddy? Can you help me?" she called from the hallway.

"Coming, sweetie," I shouted.

I started to walk out of the kitchen but stopped short of exiting completely. Turning back around, I called to her as she was facing the sink.

"Callie?"

"Yeah?" she answered, looking over her shoulder at me.

"Your ass in those pants? Sexy as hell."

* * *

I was driving to work an hour later and my body, my brain, everything, was buzzing. This thing between Callie and me was the stuff of fucking fairy tales. It blew my mind. Now that it was all out in the open I wanted the world to see us together. I wanted everyone to know she was mine.

I wanted our life together to start immediately.

When I got to the office, I called Abel, and then my parents. I invited them to dinner at Stars on the Lake. It was a favorite of ours reserved for special occasions, and it had the most incredible view. Next, I called Sophie, our babysitter, to see if she was available for that evening. When she said she was, I asked her to be at the house by five.

Even though I was buried in work, there was something I needed to do before I could concentrate on anything else.

I stopped in Saks Fifth Avenue and told the salesperson exactly what I was looking for. After rushing off, she returned with several choices for me. The one I decided on caught my eye immediately. I knew it would be perfect. Once I paid for it, and filled out the necessary things to have it delivered to the house, I left.

"Hey, baby," I said, calling Callie.

"Hey, what's up," she asked.

"Something's going to be delivered to the house later this afternoon for you."

"For me?"

"Yeah," I said smiling. "For you. I want you to have it on and be ready when I get home at six."

There was a slight pause. "What is it?"

"A surprise."

"It's not some trashy outfit, is it? I know you dig dress-up shit, but Delilah will still be up at six and—"

"It's nothing like that. I think you'll like it. Oh, and Sophie will be there around five so you'll have time to get ready."

"Are we going out?" she asked.

"No more questions. I'll just see you when I get home."

"Okay," she said, sounding uncertain.

"I'll see you then. Bye."

We hung up, and while I needed to get back to the office, I had one more stop to make. Luckily, Harry Winston's was only a few blocks away.

Chapter Twenty-One

CALLIE—

I stood in my bedroom, in my bathrobe and with a towel around my head, staring at what Aaron had delivered to the house. On my bed was a Saks Fifth Avenue garment bag with the zipper pulled down to uncover the stunning cobalt-blue dress inside. Next to it was a shoe box with a pair of heels the exact color of the dress, with shiny, red soles that meant they cost more than my car.

It was a lovely gesture. My boyfriend, who I was living with and loved, picked out a pretty dress and shoes for me. It was thoughtful and sweet. He was taking me out. The babysitter was already downstairs with Delilah so I could get ready and it was so, so nice.

It was.

But there was a small part of me that felt like it wasn't.

It was amazing, of course, but it just seemed abrupt in a way. I couldn't put my finger on it, but it just didn't seem right. I didn't even know how he knew what size I was.

I shook my head and tried to get rid of all negative thoughts. Aaron was just doing something thoughtful, and there was nothing more to it. That was what I kept telling myself.

I kept telling myself that while I did my makeup and blew my hair dry.

I kept telling myself that while I curled my hair and pinned it up.

I kept telling myself that as I got dressed, feeling the expensive fabric of the dress and the satin of the shoes next to my skin.

Over and over again.

There was a knock on my door, and Aaron popped his head in.

"Hey," he said, entering.

"Hey yourself," I said. I smoothed my hands down my dress. "Thank you so much for this. It's really too much and—"

"You look beautiful."

I winked at him. "Thanks. Looking pretty hot yourself."

He had on a dark suit, with a white collared shirt and tie. I wasn't sure where we were going, but judging by what he was wearing and what I was wearing, it was pretty ritzy.

"Where are we going?" I asked.

"Dinner."

"Okay," I said, uncertain. "I take it we're not going to Billy Boy's Country BBQ, huh?"

"No. We're going to Stars on the Lake, with my family."

"Whoa."

And when I said "whoa" I meant it. Like, as in, *Whoa, what the hell are we doing going there?*, the place that was at the top of one of the largest buildings in Chicago. I never had the luxury of going, and while it was exciting to think about, it was one more thing that didn't sit well with me.

He walked toward me and took me in a careful embrace, trying not to mess me up too much. I knew I had to stay all in place, but I was so desperate for him. I wanted him to hold me close and run his fingers through my hair, easing me in a way that only he knew how to do. Instead, he ran his hands up and down my back, sighing deeply.

His fingertips brushed up the back of my neck. "I'm so glad you wore your hair up."

"Oh yeah," I said, pulling away from him so I could look at him. "Why is that?"

"Well, not only do I think you have the sexiest neck and collarbone I've ever seen, but I got you a little something to go with your dress."

Before I could even think about what he was doing, he reached into his pocket and pulled out a small velvet box. I'd never been given anything in a velvet box, but I knew what they usually contained. Panic immediately set in.

Oh God. Please let it be Xanax in that box. A small, shiny pill to help with the panic attack that is about to ensue. Come to think of it, I'd take two small, shiny pills. Xanax and some sort of antivomit medication. Please, dear Lord, please, don't let it be...

He opened the box.

It is.

Not.

Nestled inside the box were the most exquisite diamond earrings I'd ever seen. Shaped like sunbursts and shining and sparkling from every which direction, it was a sight I'd never seen in person. I felt tears form in my eyes as I gazed at the extravagant gift, but once I saw the name, HARRY WINSTON, printed on the inside cover of the box, the tears started to fall.

"Holy shit," I said, covering my mouth.

It was too much. It was *all* too much. The dress, the shoes, the earrings…him.

"Do you like them?" he asked eagerly. "I saw these and thought you would like them, but if you want something else…"

"No," I said, interrupting him.

I fought to find the words, but nothing that came to mind sounded right. I couldn't say, "I don't belong in diamonds." Or, "This is nice and all, but don't you think it's a little soon for a gift worth thousands of dollars?"

I looked at his face, which was losing its enthusiasm as quickly as the seconds ticked on. His smiled faded, and his eyes moved from mine to the floor.

I was ruining it. The moment, the gift, and us was all going to fall apart if I didn't change my tune. It wasn't what I thought or felt, but making us okay was more important than that.

I placed my hand on the side of his face. "Look at me," I said. "They're the most perfect thing ever."

"Really?" he asked, his head slowly lifting.

"Yes, really. They're so beautiful and probably so expensive, and I've never even touched a real diamond before, and you've already bought me this dress and done so many nice things for me, and no one has ever done that for me before and… and…and…thank you."

He brought his arms around me once again and held me tight, no longer worried about possibly messing up my dress. I wanted to soak in every ounce of devotion he had radiating off of him for me. When he pulled away, he kept his arms wrapped around me, smiling with such joy I knew I'd done the right thing.

"You're very welcome," he said.

He retreated and took the earrings out of the box. He stepped forward again and then, with the gentlest touch, eased the earrings into the pierced opening in each of my ears, securing them in the back.

When he was done, he took me by the hand and brought me to the mirror. I stood in front of it as he stepped behind me, kissing the side of my neck just below my new earrings.

"You see that?" he asked.

"What?"

"That's my future in the mirror."

* * *

Aaron could sense my nervousness. I knew he did. The entire drive there, he kept one hand on the steering wheel and the other holding mine, interlocking our fingers. I knew it was only dinner with Abel and his parents. His parents had always been kind to me, but now they knew about us. I was so unsure how it would all play out. By the time the valet opened my door and I stepped out, I'd all but concluded I was thinking like a neurotic twit.

We entered through the large revolving doors, Aaron stepping in behind me and putting his arms around my waist. "I would like to remind you that I don't like surprises, and today has been a big one already."

He placed a kiss behind my ear. "This is going to be great," he said.

We exited the door and walked across the large lobby of the high-rise. At night it was quiet and empty, void of the hustle and bustle of the daytime business action. He took my hand and hit the star-marked button next to the elevator.

Once the door opened, he yanked me inside and bent down to kiss me hard. "Mmmm," he hummed against my lips.

The door closed and he kissed me again, this time with his hands on my face and his tongue swirling around mine. My body felt weightless, and I was light-headed from the rapidly ascending elevator. Or maybe it was the kiss. I didn't know.

When his hand moved from my face to my ass, I pushed against him. "Don't be getting all frisky when this door is about to open, and we'll be standing in front of your parents."

"I was testing the waters," he said.

"And what does that mean?"

The elevator rang as we reached our floor, but before it opened, Aaron leaned down. "Have you ever fucked in an elevator?" he whispered in my ear.

My jaw dropped as the door opened, and there stood Daniel, Leslie, and Abel, because of course they were there.

Oh don't mind us, Mr. and Mrs. Matthews. We don't normally walk around in public with his hand on my ass and my mouth opened. We usually reserve that for the privacy of Aaron's bedroom, which of course, is pretty much my bedroom now. Don't worry. We won't make you watch. Judging by the looks on your face, you're already thinking I was blowing Aaron, in the elevator, and your horrified looks aren't anything I'd ever care to see again.

Aaron took my hand once again as we stepped out. "Hey," he said. "Everyone's here. Great."

He shook his dad's hand with his free one, and then kissed his mom on the cheek. His mother was, for sure, wearing a Chanel suit, while Mr. Matthews had on a dark suit, his hands shoved in his pockets.

With a wave of his hand, a tuxedo-dressed man appeared, and we followed him to a circular table overlooking the lake. The dining room was small, maybe twenty tables, which were all full. I was sure it was paranoia again when I felt all eyes on us.

Abel hung back and whispered in my ear. "Everything cool?"

"No. Check out my ears. Be discreet! What the fuck?"

We pulled away, but we weren't a half a second apart before he threw discretion out the window.

"Holy shit," he mumbled loudly.

Aaron turned around. "What?"

"Callie just showed me her new jewelry and told me to shut up," Abel said.

"I said be discreet," I hissed. "I didn't say shut up."

"Whatever," he said. "Nice work, Aaron."

"Thanks," Aaron said.

Aaron's parents were quiet, standing together, and their eyes moving back and forth between us.

We all sat, Aaron on one side, Abel on the other, all of us staring at one another until menus were placed in front of us. We busied ourselves with food selections, wine pairings, and obligatory admiration of the view.

"You look lovely, Callie," Leslie said, leaning over. She was seated on the other side of Aaron.

"Oh. Thank you. It was all your son's doing."

She smiled at her son, and patted his hand. "That was very thoughtful of you, sweetie. The earrings are…"

"Extravagant," Daniel said.

His face didn't show a hint of humor, which surprised me. My anxiety began to rise again. While Daniel only said what I'd thought earlier, it was still hurtful.

"Yes," I said, reaching to my earrings. "I told Aaron the same. It's too much."

Aaron's hand found mine under the table, and I squeezed it tight. "I wanted to. She deserves it."

Daniel raised his eyes and chucked softly. "I'm sure she does."

"Daniel," Leslie warned.

"Is there a problem, Dad?" Aaron said. His grip on my hand grew tighter. "I can hardly see it as any concern of yours if I want to buy my girlfriend earrings or anything else."

"Oh, look," Abel said. "Wine's here."

We were all silent as our glasses were filled with wine the color of blood, which I was sure was the same color pooling in my mouth from biting down on my tongue so hard.

Aaron raised his glass. "To family, love, and the future."

We all took a sip, and I hoped the alcohol would be enough to chill everyone out.

"Speaking of the future," Daniel said. "You're finishing your master's soon, aren't you, Callie?"

Keep drinking everyone, especially you, Daniel.

"Bachelor's," I said. "Going part-time, along with the teaching program, made it take a little longer than most."

"I thought you said Master's, Aaron?" Daniel said.

Aaron took a long sip. "I don't think I did."

Leslie nudged Daniel. "It doesn't matter."

Abel cleared her throat. "Callie has worked so hard. I've never known anyone who worked so hard. School during the day. Working at night."

"That's right. You used to be a go-go dancer at one of Aaron's former clubs, right?" Daniel said.

I glanced at Aaron, hoping he'd jump in to defend me, but his eyes were focused on the table. He was clearly avoiding what his dad had said. Luckily for him, I was capable of defending myself.

All right, if old man wanted to go a round with me, he was going to lose. I wasn't going to be ashamed or embarrassed for anything I'd ever done. I'd been nervous about all the wrong things for this evening.

"Bartender," I said. I brought my glass to my lips and downed whatever was in my glass. "The dancers make more money, but I'm not nearly as good at dancing as I am at other things."

Abel snorted as he started taking a sip of water and started coughing. Once he composed himself, he attempted to turn the conversation around. "So, that school I've been subbing at thinks there might be a spot for me next year."

"I didn't know you were subbing?" I asked.

"Didn't Abel tell you," Aaron said. "When you guys went out that one time I thought—"

"You and Abel?" Leslie asked, confused.

"Oh yeah," Abel said. "But it was strictly business. Two education majors discussing things over dinner."

The table grew quiet again, and when the topic of Delilah came up, I thought the evening might be turning around. We enjoyed our salads, but by the time soup came out, things started to get weird again.

"So, how long has this been going on?" Daniel said, waving his spoon between Aaron and me.

"How long has *what* been going on?" Aaron said, clearly agitated.

"Well, she hasn't even worked for you for six months and—"

"I don't think it's our business," Leslie said to her husband. "They're together now and they seemed very happy."

Aaron put his arm around his mom and kissed her on the temple. "We are, Mom."

"All I'm saying is that it's been a long time since you've been involved with anyone, and I don't want to see you rush into anything," Daniel said.

"We aren't rushing," Aaron said. "We're in love."

I put my head in my hands. "Oh God," I mumbled.

Leslie's eyes opened wide. "Really?"

"Oh come on, Aaron," Daniel said. "How much do you even know about her after a few months? She could be after money, a cushy place to live—"

"What?" he barked, loud enough for people at other tables to turn to look. "What is wrong with you?"

I closed my eyes because if I didn't, if I had to sit and watch this unfold further, I was either going to cry or lose my shit.

Daniel threw his napkin on the table. "This is the same kind of infatuation you had with Lexie. The lovesick thing that made you unable to see anything go on around you. I don't want you to make the same mistake again."

"Dad," Abel said. "I'm sure Aaron knows you mean well, but I think you're a bit over the line."

"A bit?" I said softly.

I hadn't meant to say anything, but it slipped out.

"I'm worried about my son, who I think has put himself in a difficult position. You can't go from working with each other, to living together, to dating and then…living together," Daniel said.

"Well, we have," Aaron said flippantly.

"And what about Delilah?" Daniel said. "She has to be so confused. Is she going to think every nanny will end up your girlfriend?"

I stared at Aaron with wide eyes, silently begging him to put his dad in his place. But like he had the entire night, he left me to defend myself. It was humiliating.

I jumped up, bumping the edge of the table as I did, and shaking the glasses on top. "Mr. Matthews, I'm sure this is all coming from a place of love for your son, and you've been very kind to me up until this evening. I can see I was respected as an employee of Aaron's, but not as anything else. I assure you I'm not after money or anything of the sort. Everything I've ever had I earned myself. As far as Delilah goes, she means more to me than anything. I've *never* taken that lightly."

Abel grabbed my arm. "Okay, okay. Let's step outside for a second and when we get back everyone will be calm."

"I am calm, but I won't be disrespected," I looked at Aaron who had turned quiet. "No matter how you dress it up."

I grabbed my purse and yanked my arm away from Abel. "Enjoy your dinner," I said.

I hurried away from the table, as I heard whispers from other guests and the voice of Aaron rising above them. One foot in front of the other, I rushed to the elevator, so I could get away. My finger pressed the down button as I prayed for it to open as quickly as possible.

"Callie," Aaron said, running through the restaurant, causing an even bigger scene, with Abel trailing behind him. "Wait!"

The elevator door opened and I stepped in, frantically pressing the lobby button. The doors began to close, but Aaron reached it in time to stop it and stepped in. Abel ran in just before the elevator door could close.

"Both of you. Just go back," I said, tears spilling over.

"No," Aaron said sharply.

Aaron's arms were crossed in front of him, and his eyes

were watching the elevator displaying the floor numbers. We were quiet, the numbers lowering from the seventy-fifth floor, at a snail's pace, making the tension so much more uncomfortable.

"Come on, Callie," Abel said. "Just come back up and it'll be fine."

I couldn't talk. I was mortified and hurt, but most of all I was angry at myself for letting someone talk to me like that. I was mad I was crying about it all.

The elevator stopped, and as soon as the door began to open, I tried to rush through it. Aaron jumped in front of me, blocking my exit. "Can you please say something?"

"No," I said, pushing past him.

"I'll just give you two a minute," Abel said.

We walked across the lobby and stopped just before the revolving doors. I spun around to face him. "I think you should stay."

"Well, I'm not going to let you leave alone."

"You'll just leave me alone up there, right?" I said, pointing up. "You're so thoughtful to think of me now, but I think I'm capable of doing a lot of things alone."

He tossed his hands in the air. "What did you want me to do? Knock out my dad?"

"No, but you didn't do anything."

He rolled his eyes and shook his head. I hated it. It felt dismissive and condescending.

"I knew this would happen," I said.

That feeling, the nagging anxiety that circled me all day, was a premonition. Or maybe it was just my conscience trying to tell me something. Whatever it was, I should've listened to it.

"You knew what would happen?" he asked.

He squinted his eyes at me as he pressed his lips together in a tight line. I looked over at Abel, who was waving me over, but I shook my head.

"Callie?" Aaron said. "You knew what would happen?"

"Never mind. It doesn't matter. Let's just go."

We were almost out of there, when Abel stopped us. "Hold up a second, guys," he said rushing over.

"Aaron," he said. "A word before you go?"

"Not now, Abel," Aaron said.

Aaron turned toward me. "Are you ready?"

"I said I was," I snapped.

I looked at Abel and managed a smile. "See you later. Thanks for everything."

Aaron mumbled a good-bye to him and walked through the revolving door, pushing his way out of the hotel. I followed close beside him, but it didn't escape me that he wasn't trying to ease me as he did when we first walked in or didn't bother to hold my hand. Aaron passed off his ticket to a valet, who rushed off to retrieve his car, leaving us standing silent on the curb. No words were exchanged, no playful touching, but just distance in far more ways than our physical presence.

The valet pulled his car up in front of us and jumped out, rushing to the opposite side to open the door for me. I walked over to my side of the car and sat down as Aaron was on his side. My door closed gingerly while he slammed his shut roughly and peeled out of the valet line.

I waited several blocks before I spoke. "Why are you angry at me?"

"I'm not," he said as his grip on the steering wheel tightened.

"You're certainly acting like it and I didn't do anything wrong. All I did was—"

"I never said you did." he said, interrupting.

His tone was short, and he hadn't looked at me once. He could say what he wanted, but I could feel the indignation rolling off of him. We drove the rest of the way home in silence while tears stung my eyes. I couldn't wait to get out of the dress, the clothes I wore as a costume, dressing up as someone that I wasn't—someone he clearly wanted me to be.

Once we returned to his home, the silence continued, until we walked through the front door and stood uncomfortably in the foyer.

"I'm going to go pay Sophie and see how the night went with Delilah," he said, avoiding my eyes.

"Okay," I replied quietly. "I'll check on Delilah, and then I'm going to turn in after I take a shower."

"Okay."

He leaned in and gave me a quick peck on the cheek before turning to walk down the hallway. I lingered, watching him walk away and feeling lonelier than I'd felt in ages. After I heard the beginning of the conversation between Aaron and Sophie, him telling her in a phony enthusiastic voice what a great evening we'd had, the tears I had been holding in all evening came flooding out—big, fat tears escaping and running down my face.

I didn't know what was worse, that he had to lie about what a wonderful night he had or the fact he truly didn't, the reason being because of me in some way.

After going upstairs and checking on a peacefully sleeping Delilah, I went into my room to peel away my costume. I took my dress off, carefully hanging it in my closet, with my shoes placed neatly beneath it. My earrings were removed and put back in their velvet box, my fingers lightly tracing over the brilliance of the diamonds. I grabbed a pair of my old, cotton pajamas, realizing there was no need for anything sexy, considering I was definitely not going to be visiting Aaron in his room.

I threw the pajamas on the vanity of my bathroom and stood before the mirror, removing bobby pin after bobby pin which had been holding my hair in place. I turned the shower on and stepped in, not even waiting for it to heat up. The cold water hit me, chilling my skin, but comforting me at the same time. I wanted the water to wash it all away, the makeup, hair products, hurt, and embarrassment. I wanted it all gone.

I scrubbed at my face roughly, the warming water from the showerhead mixing with tears. The entire evening kept replaying in my mind, both horrifying me and bringing everything I'd suppressed to the surface. I never belonged there in the first place. It was too much, too soon, and tonight pushed us over the edge.

There was no doubt on my part where my affection lay. I was still as in love with him as I was when I woke up this morning. The scary part was, I didn't know if he felt the same.

I shampooed my hair, allowing myself to wallow and block out the rest of the world. Being in such a deep mind-set was probably the reason I didn't hear Aaron come into the bathroom until the door of the shower opened and he stepped in. I drew in a sharp breath, both surprised and relieved to see him.

"I should've shut up and I know—" I babbled through my tears.

"Shhhh," he said, cupping my face in his hands, his thumbs gently moving across my cheeks. "Please don't cry, baby. Please."

I looked into his blue eyes and saw the same softness I was used to mixed with the same confusion I felt. "Did I…we…mess it all…" I trailed off, unable to articulate what I even wanted to ask him.

He leaned his forehead against mine. "No." He sighed softly as I breathed my own sense of relief. "I don't want you to ever doubt what I feel for you."

He brought his lips to mine and I whimpered against his kiss, desperate for the reassurance. Our wet bodies pressed against each other as our kisses deepened and grew with the urgency we both found ourselves craving. Aaron moved me back, pressing me up against the wall of the shower.

"You don't have to say it back," he said. "But…I'm in love with you."

I wanted to say it back, but the words stuck in my throat.

His attention turned back on my body. He kissed his way down my body, stopping to draw circles with his tongue around each of my nipples and eventually down to my navel, pausing only to briefly look up at me for a moment. My hands gripped his water-slicked hair as he knelt down on the wet floor and brought his mouth to between my legs. I braced myself against the wall as my body tingled from the sexual intensity and the surreal intimacy of the moment. It was a culmination of the day's events, him down on his knees, confirming his love and desire for me in the only way he knew how in that moment. Sometimes there were no words.

His tongue kept a perfect rhythm against me until I came so powerfully I had to bite my bottom lip so hard I tasted blood, to stifle the screams of my orgasm. Once he knew I was done, he kissed his way back up my body, his eyes connecting with mine as he stood back up. His thumb ran across my bloody lower lip gently while he frowned slightly, trying to mend what I'd done. He brought his thumb to his mouth, sucking the blood from me into him.

"Turn around," he commanded.

And because he asked, I did. I wanted to be whatever he wanted.

Pretty dress and diamonds, perfect and sparkling...I wanted to be right for him because he was right for me.

He gripped my waist tightly and slid his dick into me, groaning against the back of my neck once he was fully in. His usual gentle, gradual moves to start were replaced by a frantic, deep tempo. It was like he was seeking out the same things I was.

Facing the wall, I tried to grip onto the smooth tiles to keep me steady, but my fingers kept slipping. My hands were desperate to hold on to something, but everything was out of reach. I knew I needed to hold on to something, anything, but I couldn't.

He leaned against my back, bringing his mouth close to my ear, his breath hot, so hot. "Tell me, Calliope."

"I love you."

Chapter Twenty-Two

AARON—

"Daddy? Daddy, did you hear me?"

"Hmmm?" I replied sleepily, still not completely awake.

I felt a tiny nudge on my arm. "Daddy, are you having a sleepover?"

"What, baby girl?"

"Are you and Callie having a sleepover?"

I stretched my arms and opened my eyes, "What are you talking..."

Oh, shit.

I looked over at Callie as she bolted upright, her eyes wild and confused.

"I...uh...guess...I forgot to lock the door last night," I stuttered.

She swatted me in the shoulder. "How could you forget?" she hissed.

"I was a little distracted, in case you forgot."

I frantically lifted the sheet and comforter, letting out a sigh of relief as I recalled us getting into pajamas, after the shower, before bed. I threw a silent *thank you* up to the universe for us not being naked and making the situation any more difficult than it could possibly be.

"So, you did have a sleepover without me?" Delilah asked sadly.

I looked at Callie.

Callie looked at me.

We both looked at Delilah.

Well, there was no time like the present.

"Come sit down here, baby girl," I said, patting the area on the bed between Callie and me.

"Daddyyyy. I'm NOT a baby. My name is Delilah," she said as she climbed up the bed.

She wiggled her way between Callie and me, giggling as she plopped down and looking up at me with her beautiful blue eyes. I was hoping I, or rather, *we*, would have more time to discuss how we wanted to handle explaining our new relationship to Delilah. We both knew there would have to be some sort of talk because if we weren't hiding our feelings from anyone outside of this house, it seemed rather silly to hide it within our own home, especially since the one person we'd be keeping it from was Delilah.

"So, yes, Callie and I had a sleepover last night. We were so tired and ended up falling asleep here. We didn't mean to have a sleepover, it sort of happened, like an accident," I explained.

I looked over at Callie, and beneath her flushed cheeks and uncomfortableness, she found the will to nod at me, encouraging me that we were doing the right thing.

Delilah laughed. "That's silly. How can you fall asleep by accident?"

"Well, it wasn't exactly an accident, but we were so tired and after we were in our jammies, we fell asleep here while we were talking."

"What were you talking about?" she asked.

"Aaron?" Callie said. "It would probably be easier to just tell her."

She was right. I needed to come out and say it, but hell, I'd never had to explain I was dating someone and relationships to Delilah before. Plus, with Callie living with us, how was I going to put it in a way she wouldn't confuse dating with getting married? I never had women coming and going through the house, nor did I date hardly at all, so if I tried to explain…

"Aaron," Callie said pinching me in the arm and pulling me from my thoughts. "Pull it together."

"Ow," I responded, rubbing my arm. "Quit it and I am pulled together."

"Look at her. You're scaring her." She gestured toward Delilah.

I looked down at my daughter, snuggled between Callie and myself, gazing up at me with confused eyes. Callie patted her legs in reassurance, and Delilah quickly grabbed her hand, intertwining her little fingers with Callie's.

I brushed my hand down Delilah's hair. "Sweetie, you know how Barbie and Ken are boyfriend and girlfriend? Well, Callie and I are boyfriend and girlfriend now."

"Oh," she said, mulling over what I said. "You mean like Nana and Grandpa?"

"Kind of, but Nana and Grandpa are married. They had a wedding. Boyfriends and girlfriends are people who like each other and want to get to know each other better. So, you might see Callie and me hug or kiss sometimes because that's what boyfriends and girlfriends do."

I paused, waiting for a reaction or comment, but at the moment, her eyes looked like they were deep in concentration. Suddenly, she looked up at me, her head tilted to the side. "Daddy?"

"Yes, sweetie."

"Are you and Callie going to get married like Nana and Grandpa, then? Because Callie could be my mommy, right?"

"Ahhh," I responded, trying to think what to say. "For now, I think…Well, I'm…What I mean is…"

"Daddy?"

"Yes, sweetie."

"Can I go watch TV?"

I breathed a sigh of relief and nodded my head, watching her scramble off the bed and dart to the door. I was beyond grateful for the brief attention span of a five-year-old and not having to explain things further.

"Daddy?" she asked from the doorway.

"Yes?"

"It's okay if you want to marry Callie, but when I'm older, I don't want you to be married to her anymore because I want to marry you, okay?"

She ran from the doorway, her tangled curls and part of my heart following with her. I fell back against the bed and rested my hand on my aching chest.

I responded. "That little girl…"

"Is amazing," Callie said, finishing my sentence. "I think she handled that conversation better than the both of us."

"Yeah, well, I wasn't getting much help from you."

She cocked an eyebrow at me. "It wasn't my place. It was a conversation you needed to have with your daughter."

"But you're part of this, too. This is about all of us, you, me, and Delilah."

I picked up her hand and brought it to my lips, kissing it while gazing at her. The events of the previous evening came flooding back to me.

I had shut down. Completely.

What the fuck was she going to think except that I was mad at her? No. It wasn't her. It was everyone and everything else. Any and everything made me question us ever taking our love outside the bedroom for everyone else to see. That, coupled with the fear that made my stomach ache that she would call it all bullshit and take off.

Her eyes. Her beautiful green eyes utterly pained over the entire evening—mostly because of my own behavior. As we stood in the hallway when we returned home, I looked at her, in her beautiful dress and sparkling earrings, and wondered how, with her looking so stunning, anything bad could happen. While rather juvenile in theory was how it seemed. Everything didn't fit anymore, everything was slightly askew, and instead of telling her what I felt, I'd connected with her in the only way I knew how in that moment.

I'd joined her in the shower and hushed her words with my mouth. It wasn't words I wanted. It was her. Only her. I wanted to taste her kisses and the warmth and softness of her skin. I needed the intangible depth of want from her. It was where I was certain of her love for me. It was where we made sense.

My throbbing erection was no match for all the lingering questions, and when I'd slid into her, our breaths caught in a moment of relief. We were together. The deeper I went, the more I craved and the more I feared. Fear that my life before her would be too much for her. Desire had little to do with reality, and while I knew she desired me, I didn't know if it would be enough considering *all* of the baggage I was bringing with me. Would the *want* she had for me be enough to sustain us? I knew if she could feel me, how we fit together so precisely, it would remind her of how much we had.

I just didn't know if it was enough.

"What are you thinking about?" Callie asked.

I sighed deeply, reaching around her waist to bring her close. "Last night."

"Oh." She bit down on her lower lip as her head dipped slightly, averting her eyes from mine. "Yeah, quite a night."

"Hey," I said, tapping her chin up. "Look at me."

The same sad, confused eyes that gazed at me last night were looking at me once again. "I'm sorry."

"I'm sorry," I said, at the same time as her.

"Look, I was an asshole," I explained. "I was never angry at you."

She sighed. "I know, but I also know you were disappointed, and that was because of me."

I wanted to tell her she was wrong, that she wasn't the cause of anything, but that would've been a lie. Everything that was happening was because we were together. It was her. It was me. It was my family. It was everyone. It was everywhere.

She fit into my life, in *our* lives. I'd never known just how much having another person to share the day-to-day things with would make me realize how much I'd been missing. How much Delilah had been missing.

She got up from the bed and walked toward the door, not looking at me. "I need to get ready."

I was getting hit from a million different directions. Every word, every move I made was forcing me into a war zone and it was blinding me.

Blind to what was right in front of me.

I was hit once again and knew what I needed to do. "Calliope."

"Yes?" she said, turning around.

"You're fired."

"Whaa…what?"

"You heard me. Now, come here."

"Aaron…I…"

"Come here."

With shaky limbs and her eyes cast downward, she moved from the bed slowly, placing herself in front of me. This, along with everything else Callie and I had gone through, could go several ways, but it was what I wanted. It was what we needed.

"You want me to leave?" she asked, tears pooling in her eyes.

I took her face in my hands, feeling her soft skin as my thumbs rubbed across her cheeks. "No, I want you to live here with me. With us."

"But if you're firing me? I don't understand."

"I don't want you to be the nanny anymore, Callie. I want you to live here as my girlfriend, not as an employee," I explained.

She started to shake her head. "What? I can't...You want...Shit. I'm turning into one of those girls who I hate, who become overly emotional idiots who can't form a sentence."

"I want you. I want only you. I've never wanted another woman more. I want you to live here, sleep in my bed, and wake up next to me because I'm in love with you. I want you here because you want to be here, not because you're the nanny."

I brought her face toward mine and lightly kissed her lips. "I want you," I murmured against her mouth. "Please say you want me, too."

"But..."

"No *buts*, please. We can figure out all the other stuff, just say yes."

Her hands that were resting on my chest began to tremble, and she no longer could hold my gaze. My heart began to sink with the realization the answer she would give me might be no. I willed myself to prepare for the rejection that was becoming more and more evident as each moment passed, but I wasn't doing a very good job. Maybe it really was too much for her. Maybe all my baggage was too heavy of a burden to want to carry. Maybe she was confusing great sex with love. Maybe...

"Yes," she said so quietly I almost didn't hear her. "Yes, I'll live here with you."

No maybe.

Yes.

She jumped onto the bed and tackled me, throwing her arms around my neck. I rolled over on top of her, kissing her mouth, smiling against her lips.

This was the answer.

"How would this even work? I mean, I need an income, and I can't, or rather I won't, rely on you solely for that," she asked.

"Well, what would you feel comfortable with?"

I'd hate to see her going back to working nights, or anywhere for that matter. She'd still be here taking care of Delilah like she had been, and my financial situation was enough to take care of whatever she needed.

She shrugged. "I'm not sure to be honest. I have some money tucked away that I've saved since living here, but with my student loans and credit card debt there is no way I can't work."

"You can still keep your salary from me," I said. "It—"

"No way," she said loudly. "If I'm not your employee, you are not paying me."

I picked up her hand. "Hear me out," I said. "It wouldn't be like that. You taking care of Delilah isn't going to change. If we are going to be together, you'll have to become comfortable with me picking up certain slack because I can, not because I think you're taking me for a ride."

I could see the wheels turning, her eyes shifted to the ceiling as she bit down on her lower lip.

I decided to press her further.

"How about you consider this, then. I'll pick up the tab for the student loans for now. It wouldn't be like I was paying you, but only helping out my girlfriend, who lived with me."

"Aaron, you are so thoughtful to offer. I'm just not sure. Your father already thought I was in this with you for money. I don't want anyone else to think that because nothing could be further from the truth."

"Of course, it isn't true, and it's none of anyone's business what we do, either. I want you to consider something, though. If you had the money to help, would you help Delilah and me out?" I asked.

"In a heartbeat," she said without hesitation.

As soon as the words left her mouth, the deal was done. I could see it all over her face. With a little more coaxing, we had an agreement.

I pressed my lips to hers before leaning back to gaze at her. "Let's go downstairs and have breakfast in our kitchen."

A short time later, just as I was setting Callie's coffee-filled Tinker Bell cup next to her at the table, my cell phone vibrated on the table. I glanced at it and saw it was the one person I wasn't sure I wanted to talk to.

My father.

"Hi, Dad," I said, answering the phone.

"Hi, son. Am I catching you at a bad time?"

"No," I said.

He cleared his throat as I walked out of the kitchen and into the hallway.

"It was quite the eventful evening, wasn't it?" he said.

"Yes, it was."

"After you left, I had a long talk with Abel. He had some

very strong words for me. I have to say, some of which were very hard to hear."

"Uh-huh."

He paused before answering, breathing in deeply. "I'm not proud of how I acted, Aaron, but I want you to know it came from a place of concern."

"I realize that, but it still doesn't excuse your actions."

"It all seemed to happen very fast. I didn't want to see you hurt again. Everything you went through with Lexie and the aftermath, it nearly destroyed you. If it wasn't for Delilah, none of us thought you'd make it through."

"And you think Callie would do the same thing to me?"

"Considering the circumstances, I may have jumped to conclusions about her, her intentions and about your relationship in general."

"I have to be honest, I'm shocked as hell you're saying this," I said.

"Well, let's just say, after last night, and the tongue-lashing I got from your mother, I had to see things at face value."

"And what did you see?"

"You're crazy in love, Aaron. I saw the way you looked at her last night, tuning out everything else around you and gazing at her, just like I used to do with your mother when we first met," he explained. "My reaction to your relationship was based out of fear. Plain and simple. I'm sorry to both you and Callie. I'd like the chance to apologize to her personally, too."

Frankly, I didn't know what went down after we left last night, but it was certainly enough for my father to come to me with his tail between his legs and apologize. Being a parent made you do crazy, irrational things. I knew this. I was going to take the olive branch he extended.

"Thanks, Dad. Do you have time for lunch this week?"

"Absolutely."

We said our good-byes while I walked back into the kitchen as Callie and Delilah were eating their waffles.

"Is…" She paused. "Everything okay?" she asked, standing and picking up her mug.

I grabbed her free hand and guided her into the hallway. "Yes. My dad called me to apologize for acting like a horse's ass. It seems after we left last night, he got an earful from everyone."

"Are you kidding me?"

"No. Pretty crazy, huh?"

"Yeah," she replied. "Well, when you were on the phone I realized we both forgot that the decorator was stopping by this morning to go over ideas for the new toy room."

"Shit, I completely forgot. Well, I think we're going to hold off on doing anything to the room right now anyway."

"What? Why?" she questioned.

"We'll do something with the playroom eventually, but I thought it would be best to hold off. You never know what the future brings," I said, smiling.

She scrunched her nose. "Eww. You don't want to turn it into one of those S and M rooms, do you? I mean, I'm all for a little spanking and kink, but a whole room, Aaron? I don't know."

"Very funny, smart-ass. All I was thinking was, what if we need an extra room someday?"

"If I move into your room, like we discussed, we'll still have a guest bedroom."

"Well, what if we decide to have a baby?" I said.

Excitement overwhelmed me at the prospect. I knew she'd want to finish school and be married, but I knew children for us wouldn't be far behind.

When several moments passed and she hadn't responded, I realized I'd surprised her. I don't know why she seemed so shocked. I had assumed it was something she thought about, but maybe it was the fact I brought it up that took her aback.

"Callie?"

She looked at me with big eyes before she dropped her Tinker Bell cup, glass shattering and coffee spewing everywhere.

Chapter Twenty-Three

CALLIE—

W hat the hell is the matter with you?" Evelyn asked. "And why do you sound like you're in a cave?"

I was hiding in my closet, calling my best friend, because that's what you did in these situations.

"He…he…he…baby…," I stuttered.

"He who?"

"Mr. Simms. My fifth-grade Algebra teacher with the bad breath and mullet. Who the hell do you think I'm talking about?" I yelled. "Aaron!"

"Aaron found a baby?"

"No, you idiot. He wants one."

She paused. "He wants one what?"

"Ev. Focus. A baby. Will you keep up, please?"

"Oh! A baby. Sorry, I was confused. Oh…oh…," she said excitedly.

I slapped my hand against the phone since she wasn't in front of me and I needed to stop her verbal nonsense. "Aaron wants to hold off on redoing the toy room in case we have a baby."

She gasped. "Is he serious?"

"I have no idea, but he sounded serious about holding off on doing the room."

"Wow. How do you feel about that?"

"I feel freaked the fuck out, that's how I feel," I replied, wringing my hands together to keep them from shaking. "I mean, I only just agreed to live here, as his girlfriend, *this morning*. Plus, I'm not even done with school yet. I'm only twenty-four…"

"Shit," Evelyn said. "I'm so sorry, sweetie. Bridget is calling me. Total wedding crisis going on. I'll call you as soon as I can tonight, okay?"

She hung up and I stood there holding my phone.

A baby? Really? Not only did the fact that the thought had crossed his mind terrify me, but the realization he was actually thinking about it in terms of placement in our home was enough to make that whole vomiting problem I had threaten to return. We *just* decided to live together.

Oh my God. If he's thinking about a baby, that means he probably already *thought* about marriage. How could he be thinking about that already? Does he want to marry me? For shit's sake, I didn't even know why he picked the blueberries out of his blueberry muffin. Why get the blueberry muffin and remove the blueberries, stacking them neatly on a napkin? Why not get the apple cinnamon and not have to perform baked-good surgery to remove the offending berry? Was it the taste he disliked? Texture issues? Not agreeable with his digestive system? These were questions I needed answered, and to get to the bottom of, before I could even consider marrying someone.

"Hey you," Aaron said, knocking on my door. "Can I come in?"

I stepped out of the closet and sat down on the bed. "Yeah."

"What's going on?" he asked.

"Nothing. I needed to…I was…Evelyn was telling me… about…blueberry muffins," I said, panicked.

"Blueberry muffins?" he questioned. He sat on the bed next to me and wrapped his arm around my shoulder. "Odd topic, but I'll go with it. Blueberry muffins: I love them."

Pulling away from his grasp, I jumped up. "Why?"

"Why what?" he asked.

"*Why* do you like blueberry muffins? Is it the muffin or the blueberry part you like? More importantly, why do you pick out the blueberries?"

"What the hell is the matter with you?" He laughed.

"Nothing's the matter with me," I said. "Is it so wrong that I want to know about your pastry preferences?"

"No, there's nothing wrong with it. It was just an unusual question, baby."

"Oh no, don't start that 'baby' shit with me. I'm trying to get some hardcore answers here. Leaving the blueberry muffin out of it now, do you have any allergies I'm not aware of? Should I carry an EpiPen for some reason?"

He looked at me blankly for several moments. "Ah. No. You don't need to carry an EpiPen. You're acting weird. Do you need to take a nap or something?"

"No. I'm sorry. I'm just…tense."

He stood from the bed, his eyes looking me over. "Maybe you need to relax."

Maybe you need to not talk about reproducing.

"I can help you with that," he said as he backed me up against the wall behind me. He pressed his body into me, bringing his lips to my collarbone.

"Um. No. Mmmm, that feels good. We can't," I said.

He placed several kisses across my chest, his lips soft as they traveled across my skin. When he reached the area below my earlobe, he nibbled the area for a few moments before he pulled away, his warm breath lingering on my neck.

"I love you," he whispered.

I closed my eyes as the weight of his words sunk in, wanting to soak them in to a place deep inside me and keep them there forever. It was so bottomless, so unattainable—in words, it frightened me.

"Are you really okay?" he asked, brushing his thumb against my cheek.

"Yeah."

He took in a deep breath, the navy fabric of his fitted shirt stretching along with it. "I know that baby comment I made earlier must have freaked you out a bit."

I rested my head on his chest, relieved he could sense what was really wrong. "It definitely caught me by surprise."

"Well, I didn't mean to catch you so off guard, but I was being honest. I think about these things."

I remained quiet once again, processing…turning it over and over…in my heart and my head. He did want a permanent commitment. He wanted a family. He wanted it with me. A wave of panic ran through me, causing me to shiver and try to recognize where all this fear was coming from. Fisting his shirt in my hands, I wanted him closer...closer... closer. I needed him. I stood on my toes to kiss him and forced my tongue to his mouth with such haste he stiffened under my grip.

"Callie," Delilah shouted from the stairs. "Is it time for the zoo?"

He smiled against my lips. "I'll guess I'll see you later. Have fun today."

One more quick kiss and he left me shaking in my bedroom. I knew I should've told him how it was all too much for me, but everything else with us was so good.

"Bye, baby girl," he said in the hallway. "Come give me a hug before I go."

There was this nagging feeling inside of me, gnawing away at all the happiness I had. The way he looked at me, revered me, was the stuff dreams were made of.

"Love you, Daddy."

And Delilah.

She was getting the family she always wanted. I loved giving her that.

There was so much good and I didn't want to lose it. It all felt too good to stop.

I didn't want to stop the good to tell him how much he was scaring me.

* * *

"Come on, Callie," Delilah said, tugging on my hand. "I see the giraffes."

The zoo was crowded, but was to be expected on such a beautiful day. It proved a good distraction from the morning events. We got close to the fence surrounding the giraffes to get a good look.

"Can you take my picture with your phone?" she asked.

"Of course," I said, digging it out of my purse. "Move over a little so I can get the giraffes in, too."

I stepped back a bit to get everything in the shot, Delilah smiling cheerfully. She had on a pink shirt, which matched the embroidered flowers on her jeans, an outfit she proudly picked out on her own.

"Ready?" I asked. "One-two-three."

I snapped the picture at the same time as my phone began to ring.

Abel.

"Come here, Delilah. Let's go walk down to the elephants."

She ran over as I answered the call.

"Hey," I said.

"Just checking in," he said. His voice was hoarse, no doubt from a late night working. "How are things going over there at the House of Sin?"

"Really, Abel?"

"Yes. *Really*."

"Stay close, Delilah!" I called after her, watching her slow down to wait for me before I returned to Abel. "Everything is," I said, "crazy. I'm beyond overwhelmed."

"Elaborate."

Delilah was a few steps ahead of me, far enough out of earshot and too engrossed in her surroundings to listen. "It's all too much. He's moving way too fast, and I don't know how to make it stop."

"What do you mean by too fast? I mean, aside from working for him, living together, and sleeping together."

"Every day it's something new. 'Callie, I put your name down as Delilah's emergency contact for her gymnastics class if they can't reach me. No need to have it as my parents anymore. That's okay, right?' Or 'Callie, when we decide to get you a new car, we'll get you one with a large backseat. No sense in getting something that won't have enough room. What do you think?' It keeps coming, more and more every day."

Abel sighed. "What do you tell him?"

"What can I tell him? No?"

"Well, yeah. You could speak up for yourself. Hell, I can barely make a crude joke or an inappropriate comment without you telling me to go to hell."

"That's different and you know it. You're a complete Neanderthal, and Aaron…well, I'm in love with him."

"So, because you're in love with him you can't say how you feel? That's seems fairly fucked up."

"Are you even listening to me? I know it is, but I don't know how to tell him without hurting him. You're the one that told me that he was all or nothing. What if I tell him I want to pull back, and he freaks out?"

"You know what? I think you want a guarantee, but that's not happening. Listen, meet me tomorrow morning for coffee. We'll get you all figured out. It'll be okay."

"I have class in the morning, but can meet you at eleven at ChiJava for a few."

"That sounds good. Look, I know—"

"Mommy? Is it time for lunch?" Delilah said, interrupting.

I almost didn't hear her say it, but as soon as it registered, I found it difficult to answer her. The breeze blew her blond curls into her face and she brushed them away as she squinted against the bright sun.

"Did she just call you—" Abel said.

"Yes."

"When did that start?"

"Now," I said, squeezing Delilah's hand. "It started now."

* * *

I didn't want what we had to stop, but it wasn't feeling good anymore. I had to tell him the truth. I had to tell him it was all happening too fast, too soon. I wasn't ready to be a mother, a wife, Mrs. Aaron Matthews. I loved him, probably more than I should, and it was what was holding me back. What started off as purely sexual had evolved into something so different, so exquisitely different, but every day I lied to him it got more and more tainted.

"Want a little pick-me-up in your coffee?" Abel asked, reaching into his jacket pocket. He lifted a silver flask out to me, but I shook my head.

We were at ChiJava, as planned, and I was ready for Abel to help me figure things out. I rubbed my temples and considered his liquor offer. A small shot might settle my nerves a bit.

But then again, I knew a horse tranquilizer was going to be my nerves' speed. I had little concentration during class, and I'd even forgotten my phone at home, which I never did. I hated putting more lies on top of lies when I told him I needed to meet Evelyn after class because of boy problems. *Her* boy problems.

"All right," he said, taking a swig from his spiked coffee. "This is what you're going to do. Put on something super sexy, like a short skirt with your garters showing. Wear it with a tight top that shows off your—"

"Are you being serious? I mean, this is your brother."

"Sorry. I got carried away in wardrobe selection. My point was to give him a distraction, mainly yourself, and that way, when you let him know things are going a bit too fast for you, he's too busy thinking about how hot you look to really process."

I gave him a dirty look. "That's the most immature, ridiculous thing I've ever heard."

"Yeah, but so are men. It's only to soften the blow. Then, you remind him of all the things you're into him about."

"I don't know."

"Look," he said, reaching across the table and picking up my hand. "I've seen him with other women, seen him married, and have never seen him as happy as he's been with you. You need to get the truth out there because ultimately it's the most important thing to him. You can do this."

"I hope so. Thank you for being such a good friend, Abel. Aside from Evelyn, you've been like my other best friend these last few months."

He laughed loudly and brushed his hand across his dark beard. "Well, I'd like to think I'm the voice of reason."

"You've been more than that. I'll always—"

Something slammed down in the middle of the table and stopped me. When my eyes focused on what it was and the hand it was attached to, my heart stop.

"You forgot your phone at home," Aaron said coldly. "I checked your last text to see if I could find out where you and Evelyn were meeting so I could bring it to you."

His jaw was clenched so tight, veins were protruding from his neck, thick and angry. The three of us were silent for a few moments; during that time, I focused on his eyes. I didn't even recognize them. The stunning blue eyes which always put me at ease were hard, almost unfocused in their anger. I watched as his eyes shifted to Abel and my hands, still being held, and the pieces all came together. He wasn't upset I lied to him about being with Evelyn, but he seriously thought something was going on between Abel and me.

I pulled my hand from Abel's. "Oh Aaron, it's not what you think."

He threw his head back, an incensed, mocking laughter falling from his lips. "I thought you might come up something better than a cliché. Then again, you both think I'm pretty stupid, don't you?"

"Listen," Abel stepped in. "You know nothing like that is going on." He stood up and put his hand on Aaron's shoulder. "Come on, let's get out of here."

Aaron shoved Abel's hand from him, stepping back and glaring at him. "Don't. Just…don't. Christ, Abel. After everything, fucking everything. Fuck, you know how I feel about her."

"Now, hold it right there," Abel said. His face began to show signs of matching Aaron's anger. "Don't make this into something that it isn't. She's your girl and we are not doing anything wrong."

"If there is nothing to hide, why the hell is that what you're doing?" he asked. He turned to me and stared.

"I wasn't—I haven't—" I said.

"Oh please," Aaron said. "Don't embarrass yourself. Meeting Evelyn because she was upset? Nice to see there was no boy problems. Who came up with that? You, Abel? Or you, Callie?"

Abel pushed against Aaron's chest, leaving his hand firmly on his brother. "All right, she lied. So did I, but that's it. It's not like we do it all the time and—"

"Whoa, wait," Aaron held up his hand. "How long has this been going on?"

I stood and reached for him, but the moment my fingers touched his skin, he jerked away. "Look, let's go home, okay?" I said. "We'll go home and talk this through, please?"

He didn't even look at me.

"I'd like to have a word alone with my brother," he responded.

"All right," I said, gathering my things. "I'll wait outside."

I walked out, the afternoon sun bright and warm in my tear-filled eyes. I wondered if I should've left them alone in there at all, not knowing what kind of scene was going on. It was as if the universe was listening to every one of my worries and thought, *You know, Callie, I think it could get a heck of lot worse. How about we give you this?* I giggled sadly to myself. Maybe I could find some humor, some sad, twisted humor in the way I'd screwed everything up.

Aaron stormed out of the restaurant, the door flung open and slammed against the side of the building. "I'll meet you at home. Delilah's at my parents'," he said.

Before I could respond, his back was turned, and he took off to his car.

He couldn't even look at me. Here I was worried about how our talk would go, and now all I could worry about was convincing him I wasn't keeping things from him.

But I was.

All the way up to the home we shared, the house that sometimes felt like it reached the clouds, a dressing of numbness surrounded my body to protect me from what I knew was going to hurt me so badly. The front door was ajar when I got there, and as I entered, I listened for him but was only met with silence. Down the hall and toward the kitchen, I still heard nothing, and I briefly wondered if he was waiting for me upstairs. No. I knew where he was.

I reached the third-floor door, opening it to a soft breeze that ran across my skin. I paused at the doorway, watching him gaze at the soft waves of Lake Michigan, his body rigid with stress.

"Hey," I said quietly.

His head slowly turned, and he greeted me not with his usual smile or excitement, but with vacant eyes. He looked back out to the lake and began speaking with his back to me.

"I shouldn't have accused you two of anything. I know Abel wouldn't do that to me."

I rushed to him, my hands lifting to touch him. "See, it's okay. We'll be okay," I said.

The moment my fingers met the side of his face, a place I had kissed over and over, he jerked away from me.

"You've been lying to me, Callie. For months and months, you've been lying about these secret meetings with my brother and I want to know why."

I took in a deep breath and closed my eyes, telling myself that it was time. It was time for everything I had been holding back, for everything I was afraid of to…

Come out.

Not knowing where else to start, I said the first thing that came to mind. "Abel knew from the start. In fact, I think he knew before we did."

I told him about that first night out with Abel and how we talked about Aaron the entire time, that same night we had made love for the first time.

I told him Abel saw in him something he hadn't seen in so long, and because he loved him, he gave me advice on how to proceed with him.

I told him how Abel comforted my fears and insecurities about our relationship so that I didn't have to burden him with it.

I told him I had been riddled with guilt for hiding things from him, that today was going to be the day I told him everything.

I told him I loved him.

Over and over again. I loved him.

He didn't interrupt, not once. He didn't so much as even nod or show any emotion whatsoever, and when I was done, he took several minutes to process everything I said.

"You know, I thought the idea of you messing around with my brother was bad," he said when he finally spoke. "But in some ways, this, what you just told me, is worse."

"What do you mean?"

He shook his head and rolled his eyes, seemingly incensed I wasn't following him. "You went to my brother, Callie. Things you should have been talking to me about, you went to Abel, and talked to him about it. How do you think that makes me feel?"

"I was trying to work through things on my own, and talking to Abel helped me get perspective so I didn't seem insecure," I explained.

"What were you so insecure about? I thought things with us were fine. In fact, I thought it was better than fine."

Tears I'd been holding in started to roll down my cheeks, hot against my skin. "We were fine, but Aaron, you're pushing, you're pushing me way too hard. One minute we were screwing around, the next we are in love, and the next you're talking about having a baby. It was too much for me."

"Then why didn't you say so!" he screamed, his tone and volume startling me. "Jesus, Callie, you let me walk around thinking you were as into things as I was."

"I was," I shouted back. "I am, but you're trying to make me into something I'm not. You're hurt that I kept that from you? I'm sorry, but it hurt me just as much that you don't know who I really am."

"What the hell is that supposed to mean?" he spat, his face red with anger.

"It means dressing me up a day after we finally admitted our feelings so you could make a point to yourself and your family. You wanted everyone, including yourself, to know you weren't just banging the nanny. I mean, you got me all fancied up in designer clothes and diamonds knowing full well your family would know I could never afford any of it. And honestly, I'm not even sure it had anything to do with money, or any of it. You wanted me to play a role and for a long time I tried to."

His jaw dropped open and he stood still. "That is untrue."

"Is it?"

"Yes, it is." He roared, "Shit, Callie! You know what? I'm not going to let you turn this around on me. If you weren't cool with going, or anything else, you should have opened your mouth like an adult and told me."

I gasped at his blatant jab at my age. "I wondered how long it would take you to blame all my concerns on my age."

"Well, it certainly is starting to show now."

"You were moving way too fast for me. I was scared to tell you because I was frightened of your reaction. Now, I can see I was right to be nervous."

"I am *not* angry about you wanting to slow things down. I'm angry that you lied." He ran his hands roughly through his hair, just as he'd done earlier, but now he held on tight to it in his two large fists. "God. It's like you don't know me at all! Like you have no clue how lying and deception and keeping things hidden messed up my marriage with Lexie. That it took me years...*fucking years*...to recover from that, and the only reason I did was because of my daughter."

"How would I know that? All you ever said was that she didn't want to be a mother. This is what I'm talking about. We barely know each other, *really* know each other."

His eyes continued to rip through me. There was no balance between anger and love there. He was all indignation. I wanted to run, as far away as I could, to stop the pain that flooded me.

But there was no place to run. I had to stand there, with his cold eyes on me, and my body trembling with heartbreak and dread.

I needed him to understand.

"Aaron," I said, wiping my cheeks of tears. "This is what you need to understand about me now. I have been working my ass off for years…years! I've never had anything of my own. Even my degree is owned by someone else until I can pay for it! So now, for the first time, I may be able to have something for myself, to enjoy the freedom I earned, but instead, I have you talking about babies and Delilah calling me 'Mommy.' I can't…"

"You should have…" he interrupted.

"I'm not done," I shouted. "I can't give any more to you than I already am because I'm still trying to figure me out. *Me*, Aaron. I don't know who the hell I am if I'm not working all the time, going to school and worrying about everyone and everything else. I know I should've told you, but instead, I defaulted to what I knew…trying to be what you wanted."

He bit down hard on his lower lip as his eyes looked to the sky. "I didn't want that. I never wanted anything different than what you are. I wanted the smart, funny, energetic woman who kicked my ass at Ms. Pac-Man and cared for my daughter with such devotion. I wanted you."

"And the sex, too, right?" I'd regretted saying it immediately as the words left my mouth, but there was an element of truth to them. The sex came first with us, and sometimes it seemed like all other emotions that followed were blurred because of it.

"Is that how you feel?" he asked. "That it was just about sex?"

"No."

"Good because don't confuse it, Callie. Good sex, no, great sex, the best sex of my life never held a fucking candle to how I felt about you."

Felt.

Past.

He shifted his weight back and forth, like the emotions were crushing him. I wanted to make it better, make it all go away, but I couldn't do that if it meant sacrificing myself. It didn't mean I didn't still love him. I still did, but wasn't going to drown myself to save him.

"I could say sorry for a million things," I said. "But the thing I'm most sorry for is that it took me this long to tell you how I really feel."

His eyes moved to the lakefront again. A chill ran through me that had nothing to do with the temperature, but with him removing the warmth he'd encircled me in for so long.

"I'm sorry it took you so long, too," he said without looking at me. "It was stupid of me to think that with all of the shit stacked against us this could actually work. So fucking stupid."

I shook my head. "It wasn't stupid. I never expected to fall in love with you, but I did. I do."

He continued to avoid my eyes, the place where I knew he'd see truth. Maybe he wasn't ready for that.

"So what do we do now?" he asked. "Rewind? We go back to how things were? I pretend you didn't lie to me about how you felt. I rewind to before I fell in love with you, and ignore the fact that the whole time you trusted my brother more than me with your feelings? I pretend you see a future with me?"

"I never said that. Of course I see a future. I wouldn't be here if I didn't. And frankly, stop acting like it was this enormous betrayal with Abel. We were talking, not fucking."

His head turned and his features had passed from anger to something much, much worse. "*You* don't get to explain to me about betrayal. It may be minor to you, I'm sure it was to Lexie when she lied, but those little things all come together. Then, without even seeing it coming, BOOM," he shouted. "It destroys everything. So, forgive me for being emotional." He drew in a deep breath, attempting to regain some type of composure. "Now, answer my question. What do we do now?"

I had no idea. None at all. I was drowning in guilt and anger and sadness. But the one thing that rose to the top of it all was how much I loved him.

"I don't know what we do," I whispered.

In two swift steps, he stepped in close to me, towering above me with his chest heaving in madness. "And that right there is something I can't get over. You didn't think about what this would do to me, or more importantly, to Delilah."

"I love that little girl more than *anything*. I did what I did, but don't you dare spin it to be like I don't love and care for her."

He bit down on his bottom lip as I saw tears form in his eyes for the first time. "Well, that's the thing, Callie. Delilah and I are a package deal. You ruin me, you ruin her."

I reached for his face and this time he didn't back away. My hand cradled the side of his face, and he hesitantly eased into my touch as his eyelids closed. Relief washed through me, knowing my touch and all he knew of my devotion to him would be enough to ease him. He'd feel it. He'd remember all we shared, that I loved him and that he loved me. He'd know this was a bump in the road, a minor detour.

He held still in my hand, every passing moment reassuring me more and more he'd understand.

Then his eyes opened.

And I knew.

I'd lost him.

"I want you out," he said almost calmly. "Now."

"Okay," I said, drawing my hand away from him. "I'll stay at Evelyn's tonight and tomorrow after we both have time to calm—"

"For good. Not overnight."

He said it so…simply, like it was *easy*. My insides were being torn apart as he decided to change our lives. Completely.

He stepped away and started toward the door. "I'll tell Delilah…something. I don't know. I need to think."

I felt like I was suffocating. I couldn't catch my breath, my eyes blurred through tears. "Are you kidding? You're not going to let me say good-bye to her?"

"No," he said without hesitation. "She's going to be devastated enough as it is without seeing you like this."

I wanted to run to him and grab his clothing, his skin, whatever was left of us...anything, to make him listen.

"Aaron," I pleaded.

He stopped. "I don't like surprises, either, Callie," he said without turning to look at me.

His final words to me were loud and clear in the slamming of the door.

Chapter Twenty-Four

Aaron—

She was gone by the time I got home.

She did what I asked and she was…gone. It should have been a relief, but all I felt was emptiness. Walking into the quiet house, no sounds of her laughter or of Delilah's who was staying the night at my parents', was a sickening reminder of what had happened. In one day, my life had been turned upside down, leaving me broken.

I went upstairs and entered her room. It looked exactly how it had before she had moved in. Empty. Peeking into her bathroom, I saw none of her things were scattered across the vanity as they had been that morning. Brushes and hair ties, perfume, and makeup were all gone; just the faint smell of her shampoo lingered. Walking back into the room, I eyed the closet. It was empty except for a Saks Fifth Avenue garment bag and shoe box directly next to it. I knew before even looking what it was, but I felt the pull to make sure. As I reached the closet, the zipper to the bag was slightly down on top, revealing the stunning cobalt-blue color of the dress she'd worn.

I sat down on the edge of the bed and lowered my head into my hands, feeling the tide of overwhelming emotions trying to drown me. Anger, hurt, sadness. The moment I would focus on one, another would flood in and replace it, all the while the same question circling through each of them.

How the hell had this happened?

How had she said she loved me, just that morning, and now she was gone? Lies. It was always lies. The path I traveled with Lexie, the lies she had interwoven into our lives, should've made me more aware of someone who would do it again. All it did was make me into a fucking fool. My head had screamed at me that getting into a relationship with her was a bad idea, but my heart screamed back louder. I'd lost the battle before it had even begun. I fought and fought, but at my weakest, my lips touched hers and I knew.

She was the one.

And now she's gone.

I was hollow.

I would deny it and try to force it away, but touching her, kissing her, making love to her only made things clearer. She was what was missing. The thing that always felt out of reach with Lexie, the ache at the core of my loneliness even after we divorced was extinguished with Callie. She soothed the pain and filled the emptiness. I felt whole and it blinded me. Now, there wasn't a hint of joy left in me. All that was left was a huge, gaping hole in my heart, a heart so damaged I didn't even know how I was breathing.

I couldn't sit in this room and look at everything that was

gone. I'd have to get rid of the bed. Maybe all the furniture. If I had to start fresh, I needed it all gone.

I'd have to ask my mom for help with Delilah while I was working. *Shit.* Here I go again. All over again. Single parenting and depending on others to help me. This was why I wanted to have a nanny, someone to live with me and take care of Delilah while I wasn't around. Someone I could count on and trust with my daughter. Callie was all those things, but it had gotten all messed up. Now, there was no way I could have someone new in the house to help me. Not only would I not confuse Delilah like that, but I just *couldn't* do it. I couldn't look at another woman, a nanny or otherwise, in this house without being painfully reminded Callie was missing from it.

With my body and mind numb, I stood from the bed and turned to leave the room, but as I passed her dresser, I noticed the box sitting there. Just like with the dress, I didn't need to open it to know what was in there, but again, I felt compelled to. I walked over and ran my fingers over the top of the small box, feeling the smooth velvet and remembering how I felt giving it to her. Excitement, nervousness, but ultimately, I felt certain. Callie was my future, just as I'd told her once the earrings were on her. I was filled with such naive belief we were on the right road, I never could've foreseen where we ended up. Now, all that was left of my future with her were the gifts I had given her, left behind, in an empty room.

I put the box in my pocket and went downstairs, stopping in the kitchen to put something together for dinner. As I stood in front of the refrigerator, I quickly realized I didn't want to eat. I wouldn't be able to stomach any food if just looking at it was making my stomach churn. I slammed the refrigerator door shut and reached into the cabinet next to it to grab a bottle of Johnnie Walker and a glass.

I didn't want to eat. I didn't want to talk to anyone. I didn't want to sit in my own damn house and remember her in every single inch of it.

I didn't want to feel a fucking thing.

* * *

"Did you hear me? Wake up!"

I slowly opened my heavy eyes and was immediately sorry I did. The sunshine coming through the windows burned my eyes, and my head felt like daggers were being shot through it. My eyes tried to focus as I noticed Abel standing above me, but everything was a blur. My hands tried to push my body off from the living room floor, but I couldn't.

"Look at you," he said. I could barely make out the disapproval in both his tone and eyes. "Passed out on the floor of your living room with an empty bottle of whiskey."

"What do you want Abel?" I questioned. My speech came out distressed and loud.

He shoved my shoulder hard. "You're still fucking drunk. Unbelievable."

"So what? What the hell do you care?"

"Actually, I don't care. In fact, you can drink yourself into oblivion if it makes you feel better, but something tells me that it won't."

I struggled to sit up, my body aching from the position I

passed out in. I climbed onto the couch and sat my tired body down. "Whatever. Get out of here."

"I will, but not until you hear what I have to say."

I chuckled. "Yeah, I'm sure you have a lot to fucking say. You have all the answers, don't you?"

"Let's get something clear," he said, bending over to look me in the eye. "You can drop the attitude. I want you to sit there, listen to what I have to say, and keep your damn mouth shut for once."

I rolled my eyes at him and sat back against the couch, letting him say whatever he had come over to say.

"I have no idea how you could've thrown her out like that nor do I have any idea what the fuck you said to make her so hysterical, to the point she's practically catatonic right now. What I do know is she had to pack all her shit in fucking garbage bags because she had no boxes or anything besides one suitcase. I also know this high-and-mighty bullshit of yours has got to stop, and I'm here to tell you, if you let her get away, you deserve every bit of what's coming to you."

I couldn't have interrupted him if I wanted to because I was so stunned by his words and accusations. I let it all sink in, and with every word I replayed in my head, every emotion I was able to process, a fiery rage erupted from deep inside of me.

One moment I was sitting there, the next I was pushing him away from me so forcefully he fell to the ground. I wanted to hit him, hurt him, not only because of what he said, but because he was the only thing near me at the moment that I could make hurt just as badly as I was. Instead I picked up the empty Johnnie Walker bottle and threw it against the wall, and shattering the picture frame it hit, shards of glass flying every-where in a shower of destruction.

"Where do you get off?" I screamed. "You don't know what the fuck you're talking about."

He got to his feet and charged toward me, getting up in my face. "I know exactly what I'm talking about, and I think you know it. Where the hell do you get off being self-righteous?" he shouted.

"Get out of my house," I said. I was trying to stay as calm as possible because reeling in my anger was the only way I wasn't going to bash his face in.

I turned from him and started to walk away, but he grabbed my shoulders, stopping me. "You know I'm right. You judged her and didn't even give her a chance to explain."

"She lied to me. For months...," I shouted, but he cut me off.

"So what? Yes, she lied about talking to me about shit, but is that such an unforgivable thing? This is what I mean about you being self-righteous, thinking you're so fucking perfect, wanting everyone around you to be the same. You don't want to hold any responsibility in what happened."

"Responsibility? She's the one who kept secrets."

"Aaron," he said, taking a deep breath and trying to get control of his own anger. "She's not Lexie."

"I know that and Lexie has nothing to do with it. In fact..."

"She's not Lexie, she didn't intentionally betray you," he repeated. "You knew before you married Lexie it wasn't right, that things didn't feel right. You told me Callie healed you and you never felt so complete with someone. She loves you,

Aaron, and you love her. Don't throw it all away."

His tone was more even, controlled, than before and it sent a chill through me. "She lied to me."

"Yeah, you keep saying that, but didn't you keep some stuff from her, too?" he asked.

"Like what?" I asked.

"You were checking her out from day one. You wanted in her pants as soon as you saw her. And even more so, you haven't told her shit about Lexie and the damage she caused you."

"Of course, I was attracted to her, but I didn't hire her so she'd be around for me to fool around with. Plus, I didn't want to bring anything with Lexie into what Callie and I had."

"But that's lying! Keeping something that huge was information she needed to know."

"I know or I knew. I was going to, but then it was too late. I was in love with her and didn't want anything to fuck it up."

"Well, Aaron, way to make it all about you."

"It's not only about me and you know it. If things were moving too fast, she should have said. Instead, she went crying to you about it, and now I have to tell my daughter she's gone. Delilah is going to be devastated. I'm not responsible for that."

"Has she ever, *ever*, been anything but amazing with Delilah? From the moment she got here, she was loving and attentive toward her. I never heard her raise her voice or anything. She didn't hurt you or Delilah on purpose. She was scared. That was it. You talking babies and marriage pushed her too hard, and I'm sorry, you should've known better."

It was like Callie's words were being repeated all over again.

I didn't think there was any way I could feel worse than I already did, but Abel was proving me wrong. The one person I thought I could count on always was the same one throwing everything back in my face.

"Whose side are you on?" I asked softly.

He breathed in deeply and was silent for a moment. "I've always got your back, Aaron. I always have and I always will, which is why I have to point out when you're fucking up. Callie's destroyed. Can you imagine how it felt to be kicked out? Completely discarded like you never gave a shit? And before you say anything, I know you're angry about her confiding in me with stuff behind your back, but you making her leave without saying good-bye to Delilah was the worst thing I've ever seen you do."

My stomach turned, the mixture of alcohol and the sickness of Abel's words. "I can't be lied to again. I've been down that road, and all it got me was divorced and feeling worthless."

"What aren't you hearing? She isn't Lexie, and if you don't get it through your head that every woman isn't, then you'll be alone the rest of your life. You keep talking about lies and deception? What were you doing going through her text messages?"

"She left her phone," I yelled. "I was going to bring it to her wherever she was with Evelyn, but instead I saw your message to her, and well, I scrolled through some other messages. You know how the rest of it went."

"Yeah, with you jumping to conclusions. Did you ever stop to think what you might have done to *our* relationship by throwing accusations around like that?" he asked angrily.

"How could you possibly think I'd ever do something like screw around with the girl you're with? Do you have any idea how insane and hurtful that is?"

"I know you wouldn't, but in that moment it seemed—"

He held up his hand to stop me. "I've never fucking lied to you. Ever. How you could jump to a conclusion like you did, I'll never know. And you can say whatever the hell you want, but you invaded her privacy. So what if she didn't have her phone? You knew she'd be home soon, or when she realized she didn't have it. I think you were snooping around, and you found exactly what you were looking for. A reason not to trust her because you'd been waiting and watching for it."

"I've had enough! Stop!" I shouted, pushing my palms into my eyes in angry frustration. "You think I wanted this? Do you think I'm not torn up inside because she's gone? She was it for me. There has been nothing, *fucking nothing*, except for Delilah in my life for years, and Callie walks in and changes my life. So, don't try and pretend you know better than me because you don't."

I moved myself onto the couch and threw my hands across my face. Pain, from my head, my heart, fucking breathing, caused me to gradually fall apart. I was so angry and the only person around I could take it out on was standing in front of me.

What the hell did Abel know? He didn't know how deep it ran for me with her. How when she smiled, a heat warmed across my chest. How when I saw her with my daughter, who I thought would be her daughter one day, a peace I hadn't felt since the day Delilah was born came over me. How I could barely acknowledge the idea she wouldn't be in my life any longer. He didn't know.

I didn't even know anymore.

Why didn't she just tell me? If it isn't want she wanted—if I wasn't what she wanted—why didn't she say so?

It was then it hit me. Maybe it was me she didn't want.

The weight of those words crushed me as I forcefully rubbed my eyes to stop the burning tears from emerging. Abel moved next to me and rested his hand on my back, an attempt to remind me I wasn't alone.

We sat like that for I don't even know how long. His hand never left my back, and I knew it was his attempt to make peace.

"Take a shower, sober up, and go pick up your daughter," he said. "And if you want to talk, call me."

"Yeah, okay."

He got up and left, and I didn't even watch. I knew I was alone again.

After an hour-long shower and an almost full pot of coffee, I left the house to go pick up Delilah from my parents'. The entire ride there I went over and over in my mind what I was going to say. By the time I walked through the front door, I didn't know if I could do it. All I wanted to do was come clean with my parents, to unload the truth, but I couldn't. I couldn't hear "I told you so."

"Hey there," I said, entering the kitchen.

"Daddy," Delilah said, running to me.

I swept her up in my arms, squeezing her tight and brushing my hand over her soft curls. I'd had no idea when I dropped her off the day before all that would've transpired. I swallowed the lump that had formed in my throat and put her down when I noticed my parents looking at me oddly.

"Hey, sweetie. Why don't you go get your things before we go, okay?" I said.

"Okay."

I waited until she ran out of the kitchen before facing my parents. Just like I always knew when Delilah wasn't feeling well, my own parents knew when something was wrong with me.

"You look exhausted," Mom said. She set a plate of cookies on the table and sat down next to my dad.

"Long night," I said.

"Where's Callie?" she asked.

I closed my eyes and silently reminded myself that the faster I said it, the faster it would be over. Then I could leave. My eyes opened, and I lied.

"Callie's mom fell down her basement stairs. She banged herself up pretty good, so Callie flew out to California to be there."

"Oh my goodness," Mom said. "How is she? Did she break anything?"

"I don't know a lot of details, but there were some broken bones. She'll be okay, but Callie is going to stay out there awhile to look after her."

"How long?" Dad asked. "What about her school? Didn't the semester just start?"

I shrugged. "I don't know. I'll find out more later, but Delilah doesn't know yet and I don't want to tell her until later."

"Of course. And it goes without saying, I'm happy to look after her until Callie gets back," Mom said, standing back up. She stepped over to the counter and picked up a pad of paper and pen. "I want to send flowers. Do you have her mom's address?"

I shook my head. "I'll get it to you, but it's not necessary."

"Well, we know it's not necessary, but we want to," she said.

I rubbed my hand across my forehead, trying to massage away a headache. "Yeah. Okay. I need to get going."

I started to head out of the kitchen, but Dad stood and stopped me. "This must be a lot to take in. You okay?"

Concern was written all over his face, along with Mom's who came up behind him. Having to lie about the situation to them was bad enough, but knowing that they were probably seeing right through it was more than I could take.

I'd tell them the truth. I'd tell them tomorrow or maybe the day after that.

"Yeah. I'm okay," I said.

* * *

Ice cream. Ice cream would soften the blow for Delilah. So, that's where I took her.

"Baby girl?" I said, as we sat at Scoops.

She looked up from her sundae, chocolate smearing the sides of her lips. "Hmm?"

"When we get home, Callie isn't going to be there," I explained, a large lump in my throat making it difficult for me to talk. "Her mommy fell and she had to go help her feel better."

"Where is her mommy?"

"A place far away from here."

She scooped a large bite of ice cream into her mouth. "When I was sick, Callie gave me ginger ale," she mumbled. "Did she give her mommy ginger ale to make her better?"

"I don't know, sweetie."

"Daddy?"

"Yes?"

"Can we go to the pet store after this?"

I breathed in deeply, briefly relieved she wasn't asking more questions. I knew, in the days that followed, there would be many more. "Sure."

"Daddy?"

"Yes, baby girl?"

"Is Callie going to come home soon?"

For the first time all day, I didn't have to lie to anyone, most importantly my daughter. "I don't know."

Chapter Twenty-Five

CALLIE—

Callie? Come on, sweetie, wake up."

I felt a small hand on my lower back, rubbing soothing circles and trying to gently wake me up. I could tell before I even opened my eyes that it had to be late afternoon. My head had that weird fuzzy feeling you get from sleeping too much, and the sun hitting my closed eyelids wasn't as strong as morning rays. Still, I didn't want to open my eyes, regardless of the time.

"It's almost three in the afternoon. Do you have something against sunlight these days or do you just prefer to wallow at all hours?" Evelyn asked.

Her daily motivational speech was neither uplifting nor welcome, but considering how beat down I felt, I didn't have the energy to tell her to fuck off.

"It has been almost three weeks," she said.

When I still didn't respond, she sighed loudly and sat next to me on the bed. "I'm not trying to be insensitive, Cal."

"Well, you are," I said.

I rubbed my eyes and slowly sat up, my back cracking and achy from all the time spent lying in bed.

"Sorry," she said. "I'm worried. You shouldn't let what he did to you affect you like this. Consider it a blessing that he showed his true colors."

"Give me a fucking break," I barked. "You'll be very happy to know I'm going back to school today and starting work tomorrow. Happy?"

I really had no business being angry with her, considering how amazing she'd been to me. I showed up at the apartment, crying and with all my stuff after Aaron kicked me out. She held me while I cried, listened when I talked, and ultimately when I retreated to my bedroom to stay hidden, she let me be. Well, at least until recently. I was sure at some point my moping turned into depression and depression turned into a full-on emotional breakdown which concerned Evelyn. I didn't know what to categorize my state of emotions as because all I felt was empty and numb.

Nothing.

No smiles or joy. No little girl laughs or matching shoes. No kisses. No feeling his warm breath on the side of my face in the morning. No intimate touches. No looks of longing and goofy jokes.

No I love yous.

It hurt more than I could have ever imagined, more than I could even comprehend. All the love and affection I felt from him was equally replaced with pain and anger.

Evelyn rested her hand on mine. "I'm glad you're going back to school, sweetie, but what work are you going to?"

I threw the covers of the bed off me and pushed myself out of bed, past her. "Venom," I responded quietly.

"What?" she exclaimed.

I walked across the hall to the bathroom, calling back to her before shutting the door. "Calm down. It's no big deal."

"No big deal?" she asked. "Why the hell would you go back there? What…you miss the shitty hours and drunken slobs?"

I turned around in the doorway. "No, Evelyn. I don't miss anything. Not the puke-filled bathrooms at the end of the night and the polyester tank top I have to wear while serving horny frat boys. No, I don't miss it, but since my boyfriend kicked me out and I lost my job, I don't have a lot of other options."

Tears welled up in my eyes, mostly from anger at the entire situation, but also from the sheer humiliation. Having to grovel back to a shit job just so that I could pay my rent and stay up to date on all my bills was nothing I'd expected or wanted to do, but I had few options until I finished school, which was still another semester away.

"I didn't mean to upset you," she said. "I just don't want to see you have to work there again. Maybe you can find something else…like…maybe you can look for another nanny job?"

I shook my head. "I can't."

"Well, it's a good résumé builder and I'm sure—"

"I said no!" I shouted. "Damn it."

I slammed the door to the bathroom so hard the frame shook. Then, I sat down on the toilet and cried.

I went to school that day, but as I sat in the classroom, I

didn't know how I got there or what I was listening to, my notes filled with gibberish and swirls. But I went back the next day. And the next.

* * *

Being behind the bar at Venom came right back to me, not comfortably or welcoming, but familiar. Stale cigarette smell, beer, and sex was still the theme, clinging to my body like the drunks I served. Plastic smile to match my practically plastic clothes, both worn well enough on me to give the patrons what they wanted. It felt cheap as it always had, but the difference now was it felt deserved.

Every day I moved, one foot in front of the other, trudging through what felt like wet sand, knowing the only saving grace would be when I could return to my bed and pray for it to swallow me up. It would be quiet and dark and nothing to think about.

I wouldn't have to think about him.

It got colder and colder out, no longer fall, but early winter. We had an early snowfall, before Thanksgiving even, and it turned the city and everything around me gray. It wasn't white, it was gray, melted, muddy, and definitely not white.

No.

No more tears. If I could control nothing else, I could control that. At least that's what I told myself.

I was sitting at Starbucks and should have been doing research and a paper for school, but was reading the gossip sites instead. When my phone rang, it took a moment for me to register the ring tone as him calling. I never bothered to change it since he never called, but it shouted from my phone. I hadn't heard it ring with that tone in over three months. There was hesitation to answer it, but the need to hear his voice was greater. Far greater.

"Hello," I answered tentatively.

"Callie! It's me! Delilah!"

My breath…the air…everything stopped while my heart began to beat so fast it felt painful. There was no one around me, there were no noises, and her tiny voice was all I heard. She sounded the same as she always had, but not hearing her for so long made her voice sound different.

"Callie? Daddy helped me call you." She paused as I tried to compose myself before answering her, wiping tears frantically off my face with cheap brown napkins. "Do you remember me?" she asked nervously.

"Of course!" I exclaimed. "Oh, Delilah, I was just so surprised…you surprised…"

"Do you have the sniffles?"

"Yes," I lied, quietly trying to blow my nose. "How are you? I'm so happy you called!"

"Is your mommy better yet?"

A sick mom. That was what he told her.

"She is, but not all better. I miss you so much, sweetie. What's happening? Doing anything fun?"

"I lost a tooth and Nana took me to see *Mary Poppins* and not the fake one in the movie, but the real one onstage and she flew up high and over us and Daddy says it's too cold now for me to wear my pink shoes that are like yours, but did you know that I was in a play at school and Sam at school got turkey pox disease and do you know what that is? He got itchy like when you're outside in the summer and the bugs get you."

The pink Toms. Mine were thrown out as soon as I unpacked them.

"It sounds like you're having so much fun lately. How's school?"

"It's so fun," she said. "But I miss your pancakes. When your mommy is better, will you come and make pancakes? You can have sleepovers with Daddy again if you want and…"

She trailed off and I heard him. It was super faint, but I still pressed my ear as tightly to the phone as I could, hoping that would make his voice clearer. Closer.

"Daddy said I have to go now."

"Oh…okay," I replied, my voice quivering. "You can call me, anytime you want, okay? Anytime. I'm so happy to hear from you."

"Callie?"

"Yes?"

"Um, will you send me some pancakes that you make because Daddy doesn't do it right and Nana can't make shapes like you so can you send me some?"

I swallowed deeply. "Of course I will, sweetie. I'll figure out how to get them to you as soon as I can, okay?"

"Okay! Daddy said I have to go now. Bye!"

The phone went dead before I could even say good-bye.

As soon as I could process all of it, I wondered how I was going to get the pancakes to her. There was no way I could go to the house even if he wasn't going to be there. Just seeing the home I'd been living in, recalling all the memories, was something I didn't want to revisit.

I decided to figure it out later. Even if I had to send it by private messenger, I would because I promised her, and if I could give her nothing else, I could keep my promise.

I went to three different stores and bought as many pancake molds and shapes as I could. I made banana pancakes, and when I was almost done, I remembered she also liked my blueberry ones, so I made those, too. Since there was so much leftover batter, I decided to make regular, plain ones as well. I had multiple pans, along with a griddle, going all at the same time because I didn't want them to be sitting around a long time. Evelyn had offered to bring the pancakes over to the house for me and promised to be on her best behavior.

Evelyn was standing by, wrapping each batch tightly in foil and placing them in an insulated carrying case for me. Once I was sure everything was perfect, I wrote a short note to Delilah, placing it inside one of the new books I was giving her, and sent Evelyn off on her way.

When she came home, she told me Delilah was so surprised and excited about the pancakes and books. I got a phone call that night from Delilah, thanking me. She continued to call me every week thereafter.

* * *

The new semester, my final semester, started, and for the first time in almost four months, I felt fleeting twinges of hope. I was student teaching during the day, working at Venom at night. I never stopped thinking about him, and while I could ask Abel anytime how he was or if he was seeing anyone else, I didn't. I was finally starting to make peace with the fact that although I had messed up in the relationship, he did something far worse in my eyes.

He left me.

No discussion. No working it out. No listening to my side.

His reaction was hasty and showed me what kind of value he placed on both our relationship and myself. Every day which passed that I didn't hear from him showed me I mattered far less to him than I thought I did, and that was what hurt me the most. I could get over the breaking of my heart, but the breaking of my trust, my respect, would take a long time.

It didn't make me miss him any less, though.

One evening, I was exhausted from teaching and working and I had a rare night off. Evelyn was working late, so with the apartment to myself, I ordered Chinese food, enough to feed me and twelve of my closest friends. I was going to eat every bit of it myself. Anyone who said stuffing your emotions with food was wrong never had the fried dumplings and egg rolls from Dee's, our favorite Chinese place. If a food orgasm was the closest I was going to get to any orgasm, I was going to welcome it. While I giggled to myself over the metaphor, the pit in my stomach of sadness alerted me to the truth in the entire joke. I rubbed small circles over my stomach, soothing the pain and realizing, even after all this time and even though it wasn't as prominent, it was getting better.

Getting better. Not healed.

The knock at the front door startled me for a second before I realized it was probably just my food being delivered, and they were let in by someone else coming or going from the building. I threw a hoodie on over my braless tank top in order to not give the delivery dude a free show and pulled up my sagging yoga pants. Walking quickly to the front door, I stopped to pick up my cash on the table when they knocked again harder.

"I'm coming!" I shouted.

I unlocked the door and flung it open.

It wasn't the delivery guy.

It was him.

Aaron.

I thought I was forgetting his eyes, the color so blue that I lose myself staring into them, but no. They were exactly how I remembered. Everything was exactly how I remembered, his lips, his slightly curled hair, even his broad shoulders—it was all him.

We stared at each other for a few seconds or a few minutes, I couldn't really tell how long it was because I was too busy taking in his face, his presence, and trying to resolve the fact that he was standing right in front of me.

"Hi," he said. "I'm sorry to just drop by like this."

His body swayed slightly as he shifted his weight back and forth, and he looked toward the floor, awaiting my response.

"You're here?" I asked. It wasn't meant to be a question, but that's how it came out—as a question.

"Yes," he replied. "Delilah made something for you for Christmas. I know it's kind of belated but…"

He trailed off and reached into a small gift bag he was holding. He pulled out a pile of colorful construction paper, stickers, and crepe paper held together by ribbons.

"You could have mailed it and saved yourself the trip." The words stumbled out of my mouth and none of them were the ones I wanted or should've used.

"Well, I had this, too," he said pulling something else from the bag.

A Tinker Bell mug, just like the one that I had dropped.

An ache in my chest, starting with a slow burn, began to multiply rapidly as I recalled how many mornings he made my coffee in that mug.

I shook my head free of angst. "Again. You could've mailed it," I repeated.

"I know, but…" He stopped and reached his free hand up to hold on to the doorway, his eyes cast downward. He waited to say anything else.

I waited, too, because I didn't know what to say.

His eyes cautiously moved up to meet mine. "Can I come in?"

I nodded and stepped away from the doorway to allow him in. He walked in and stood awkwardly next to the door. I closed it behind him, his hands fidgety and making the crepe paper rustling the only sound between us. I took a deep breath, realizing I was probably coming off like a heartbroken teenager to him, all quiet and standoffish.

"Do you want to sit down?" I asked.

"No thanks. I can't stay and I'm sure you have plans on a Saturday night." He looked at me almost earnestly, hopeful that I would deny any plans. I decided it was better off, him just thinking whatever he was thinking. Except when my intercom buzzed, alerting me someone was here, I realized my food was in fact being delivered and my cover was probably blown. I excused myself for a moment and buzzed the delivery guy in.

"Sorry, I'm having some food delivered," I explained.

"No problem," he said. "I'm sorry I'm interrupting."

I nodded my head, and once again, we stood in awkward silence. He looked around the apartment, eyeing framed pictures and books lying around. It hadn't occurred to me until that very moment that he had never been here. I mean, why would he have been?

There was a knock at the door, and as soon as I opened it, I realized just how much food I did in fact order. I shoved the money I was still holding in my hand at the delivery guy and took the two large bags of food from him. I could feel his eyes follow me as I carried the bags to the kitchen and set them down.

I turned around in time to see him place the gift from Delilah on the coffee table and then shove his hands in his pockets. The ache and sadness I had in my chest since he'd arrived, or rather…ever since we had been apart, burned even more intensely. He was familiar, but I felt like he was a stranger.

"You're expecting someone," he said, gesturing to the bags on the counter. "I'm sorry for not calling."

He rushed to the door and was about to walk out without a word. "Hey, hold up," I called out, enraged at his gall. "What? Not even a good-bye? Wow. Twice in a row. Classy, Aaron."

He stopped just short of the door and turned around. "You're obviously waiting for someone so I'll leave before I cramp your style."

"Are you serious? Coming over here and storming out? I'm sorry but you can do that at your house. Don't come to mine and do it, too."

I felt the heat, the anger, the hurt…everything I'd suppressed starting to rise to the surface. All these months, with the last words he ever spoke to me fresh in my mind, had been painful, even excruciating at times. He made me leave without a word to Delilah who had become everything to me, and the ache I had from being away from her was something I'd never forget.

He stood still in the doorway, staring at me harshly, which proved to only further my anger. "I think it's best I leave because seeing you have a date, or whatever you're doing, is something I don't care to see."

"Then you shouldn't have come over at all. What I do or who I date is absolutely none of your concern. You made that perfectly clear to me when you threw me out."

"You're right. It isn't my business, and I didn't come over to argue with you," he said quietly.

"Why did you come over, then?" I snapped. "It certainly wasn't to just drop off something from Delilah."

"I wanted…"

"What?" I shouted. "Spit it out. Why did you come here? Was it just to see how miserable I was or if I was dating someone else?"

"No, of course not," he responded incredulously.

"Then what?"

He took a deep breath and blew it out strongly, his eyes focusing on the ceiling instead of me. "I wanted to see you," he whispered.

His soft tone, the words laced with truth, felt like a punch in the gut to me. I had heard his words before and I believed them, but now, I knew I couldn't.

"I don't know how you want me to respond to that," I replied irritated.

He shrugged his shoulders. "Do you think about me, Callie?"

Tears pricked my eyes, but I knew I couldn't, wouldn't, let him see me cry. "Don't do this to me, Aaron."

"Do what?"

"Come here! After all these months and say these things. You kicked me out like I was fucking trash, without a word, without a discussion. So, forgive me that I'm not as welcoming as I should be."

His jaw hung open, and I was shocked that he seemed so surprised at my reaction. I almost wanted to laugh at him to show him how twisted his thinking was, but I couldn't. The gaping wounds he just tore open by simply being in front of me were enough to keep me stone-faced.

"I'm sorry."

I shook my head. "You know what, Aaron? There was a time when I would've been anything you wanted me to be. I would've put on fancy dresses and pretended to be comfortable with it. I would've let you crowd me, and put our relationship on fast-forward. I even would've allowed you to be angry at me for not telling you the truth about Abel, but you don't get to say sorry and have it all be okay. Do you know why? Because it's not fucking okay. You held back from me, too. Whatever you went through with Lexie was still there with you. The baggage was dragged right into the middle of us."

He winced, surprised at my words and the power behind them. I wasn't even sure I'd ever cursed around him before. I watched as his eyes scanned my face, looking for the girl he thought he knew. It hurt my heart to see his pain, but I knew that if I didn't stand up, didn't speak the truth, then it would've been my pain all over again.

"I know it's not okay," he said quietly. "I know, but I couldn't go the rest of my life and not apologize for it."

He took a couple steps toward me, but stopped short of getting too close. "I'm sorry. For what I said. For how I treated you."

I shook my head because I couldn't hear anymore. I couldn't hear apologies or look at him and see the eyes I fell in love with, that I was still in love with, without begging him to stay with me.

"It's too late for an apology. Get out," I said.

He raised his eyebrows to me and crossed his arms in front of his chest. "You didn't like getting dismissed by me, and I don't like it any more than you did."

"How dare you?" I screamed. "How dare you throw that in my face."

"Shit," he yelled. "Damn it. This…this isn't how I wanted this to go."

My emotions betrayed me and the tears began to fall as I stared at the floor.

"Calliope, look at me, please," he asked softly. "I know I reacted badly when I found out about things you were keeping from me, but I hope you understand, that you realize, how upset I was. Finding out you were telling Abel things, things I had no idea about or how you felt about them, made me doubt the trust I thought we had."

He paused briefly, looking at me with such a hopeless expression.

"I doubted you," he continued. "I doubted your feelings for me, and I shouldn't have done that without hearing you out. I felt…betrayed and confused and a flood of emotions from the time I was with Lexie, and I took it out on you."

"Lexie," I said, shaking my head. "She was always the other woman in our lives, wasn't she?"

He looked at me confused. "I don't understand."

"You know," I said. "I always wondered about Lexie. You never even told me the whole story about her, but from what I do know, I can't understand how you loved a woman like her and then a woman like me."

"We were married. We had a child together," he said. His face reddened before continuing. "Can you blame me for having some baggage?"

I didn't hesitate to answer. "Yes. Yes, I do blame you because you're still not being honest. What was it, Aaron? What did she do to you?"

"She left me!" he roared. "She left her daughter without a fucking care in the world! I came home one day and all that was left of her was a note. She didn't even want to see Delilah ever again. So, there it is. That's the baggage."

I watched as his chest heaved in residual anger, and I watched as he slowly worked his way through it. When I thought he was ready for it, I said my piece.

"I'm sorry, Aaron. And I'm sorry for Delilah. I can't imagine how awful that was, but I'm also not her. I'm not Lexie, but you kept waiting for me to turn into her."

His eyes looked around the apartment. He stared at framed pictures on the wall and my grandma's Tiffany lamp before squinting at something in the kitchen. With slow steps, he walked to take a closer look. As he approached the refrigerator, I knew what he had seen. The several things Delilah had colored for me decorated the front of our refrigerator.

He stood in front of the drawings, smiling sadly. "You have been more of a mother to her than Lexie ever was. I should've told you before. I should've told you a lot of things before."

My mind screamed to tell him to leave, but beyond the screams was the quiet voice that told me I needed more. I wiped away the falling tears and stared at the ceiling to keep more of them contained.

"What else should you have told me?" I asked.

Even though my eyes were closed, I heard him moving closer. "I should've told you that I'm not perfect, and I didn't expect you to be, either. I should've told you it wasn't all about sex, that I fell in love with your smile and your boundless energy. I should've told you I'm a hotheaded, stubborn asshole, that there'd be times I need to be put in my place. Mostly," he said, close enough for him to brush his hand against mine, "I wish I told you about my past earlier. I thought I was ready, but I wasn't. Putting everything in fast-forward was my way of making sure I kept you."

I shook my head, unable to understand his reasoning. What had taken so long? Why now?

I couldn't think of all the questions spinning around my mind without considering what my role was in all of this. As much as I wanted to put it all on him, I couldn't. The things I kept from him were the catalyst and his reaction was the result. Two parts that made the whole big fucking mess.

I lifted my head to look at him. "I shouldn't have lied," I whispered.

He was right in front me, so close I squeezed my eyes shut to keep from looking, but it didn't matter. I *felt* him. The energy, the heat, from his body that had always been my downfall was penetrating me, taking over and dragging out all the emotions I'd tried so hard to bury.

His hand left mine and moved, so gingerly, to palming the side of my face while his thumb brushed away the tears.

It was him and his touch, and he was here.

I shook my head against his touch and hesitantly eased myself into his hand. "I want…but…"

His lips, soft and warm, pressed to my forehead. "Tell me," he breathed against my skin.

"I want to forgive you and I want to forget," I answered, pausing briefly. "I want to, but I can't."

"I know," he whispered, holding my face in both of his hands now.

His smell, the smell that was only his was surrounding me

along with his sweet breath. He kissed my forehead again, then my temple and my cheek while my tears streamed down between his fingers. I knew I should tell him to stop, tell him to leave, but I knew once I did, that would be it. He would be gone for good.

"Are you waiting for someone else tonight? Or any other night?" he asked as he ran his nose along my jawline, making my skin erupt with heat in a way that only he could.

"No."

He lifted my face so I was staring at him, our mouths inches apart. "I hope to hell you can forgive me, but if you can't, I understand."

It would have been so easy, so very easy to just tell him I did understand and all was forgiven, but it would have been another lie. I would never be able to live with myself, or look him in the eye, if I let what he did and all he said be forgotten. But I couldn't.

My heart was breaking all over again.

He didn't ask for a response; my silence and my tears told him everything he needed to know. "Shh," he muttered. "Please don't cry. Please."

He brought my mouth to his, brushing his lips against mine hesitantly and waiting for me to tell him it was okay. I didn't.

I pushed him away from me with both hands and watched him stumble back. His determination was fierce, though, and he came right back to me, sweeping his hands through the back of my hair and pulling me toward his face. I wanted to hit him…slap him…scream at him to get away from me, but my heart, the heart that hadn't been whole since he left me, was winning the battle. Suddenly it wasn't a question of anger or hurt, but finally putting it all to rest.

I wanted him to put his healing hands and lips on me and make it better, to say good-bye to me in the only way we knew how.

"Please," he begged.

He wasn't asking me in words if it was okay to move forward, and when I pressed my lips to his, I wasn't answering him in words, either.

His lips moved cautiously with mine while he voiced tiny moans, the sound both arousing and agonizing. Like we had so many times in the past, we let the physical lead our emotions, and while I knew it could lead to only more hurt, I wouldn't stop.

I gripped his shirt tightly in my hands, pressing myself into him as hard as I could.

I knew it wouldn't be close enough until his skin was on mine, our bodies wrapped up in each other, and reminding me of everything I'd lost.

"I missed you," he murmured against my lips. "I'll miss you so much."

He bent down and picked me up, never breaking our kiss until he started carrying me toward the bedroom. I wrapped my legs around his hips and my arms around his neck as I directed him to mine.

"Are you sure?" he whispered as he laid me across my bed.

His knee nudged my legs open for him to get close, and he pushed up from his arms above me. I looked at him, his beautiful blue eyes, now sad and dark. I hated it. I hated that those same eyes once sparkled and delighted in seeing me.

"I'm sure. Just slow, okay?"

Every layer of clothing, every touch, every kiss was excruciatingly gradual. It wasn't about frantic movements or pleasure as it had once been, but about the vehement desire to dull the pain. It could have been minutes or it could have been hours, I didn't know. I didn't care. Every feel of his body under my fingertips, I was committing to memory. I had to remember all of it, all of him, because it was going to be over and there would be nothing left except memories.

Our naked bodies clung together, desperate and wanting, and when he pushed himself into me, we gasped at the sheer mix, the precious combination of pleasure and pain. We knew each other's bodies so well, recalling with instinct how to move together. It was lazy and deliberate, our skin damp with sweat and salt of our tears. Everything in me screamed violently this was making it worse, making it easier for me to tell him to stay, but I didn't care. I had him now, and in mere minutes, I wouldn't anymore.

I loved him, but I hated what we did to each other. We had lied and hurt each other and love doesn't make that go away. Love doesn't conquer all, just like Aaron said and contrary to how the saying goes. I felt like an asshole for believing my whole life that it would.

He moved above me, deeper and deeper with each thrust. It still wasn't close enough. He'd never be. When he couldn't take it anymore, he came inside me, his warmth pouring into me and marking for the last time what was his. He stayed inside me as he rolled us to our sides, unwilling to break the connection for fear of the spell being broken. We laid together like that for a long time, until our breathing normalized and bodies chilled.

With one more kiss to my cheek, he moved from me to sit on the edge of the bed. I watched him pull his boxers and jeans on, and when he turned to grab his shirt, I saw it. There was a new tattoo. Extending from his existing tattoo on his side was musical notes, and long cylinders with steam coming out. All of it was coming from the inside of the scroll tattoo, scattering what was once his blank page.

"New tattoo?" I asked, my voice hoarse from crying.

"Oh yeah," he replied, pulling his shirt on over his head. "About a month ago."

"What does it mean?"

He stared at me hard. "You know on old-fashioned merry-go-rounds they have the steam whistles that produce the music? That is pretty much what it is."

"You know I remember when I was little, my dad would tell me of—" I gasped, and covered my mouth realizing what he had done. "Oh my God."

A small smile lifted his face, his spirit, but it was brief. "Calliope will always be part of my story."

I was stunned and silent as I tried to process. The steam instrument is called a calliope.

I watched him walk toward the door. He stopped shy of it and reached into his pocket, pulling out a small velvet box that I instantly recognized.

My earrings.

He placed them on my dresser. "I gave you these as a gift,"

he said, tapping the top of the box, "and I want you to have them."

I opened my mouth to protest, but he shook his head at me immediately, letting me know any attempt at refusing would be futile.

"Good-bye, Callie."

I peeked out my window in time to see him reach his car parked in front of the building. As if he knew or hoped I was watching, he looked up at me and smiled sadly. Then in a flash, he was gone, leaving only the sound of his car taking off down the street. I strained until I couldn't see it anymore.

Then there was nothing.

Chapter Twenty-Six

AARON—

I sped away in my car and away from her, leaving my heart and what was left of my sanity behind. Once I was down the street, I pulled over, knowing full well I wasn't in any position to be on the road when I was so upset. After I'd stopped, I turned off the engine so I could process what the hell happened.

What the fuck did I just do?

I pounded my fists against the steering wheel, feeling sick for fucking up the last time I was probably going to see her. All the planning out in my head what I was going to say, all the fucking therapy I'd gone through in the past four months, and I still managed to mess it up. It's exactly what I didn't want to happen, but seeing her, how the hurt was still so fresh on her face, I lost all of my purpose.

I told her so many things, but the one thing I didn't was that every day I regretted what I had done and how I treated her when she left. The days and weeks after she left I drowned myself in self-pity and anger. It wasn't until I was confronted by the last person I expected to help me that I started to see things in a different light.

***

I sit in my office at the Regency building, drowning in e-mails and unreturned calls. It's been a month since Callie left, and I am only beginning to dig myself out of all I have neglected.

A knock on the door brings me out of focus, and I see my dad step inside, closing the door behind him.

"Hey Dad," I say, standing up. "Did I forget we were meeting?"

He hugs me, patting my back firmly. "Nope. I was in the neighborhood and thought I'd stop by to say hello."

He clears his throat and jingles the coins in his pocket with his hand.

I narrow my eyes at him. "Have a seat, and then tell me why you're really here."

"I need a reason?" he asks.

"Of course not, but I can tell you're lying," I say, sitting back down. "Ever since Marshmallow the guinea pig died, and you told me it ran away, I've known you lied when you do the cough-coin-jingle combo."

He sits down with a sigh. "Did you and Callie break up?"

I've let my parents think, ever since she left, she's with her mother. I know I must come clean eventually, but keeping up the charade for the time helps me keep my head above water.

At least I could put an end to one lie.

"Yes," I say. "Did Abel tell you?"

"*Yes, but don't be angry with him. Your mother and I knew something was going on, and we were concerned. He was worried, too.*"

"*I know,*" *I say.*

After several moments of silence, he asks me the question I know will come next. "*Why didn't you tell us?*"

"*And hear the dreaded 'I told you so?'*" *I reply.*

"*I wouldn't have said that, and I won't now.*"

"*I have a hard time believing that,*" *I shoot back.*

"*Are you going to tell me what happened?*" *he asks.*

I shrug my shoulders "*Same ol' same ol.'*"

"*What does that mean?*"

"*It means, I should have learned my lesson from Lexie, but obviously I didn't and let another woman blindside me.*"

He lifts his eyebrows in surprise. "*She took off?*"

"*No, I told her to leave.*"

"*Wow,*" *my father says, tilting his head to the side in confusion.* "*She must've done something pretty unforgivable for you to ask her to leave.*"

"*She…lied to me.*"

"*Was it another man?*"

"*Yes, it was Abel.*"

"*What?*" *he questions, raising his voice.* "*Abel and Callie were having an affair?*"

I lean back in my chair, already exhausted by the conversation. "*Not exactly. I found out they were talking and meeting sometimes behind my back.*"

"*Did you think these talks and meetings were of a romantic nature?*"

"At first I did, but then I realized I was wrong. I guess Callie was feeling insecure about our relationship, and instead of talking with me about it, she went to Abel."

He nods his head again, his face void of any measurable emotion. "I see," he says.

Something in his tone, the indifference, makes me angry and heat begins to rise through me. "There was more than that, Dad," I add in an attempt to defend my actions.

"Well…that's too bad," he replies. "After overcoming the shock of seeing you and Callie together, and getting past my initial worry, it seemed like it was the real thing. Honestly, I'd never seen you happier."

I fight the urge to laugh because he is being so obvious.

"If you have something to say, which you obviously do, I wish you'd just say it."

"You're right. I do have something to say, but considering how upset you are, I was going to keep it to myself. The last time we had a disagreement about your love life with Callie it didn't end well. I was being a little more conscientious this time, but since you want to hear it, I'll tell you." He pauses briefly before continuing. "I know how difficult the breakup with Lexie was for you, and you probably have a lot of residual hurt from that, but if you don't get past it, you're going to ruin every single relationship you have, both with your family and significant others."

"That is completely untrue. How can you even say that to me?"

"Because you're my son and I love you."

"Oh, please," I say, rolling my eyes.

"That," he says, pointing a finger at me. "Right there. That's *exactly the kind of attitude I'm talking about. You think you're the only one who's had it tough? That has trust issues? You're going to let one bad experience ruin your life? Fine. Let it, but you'll regret it. I worried about the consequences of this relationship because I knew you'd be watching for any hint of less than perfection, and once you saw it, you realized she was just that. Not perfect."*

"I didn't need perfection. All I needed—all I wanted—was honesty."

"I hardly think talking to your brother and having coffee with him was such a huge breach of trust and a reason to break up with her."

"I told you! There is more to it than that."

"Yes, you did, and I don't even know what that is. It's not for you to explain or for me to understand. It's between you and Callie, but I'll tell you this, Aaron. Your mother and I haven't been married for almost forty years by chance."

"Yes, I know," I say. "Marriage is hard work. Ups and downs and all that bullshit."

His face softens. "I met your mom when we were both so damn young. We didn't know which way was up and which way was down, but I knew... the moment I saw her... there was no one else, there would be no one else. And that's what you hold on to, to make it work."

"Yeah, well, that's nice and all, but sometimes things are more complicated than that."

"Only if you want them to be. You have to think to yourself: Can I live the rest of my life without this person? I know I couldn't, so you work through the hard stuff. Maybe you need to *ask yourself the same question. Can you live the rest of your life without her?"*

He sits quietly, staring at me, for several minutes before he stands. "Love you, son."

* * *

Then he was gone, too.

The months that followed were predictable and common. Delilah, work, and putting up a convincing front were my daily objectives. For the most part, I was able to keep it up pretty well, but there were times when I would come across something of hers, a hair tie in one of my bathroom drawers or a T-shirt left in the laundry room, and my mind would be flooded with memories.

All of the what-ifs.

So many what-ifs.

The more I considered the fact that I might've made a mistake, the further I slipped into a place so dark my skin would crawl with fear. There was hurt and sleeplessness and guilt and too many fucking feelings for me to separate them all. It got to a point where I decided to take my father's advice and stop playing the martyr and get some help. I started seeing a therapist and talking out all the things I'd buried for so long.

Time marched on. Through the fallen leaves and snow-covered streets. Through Thanksgiving and Christmas and New Year's. Time moved forward.

But I stayed still.

I married Lexie when I knew I shouldn't have. I pushed

her and tried to get her to mold into the perfect wife and the perfect mother when she simply wasn't capable of it. I used the excuse of her leaving to stay closed off, and when I met Callie, the lid got blown off. Sex and emotions manifested and it was so fucking good, I ignored what was staring me in the face. I simply didn't know Callie. I knew her body and her kindness. I knew her love for my daughter and her free spirit. I knew her determination and fierce desire, but I didn't know *her*. So much of that was on me, too. I saw how I could have the family for Delilah and myself that I always wanted with Callie. I pushed and tried to mold her into what I thought we could be. I never stopped to ask her what she truly wanted.

I'd have to make do with the fact I never would and that was the worst part of everything.

No. Actually, the worst thing ever was realizing I was the one who told her to leave.

Time moved forward, but I stayed still.

Then one day I realized I was starting to forget things…the smell of her freshly shampooed hair and the taste of her skin just above her collarbone. It made me wonder if it was ever real.

I tried and tried to keep my resolve up, through hearing her voice talk to Delilah so often, through the lonely nights, through all the therapy in which I was realizing and taking ownership of where I went wrong, until one phone call with Abel blew it all up in my face.

It was an unseasonably warm March day and I was sitting at the park, watching Delilah run and burn off the energy she'd stored away during the long Chicago winter. I was fiddling with my phone when a call from Abel came through. We certainly hadn't been talking as much since what happened, so I was surprised he was calling.

"Hey Abel," I say, answering.

"Hey. What's up?"

"Nothing too much. At the park with Delilah. How are things going?"

"No complaints. Delilah's good?" he asks.

"She is. She loves going to preschool and Mom's been a big help after recovering from surgery."

"Are you going to look for a new nanny…or…someone to help you out?" he asks hesitantly.

"Eventually, but I think…well…I guess," I drift off, choosing my words carefully. "I'm not ready for that."

His silence speaks volumes. Maybe it's because he's my brother or that I know he'd never want to hurt me, but I know he understands me.

Then he tells me so.

"I understand," he says. "It sounds like a wise move for right now."

"Thanks."

We haven't spoken of Callie since the day after she left. The same day he came over and found me shit drunk and drowning in my own self-pity. So many times since then I want to ask him how she's doing. Even at my most angry, I wonder, but never ask. If I did, it would be, in some way an admittance of guilt.

Now? It's time and I need to move forward with it.

"How is she?" I ask.

"Callie? She's…well."

The hesitation he uses, along with his tone, don't settle well with me. "Well?"

"Actually, I don't see her very often. School and she's busy at night so…yeah."

Nausea rolls through me and a lump forms in my throat. If she's never home in the evening, it could only mean she's out, with someone. "I see," is all I manage to respond.

"Considering the circumstances, she had to go back to working nights…at Venom."

"What? Why would she do that?"

"Why do you think?" he replies, his voice raising. "She needed a job."

I fight the urge to question him further because as much as I want to know, as much as I need to know, I lost that right when I asked her to leave.

"She's graduating soon. She got a job already, too. She just found out, I guess. I don't know the details, but the school she's student teaching at loves her and offered her a job for next fall."

I let my eyes fall shut, feeling such an overwhelming sense of happiness and pride for her, for all she worked so hard for. "That's really great," I respond.

We're quiet for a minute, each of us waiting for the other to talk, and letting the tension diminish.

Abel clears his throat. "So, I'll talk to you later, okay?"

"Yeah. Maybe drinks some night this week?"

"For sure."

Later that evening, I was tidying up in Delilah's room while she spent the night at my parents'. I stripped the sheets off the bed to wash them, and as I removed the mattress cover, the mattress shifted and I noticed something underneath. A picture and something on multicolored paper, half on the bedspring, half on the mattress. I pushed the mattress over so I could retrieve the items, wondering why it was there.

I pulled it out and once I recognized it was picture of Callie, Delilah, and myself, a pain shot across my chest. I had no idea where she got the picture from or how it ended up there. The other thing was a Christmas card she'd evidently made for Callie and never told me about. For whatever reason, Delilah was hiding it under her bed, making sure I'd never see it. I sunk to the floor.

The picture. The card her little hands made, but were too afraid to tell me about, left me frozen and sick.

I'd fucked up.

I needed to make it better.

I grabbed the earrings she left behind, along with the card Delilah made, and took off. I rehearsed on the way there what I would say, how I would ask for forgiveness and plead with her to talk it out with me like we should have so many months ago. But the moment I stepped back into her world, nothing went as I planned.

None of the words came out right. I panicked when I thought there was another guy coming over. She was so mad at me still. It was like walking into a tornado, everything out of order and spinning around madly.

There were movements and words and I tried to reach her, but she had already decided.

It had been too late.

I looked up at the sky as tiny droplets of rain began to fall, dragging me from my recollections and alerting me to where I actually was.

I had to go back.

I couldn't leave it like this. My father's voice was ringing in my head, "Can you live the rest of your life without her?"

No. I didn't want to. Not after seeing her face and knowing I couldn't live the rest of my life without seeing it again.

Things didn't need to be complicated. Not after realizing the role I played in things not working out. Not after the awful things I said to her.

Not after seeing the pain in her eyes, hearing her tell me it could never work between us again, and not telling her I didn't need to be her lover or her boyfriend, I just needed her in my life.

Not after leaving her right after making love, leaving her to think that was all I wanted or had ever wanted from her.

It didn't have to be perfect. I only wanted us to be.

I ran back to my car and raced back to her apartment. There was no rehearsing as I had done earlier, no thoughts of exactly what would happen. It just needed to be authentic. It needed to be honest, complete, me.

Before I had another thought about what I was doing, I was at her door, praying she would open for me. The light footsteps on the other side of the door let me know someone was coming.

Then she was there.

"Are you okay?" she asked, concerned.

"Blueberries," I blurted out. "They stain my teeth."

"What?"

"You asked me once, you wanted to know why I picked the blueberries out of my blueberry muffin. They stain my teeth, but I still like the blueberry taste."

She continued to look at me, a mixture of concern and confusion.

"I spent a semester abroad in France and I got arrested for streaking across the Fountain of Versailles." I paused to gauge her expression, but it was still too cryptic for me to discern. "I've never told anyone that."

"Aaron…"

"I lost my virginity to Mandy Fernberg when I was sixteen in the backseat of my father's BMW. Also, I was so messed up after Lexie left, I was on antianxiety medication for years."

Her eyebrows lifted, a sad smile lifting the sides of her mouth. "Mickey Mouse pancakes."

"Huh?" I asked confused.

"That first morning when I made Mickey Mouse pancakes for breakfast. I saw a prescription bottle in the cabinet, but never saw it again."

"I moved it," he whispered. "I stopped taking it soon after and I was going to tell you, but I had, I have, so many other things to tell you."

She pressed her lips together tightly and shook her head. "What are you doing, Aaron?"

"What I should have done when I first came here. What I should have done months ago."

"What are you doing?" she repeated slowly.

"I don't want to leave tonight, Callie, without you knowing, without telling you, how I feel."

"But…look…"

I reached across the open doorway and took hold of her wrist. "We don't have to forget about everything and pretend like nothing happened. We both messed up, but we can both make it better. I don't want anything else but you. I don't want you to be my nanny. You don't even need to be my girlfriend. I just want…to get to know you. I want to take you on a date, on many dates, and I want to know you, and I want you to know me. Remember that day at Wildberry? When you mentioned your dad for the first time? I promised myself I'd ask more questions, learn more about who you were, but I didn't. I told myself I would explain to you all about Lexie and what her leaving did to me. But I was so wrapped in who we were, where we were headed, and I thought we'd have time. I always thought there would be an endless amount of time. I took that for granted and I'm so fucking sorry."

Tears pooled in her eyes and she attempted to shake her head no, but stopped.

"Please. It wasn't our imagination. I want this. I want us, and I want us to get there together, how we should have gotten there to begin with." My hand still gripped her wrist, unable to let go. "Please let me in," I pleaded.

She let out a small cry, tears rolling down her perfect face.

After a deep breath, she took a step back. I waited for the door to slam shut, but in true Callie fashion, she surprised me once again.

She stepped out of the doorway and held the door wide open for me. A tiny smile lifted the corner of her mouth slightly. "Okay, I'll let you in," she whispered.

Chapter Twenty-Seven

CALLIE—

I couldn't shut the door, shut him out, knowing I'd regret it for the rest of my life if I did.

I couldn't pretend that what I felt from him was an illusion or that it was wrong. I couldn't want him and not want him at the same time.

I couldn't tell him I wouldn't forgive him when I wanted the same forgiveness from him. I couldn't.

So, I let him in.

I'd never seen him look so vulnerable, yet as honest as he did in that moment. It was as if the raindrops soaking his skin and clothes had washed his entire facade away and what was left was just him. Just Aaron. His eyes were different than they had been just an hour prior when he left me. They were clear and open, looking at me, actually looking at me, and they looked relieved.

"Can we sit down?" he asked.

I nodded and followed him to the couch. I sat at one end,

grabbing the throw blanket that was hanging across the back of the couch, and he sat at the other. After I wrapped myself up in the blanket, I fiddled with the yarn at the end and focused on anything but him.

"Callie?" he whispered.

"Yes," I replied, avoiding his gaze.

"What are you thinking?"

I sighed deeply. "I'm thinking…that…we, everything, is really messed up. We messed up."

"I suppose we did, but I have to be honest." He paused for a moment before continuing. "Callie, can you please look at me?"

While it was probably the polite thing to do, I knew that looking anywhere in the vicinity of his eyes, his face, was usually my downfall.

Or the dropping of my pants.

It was how, like I'd just told him, we really messed up. We let the sex guide us and somewhere along the line we fell in love. Unfortunately, communicating with me in any other way besides in bed was something we never completely established.

It was the way we said hello and ultimately the way we said good-bye.

Or so I thought.

"Calliope?"

"I'm scared, Aaron. So much has happened and I don't know how we can fix it," I said.

"Neither do I, but I'm willing to try." He paused and looked down. "Are you?"

How did I explain to him that, yes, I wanted to try to fix us, but I was scared out of my mind. I was starting a brand-new life, a life in which I wouldn't have to be dependent on anyone for the first time, and that meant I wanted to wipe the slate clean of all my screwups of the past. While I didn't want to consider what we had a screwup, I knew all the lying and deception weren't some of my proudest accomplishments.

"I don't know," I answered honestly.

"I understand. I really do, because even though I don't know how to make this better, I know I want to try. I know because I can't imagine living any more of my life without you in it."

He paused to gauge my reaction, which I'm sure looked something like I had gone a few rounds with Mike Tyson. I was tired, beat down, and my head was just swimming with confusion. After a nod of my head to let him know I was listening, he continued.

"I came here tonight to tell you that, to tell you so much, but I messed up. Again. Seeing you, after not for so long, and thinking you might be with someone else, that I was too late, made me lose my entire reason for coming here in the first place. Then…I don't know…we…just…"

"Fucked?"

"Well, yeah," he chuckled sadly. "Although I didn't want it to seem so crude."

"Well, let's call a spade a spade, right?"

"I know that's how it looks, but I'm telling you the truth. I didn't come over just to do that. You have to believe that."

We were quiet for a minutes, allowing everything to sink in.

"I was waiting to not trust you," he said, not waiting for me to answer his question. "I mean, I didn't realize at the time I was doing it, but in retrospect, and talking with Diane, I was able to…"

"Wait," I interrupted. "Who is Diane?"

So help me God, if he has another girlfriend or a new nanny he's banging, I'll grab the closest thing I can find and beat him until he is stuttering like a crack addict on a bumpy L route.

"Diane is…she's a therapist I've been seeing," he replied nervously.

"You're seeing a therapist?"

"Yeah."

"Wow," I said.

He shifted uncomfortably while wringing his hands together roughly. "Does that make you uneasy?"

"No, it's surprising, but it doesn't make me uneasy."

He nodded. "I can see that. No one was more shocked than I was that I was actually doing it, but my dad gave me a good verbal ass-kicking and…"

"Your dad? I mean, sorry to keep interrupting you, but… your dad was the one who told you to go to therapy?"

"Strange, right? Yeah, I mean, he pointed out what a fuckup I was being, and for the first time ever, I listened and realized he was right."

"So, does that mean he knows about what happened between us?"

"He didn't at first, but yes, he does know. Everything."

I almost wanted to laugh out loud at the irony. Daniel, who had put up such a fuss and caused so much stress, was the voice of reason.

"Do you feel like talking about some things helped?" I asked.

He took his time responding. "Yes," he answered.

I wanted to ask him what he learned or how it helped. I wanted to know what he told this Diane person about me and what she said about me in turn. I wanted to be angry that it took an outside person to get some shit through his thick head, but in the same breath, I wanted to praise him for not wallowing and for taking charge.

"What are you thinking?" he asked.

"I'm thinking…wondering…if I'll ever understand you."

He looked sad, so totally defeated. "It hurts me, more than you know, that you feel that way."

"I'm sorry. I…"

"No, let me finish. Callie, I have to be accountable for my role in all this. I could point fingers and say it was all your fault, but that wouldn't be fair because I know the truth. The truth is, I wanted you the same way you wanted me, and it scared the shit out of me. I was so scared of losing you, to realize you wouldn't want me anymore, that I didn't want to consider anything else." He paused and took a deep breath. "I never should have hired you. I knew there was something between us that first day, that first minute, we met. I should have thanked you for your time, and before you left, I should have asked you for your number and asked you out to dinner."

I'd known it would be difficult to hold tears at bay, but it was impossible after what he'd just said. It was shocking and honest, and if there was going to be any part of us that healed permanently, I'd need to be as truthful. Funny thing was, I believed I had already been honest with myself, convinced with the new job and moving out, that I was almost over him. After tonight, I knew nothing was further from the truth. Lying to myself was so much worse than lying to him or anyone else. It was time to lay it all out on the table.

"Can we agree," I choked through tears, "we were both wrong? I mean, there's no way to get past all the bullshit without each of us admitting things."

"Yes," he said. He shifted his body toward me and slid closer, but not close enough to touch me.

"I never felt like I was living, really living, until I was with you, and it scared the shit out of me. Here you were, this amazingly brilliant, beautiful man and then there was me. I never felt I would measure up. I was this young twit who had no business being with you in any real sense…in any real kind of relationship. I didn't want you to know how freaked out I was, so I went to Abel and told him everything I should have been telling you. How I felt about you and how the pushing and eagerness to get married freaked me out. It all happened too fast and I know I should've said so. That is all on me. My voice was lost among all the confusion, and it shouldn't have been. I've had to stand tall for a lot of things in my life, and this was the one time I went silent. I won't, I can't, do that ever again."

"There was too much for anyone to deal with coming into a relationship with me. Delilah, Lexie, my dad, but you handled it all the best you could, better than I did myself." He stopped and hung his head. "Fuck. I never wanted you to feel, never ever, you weren't what I wanted, that you didn't measure up in some way."

We sat quietly for a while, well, semi-quietly. I was a sniffling, sobbing mess, but in an attempt to try and hide it, I was snorting up the most disgusting sound imaginable. It was as if we were comforting each other, understanding, without touching.

It was a first for us.

"How's Delilah?" I asked.

The corners of his mouth lifted up into a smile, the same familiar smile he always had when he heard his daughter's name. "She misses you. The phone calls and pancakes help. Thank you for that, by the way."

"I've enjoyed doing it. I miss her a lot, too."

"Well, that leads me to the biggest apology I have to make to you," he said sadly. I saw tears pool in his eyes, and it was enough to make me start sobbing all over again. "Making you leave the way I did, so abruptly, without discussion and especially without letting you see Delilah, is the most reprehensible thing I've ever done in my life."

I drew in a sharp breath, both from remembering all the pain his actions caused me and also from how much he had been beating himself up over it. I wasn't ready to just say, "Oh...it's all right. I understand," because I didn't. If we were talking about true honesty, I wasn't going to appease him to make him feel better, no matter how horrible he felt.

He didn't wait for me to make him feel better, though.

"I know she's told you, but she started ballet lessons," he said. "It's the most adorable thing ever. She gets such a serious look of concentration, and she tries so hard, but coordination is really not her thing."

"So cute," I replied, wiping my nose on my blanket.

"It is." His eyes were thoughtful and he bit down on his lower lip. "Would you like to, maybe, come see her dance, with me, or you can meet me at the studio?"

"Well, I think…"

"I mean, you can think about it and let me know. You can call or e-mail or whatever. It's not like you have to decide right now because I know there are a lot of things to consider, and after this evening, I wouldn't blame you if you couldn't or wouldn't."

"Yes, I would like to go. I'd love to see her," I answered.

He breathed a sigh of relief and inched himself closer to me once again, close enough for our legs to be bumping. I looked down at where we were touching, feeling the same heat and energy I always had whenever he was close. It made me want more, to feel more of him, to remember how good it used to be, but for the first time, I thought with my head and not my heart. Or my lady parts.

"Are you okay?" he asked.

I nodded. "I'm okay. Just so much to think about."

"I get that."

I was scared to go where I was about to go, but he had to know how I felt. If there was any hope at all, he had to understand. If he didn't, then I'd walk away knowing I was honest and true to myself.

"I'm not ready to be with you again, Aaron. I'm not sure I ever will be," I said.

"I understand," he replied. He frowned. "I know the damage is done."

"I wasn't done with what I was saying."

"Oh, sorry. Go ahead."

"I'm not sure what the future holds. I'm about to start a whole new life. Graduation, new job, new apartment, and for the first time, I'm going to be standing on my own." I stopped briefly to choose my next words carefully. "I'm not sure how the real us would be together. We've been putting up a facade for so long…"

"Callie, please," he pleaded. "This is…painful…I get it. It's too late. I get…"

"Can you shut up for a second and let me finish?" I snapped. It was time for me to be me.

"Sorry," he said, embarrassed.

I raised my eyebrows to let him know I was serious about him letting me finish my thoughts. "I can't forget about the past and I have no idea what will happen in the future, but what I do know is what I felt for you wasn't my imagination. I felt real emotions and real pain, and I did not imagine it. I'd be stupid to deny that because, while I might be a total bubble brain about some shit, I know what is between you and me doesn't happen every day. So, I want to know you. The real you, and I want you to know the real me."

He had the slightest hint of a smile. "Really?"

"Yeah, really."

He reached out to me, but stopped short of hugging me. "Can I?" he asked.

Remembering my downfalls—his touch, his smell—and how I usually lost control of any sense being close to those things, I was apprehensive. However, if it was time to start new, baby steps were going to have to be made.

"Yes," I replied softly.

He smiled before wrapping his arms around my waist and bringing me into him. A breath of relief, or maybe optimism, left his lips and warmed the side of my neck. I settled into his body, laying my head on his shoulder and just let him…hold me. All questions wouldn't be answered in one night, all wrongs not made right, but in that moment, it was the start of something new.

He rested his forehead against mine and we sat, quiet and still…until the front door slammed.

And the screaming started.

"What the *fuck* is he doing here?" Evelyn yelled.

Aaron and I pulled away from each other quickly, like two teenagers caught making out by our parents. Evelyn pounded into the living room, standing before us with her hands on her hips.

"Are you going to say anything?" she repeated. "What the hell is going on?"

Aaron stood up, nervously running his hands through his hair. He turned his body toward Evelyn. "I love her."

"Yeah, right. Why are you here in the first place?" Evelyn said. She whipped her head around and directed her rage at me. "Cal?"

"He stopped by to drop something off Delilah made for me, and we started to talk and stuff," I replied.

"What?" she shouted. "How could you let that asshole into the front door after what he did to you?"

"I think it best I leave you two to talk about it on your own for now. Evelyn, I have no idea what you must think of me. When things calm down, I'd like the chance to explain," Aaron said, standing. "I'll talk to you later, Callie."

"You'll what?" Evelyn said. "Oh, you've got to be kidding me. You're going to let him walk back into your life after all these months?"

I stood up to face her. "Evelyn," I said as calmly as I could. "I love you. I couldn't have gotten through these last months without you, but for right now, I need to sort this out on my own. I need to sort through it all with him. We can talk about this after he leaves."

"Why don't you want to talk about it now?" she said. "You don't want him to know the truth?"

"He *knows* the truth, Evelyn," I replied, anger bringing tears to my eyes again.

"Well, great," she said. She plopped herself down on the couch and folded her arms. "So he knows how I was sick with worry after he threw you out like trash? Does he also know you missed weeks of school and almost fucked up graduating because you were so devastated? Does he know you had to grovel to your creep of an ex-boss for your job back? Did you tell him—"

"Enough!" I screamed. "I'm sick of it. What I do or who I do..."

"You DID him?" Evelyn asked.

"Shit," Aaron said under his breath.

"Aaron, you don't have to answer that," I shouted. "It's none of her business. Why don't you go ahead and go home? I'll talk to you later."

"You did!" Evelyn said. "You slept with him?"

I sighed loudly. "Would you excuse Aaron and me for a minute?" I didn't wait for her to answer before I crossed the room and followed Aaron out the door. Once we were in the hallway, we looked at each other, both horrified at the reaction we'd gotten.

"I'll talk to her and she'll chill out," I explained. "She's... well, I put her through a lot."

"It's understandable and deserving." He grabbed me around the waist again and hugged me tightly. "I'm so sorry, Callie. I promise you'll trust me again." He whispered into the top of my hair.

"Me, too."

And though that's how the night ended, it's also how the new start of us began.

* * *

I'd be lying if I said the two months between the night Aaron showed up at my doorstep and my graduation was easy. It wasn't easy at all, but it was the most comfortable and content I'd ever felt in my entire life. Shortly before I graduated, I moved out of the apartment I shared with Evelyn, partially to be closer to my new job, but more importantly, because I *could*. I'd saved for months to be able to do it, and once school started, I'd be doing just fine. For the first time ever, something was mine, and I didn't have to lean on anyone else to help me. It was freeing and cathartic. I felt like I did as a child, running and running, but never being out of breath. I could breathe so deeply, so satisfying now, I never realized how long I had been holding it.

With moving, finishing school, and starting a new job, things were frantic, but somehow I made time to start dating again. Someone new. He looked the same as he always had, but Aaron was new to me all over again. When he showed up for our "first" date, he was nervous and awkward, standing in my doorway with a bouquet of wildflowers. We went to dinner and to a movie that he let me choose. He walked me to the door and gave me a quick peck of a kiss.

He left me with butterflies…

And searching through packed boxes for Trix.

We went out again the following week and twice the week after.

I met up with him and Delilah at the zoo one day and had been to her ballet practice twice.

On our fifth date, we made out in his car for forty-five minutes, and I let him go to third base.

He told me in painful detail about his relationship with Lexie and how the aftermath of her leaving affected him. In kind, I explained to him more about me, about how my father's death impacted my life daily.

It was strange and unconventional and made no sense to anyone but us what we were doing. Giving the term *starting over* a very true meaning.

If I hadn't known him before, I would fall in love with him. Instead, I was falling in love with him all over again.

When I graduated, he was there, along with Evelyn and Abel. I wore my earrings Aaron had given me to the ceremony, and later that evening, when we were all having a celebratory dinner together, Aaron caught me staring into the mirrored wall next to us.

Evelyn was giving Abel a dirty look. "Really? That's your pickup line? A goldfish has more game than you," she said.

"Feisty," he said, nodding his head. "I like that."

I laughed before I turned my attention to Delilah. Her precious face smeared with chocolate cake, talking animatedly with our server and giggling.

I gazed at Aaron and now I knew, with all my heart, we were in the right place. We may have messed up, taken detours, but we were on the right track and where we should be.

His fingers brushed against my neck. "What are you staring at?" he whispered in my ear.

I repeated the words he once said to me. "My future. My future is in that mirror."

Acknowledgments

The name Melissa Marino wouldn't be on the cover of this book, or any book, if it wasn't for the faith and encouragement of my Super Agent and fellow Kate Spade enthusiast, **Kimberly Brower**. Kimberly, you took a chance with me and believe in every word I write. Thank you for always knowing by your secret agent powers the moments to say, "Good but you can do better," or "Don't panic." Grateful doesn't even cover the gratitude I have for you.

I've been blessed by having not one, but two editors at Forever Romance who loved this book enough to work tirelessly on its behalf. So many thanks to **Megha Parekh** whose excitement for this series made my hopes and dreams for these characters come true. **Lexi Smail**, your endless eagerness, keen eye, and *The Bachelorette* shouty caps make my life, my work, a delight. Also, **Yasmin Mathew**, **Kathleen Scheiner** and the entire team at Forever Romance for making this book more amazing than I could've ever imagined.

Brighton and **Anna**, thank you for aiding in the original version. I have never forgotten all the input and hand-holding you did so many years ago.

My writer friends turned life friends: **Sarah Cannon, Carla Cullen, Rachel Goodman, Tara Sue Me, The Wolf Pack**, and **Ann Marie Walker**. Each and every one of you has encouraged me in countless ways.

My sweeties and two of my biggest cheerleaders, **Lo** and **Christina**. There was a time I was ready to give up, and you two sat across from me as we ate maple bacon doughnuts to tell me to keep pushing. You told me I was almost there. I trusted you and you were right. Thank you for your friendship and for celebrating every tiny publishing milestone with me.

Nina Bocci. My dear Nina. Absolutely none of this would be possible without you. A lifetime of lip glosses are owed to you.

My soul mate and boob-bumper, **Amy E. Reichert**. You virtually hold my hand daily, filter hysterical FaceTime calls, and encourage cocktail hour(s). Thank you for pushing me creatively and reminding me I can do anything. Your spirit is one of my most treasured joys.

To my lobster muffin, **Sarah Wells**, who calms my crazy, reminds me of my strength, reads countless words, and has never made me doubt why she is my person. Thank you for being the Rachel to my Monica.

All the creatives, teachers, and staff at **StoryStudio Chicago** who guided me in my early days and read drafts that were far from readable at that point. Also, enormous gratitude to **Jama Kehoe Bigger**, director of Midwest Writers Workshop, and the entire faculty of this life-changing conference. MWW is the creative kick in the butt I've needed every year, and the people I found there have made my journey so much more enjoyable.

So Twisted would not be a book if not for the community of amazing readers, writers, and human beings in the fandom that embraced the original and gave me more than I could ever give them. ::pats my heart:: Twi fandom. You are some of the most dynamic women I've ever known, and I carry you and all we've shared in my heart forever.

When I told my very conservative, very religious father about this book, his response (after I explained to him he would probably be uncomfortable reading it) was priceless. "Melissa. I trust you know what you think I can handle. In that case, let me get a pen and write down what the book is about so I know what to say when I brag about it." I won the parent lottery with him and my mom. Both have supported every decision I've ever made with love and solid advice. I wouldn't be the woman I am today without you, Mom and Dad.

To my two boys. L, the fact I'm even writing this acknowledgment is proof that your unwavering faith and stern talks, when I struggled, to pull up my big girl pants is how I reached my dreams. I simply couldn't have done any of this without you, and I will never, ever forget that. J, you are never allowed to read this book because your father and I simply don't have the funds for the kind of therapy you will need after. Thank you, my darling, for being proud that your mom is "a mom who writes books" and for making me know boundless love.

And lastly, to the original DILF and Nanny. When I asked the night we met, "If you're out with the nanny, who is watching the kids?" DILF answered pointedly, "I had to hire a fucking babysitter so I could take out the nanny." Both of you—and I—had no idea that a story would be sparked and lead to this. I thank you and wish you continued happiness.

Evelyn Owen, a career-minded wedding planner and serial dater, meets her match in Abel Matthews, a womanizing bartender. But their hot and heavy romance is cut short when Evelyn is sent off to open a West Coast location. When Evelyn comes home a year later, she's shocked to meet her newest client: the groom Abel.

Please turn the page for a preview of So Screwed

Available Early 2017

Chapter One

EVELYN—

I glanced at my phone as I flung the glass door open and hurried inside, wondering what the appropriate length of time was to stay at the funeral of my best friend's boyfriend's father's mother. It wasn't like I'd ever met the woman. The fact that I was there at all should've been enough of a gesture of support without worrying if a condolence and bolt was out of line. After unbuttoning my coat, I smoothed my hands down the front of my skirt as I shook my head to fluff my long blond hair. I followed the muffled sounds of the bereaved conversing and entered the stuffy viewing room.

Why did funeral homes always have a weird smell? Was it from all the flowers and fresh dry-cleaned clothes of the family? Was it from the embalming? Was it too morbid to even be thinking about as I stepped around the others, waiting to get myself to the front of the line? Probably.

Mr. Matthews stood next to the open casket of his now deceased mother as he chatted quietly with another older gentleman. He removed a handkerchief from the pocket of his dark suit jacket and dabbed his eyes.

Yup. Get that all out of the way now. No tears with me. I can't deal with almost strangers crying.

My eyes scanned the room around me, looking for a familiar face or even an unfamiliar one I could stare at for a moment. Anything to avoid the dead woman to my left. The gentleman talking to Mr. Matthews walked away, and I waited a few seconds before stepping in.

"I'm so sorry for your loss," I said to Mr. Matthews. "I'm not sure you remember me. I'm Evelyn Owens, Callie's friend."

"Of course I remember you. Thank you so much for coming, Evelyn," he responded, nodding his head and grabbing my hand. He turned to his mother. "She was a wonderful woman."

"I'm sure she was."

He kept staring at his mom. I stood quiet, as he continued holding my hand, wondering how long I had to stand there.

Wasn't there a way to make these things less awkward? No one ever knew what to say or do. There had to be a way to lighten it up. It wasn't like it had to be a full-out bash. Just something to break the ice enough—something more like a wedding. Weddings I was good at.

"So, how are you, Evelyn? Has any lucky guy caught you yet?" Mr. Matthews asked.

And just in case awkward wasn't enough, the inevitable inquest into your love life from the father of your best friend's boyfriend should slide you right into face-peeling uncomfortableness.

He took my silence as an invitation to press the issue.

"I still have a single son," he said.

He dropped my hand and waved it with authority above my head. No doubt inviting himself into matchmaking.

"Oh, Mr. Matthews. I've met…"

"Excuse me, kids," Mr. Matthews said stepping away as I felt a brush against my lower back.

"Evelyn," said a low voice behind me.

I turned and lifted my head because he was that tall. The few times we'd met before I'd taken notice of his stature, but standing next to him served as a reminder.

Mr. Matthews's youngest son, and award-winning eye candy, was dressed in a slim blue suit tailored to perfection. His dark pompadour and closely shaved beard made his blue eyes stand out in contrast. The entire package was quite startling.

"Abel," I said. "I'm so sorry for your loss."

"Thanks for coming to pay your…respects."

His eyes scanned up and down my body with deliberate aggression.

"God," I hissed. "Your dead grandmother is laying there." I stabbed a finger in her direction. "Can't you check me out some other time?"

The corner of his mouth lifted into a tiny grin while his eyes found mine. *Dimples.* They were just visible from beneath his beard, extending onto the smoothed skin of his cheeks.

He was hot, but blatant cockiness wasn't a flattering look on any man outside of the bedroom.

"It isn't exclusive to today, Evelyn. I check you out every time I see you. How could I not? It's you who hasn't wanted to pursue anything."

"And now I remember why."

"Come on," he said, touching my arm. "I think you and me together would be what Grandma Dorothy would've wanted."

He was a handsome, handsome guy. I'd give him that. No doubt a line of panties dropped wherever he went. Hell. I would've maybe dropped mine if I didn't think it would cause drama. My best friend's boyfriend's brother? Not ideal.

"Ev," Callie, my best friend, said, coming up next to me. She took me in a hug as her boyfriend, Aaron, came up next to her. They were one of those couples others hated. Strikingly good-looking, her with her long auburn hair and perfect skin, and him tall and built just like his younger brother, with a smile that warmed up a funeral home.

I stepped over to Aaron, and squeezed his hand. "I'm so sorry," I said.

His eyes shifted between Abel and me for a brief moment. "You're a sweetheart for coming."

"You are two of my favorite people," I said. "It's what friends do."

Aaron and I had our differences in the past when Callie and he had their troubles. I wasn't happy with him for a long time because of the way he handled things when they broke up, but ultimately, they made up. Over the last year, I've seen how much he made her happy and that made me happy.

Abel cleared his throat. "Want to make it three of your favorite people?"

Handsome *and* ballsy as shit. It was appealing, but the undercurrent of douche bag was a bit too prevalent for me to take him completely seriously.

"I have to run and get back to work but wanted to stop by," I said.

"I'll walk you out," Callie said, linking her arm through mine.

"Thanks again, Evelyn," Aaron said.

"You'll all be in my thoughts," I replied. I turned to Abel. "Sorry again."

Callie and I started to walk away, but Abel's hand on my arm stopped me. He stepped close, hovering over me. "How about a drink later?"

"I don't think so," I said.

Callie remained quiet, but the tug on my opposite arm began to pull harder. Abel was trying to catch me as Callie tried to save me.

"Please," he begged, batting his dark eyelashes at me. "I'm in mourning. You wouldn't want me to be all alone, would you?"

"Abel." Callie sighed. "The list of phone numbers you have of willing ladies is the size of the first draft of the Bible. Quit creeping on my best friend."

"Are you trying to cockblock me at Nana's funeral?" Abel snapped.

Callie yanked on my arm and tugged me away. "Really, Abel?" she said over her shoulder.

I chuckled because I appreciated the persistence on his part, but Callie's response only solidified my decision. We left the room and headed for the exit with her shaking her head the entire time.

"Sorry about him," she said. "He's about as civilized as a toddler on a sugar rush."

"It's oddly charming."

She stopped in her tracks and spun around, placing her hands on her hips. Her eyes narrowed like she was looking for some hidden message behind them.

"Oh, shit," she said. "Please don't."

"Don't what?"

"Bang my boyfriend's brother."

And like any best friend could, she read me like a book. It wasn't something I would do, though. I had boundaries.

"I'm not," I promised. "I won't."

About the author

Melissa Marino is a full-time writer and part-time Storm-trooper collector. When she's not writing, you can find her watching *Friends* reruns, mastering her cupcake frosting swirl, and hunting for the perfect red lipstick. Melissa lives in Chicago with her husband, son, and very opinionated dachs-hund.

You can learn more at:
melissa-marino.com
Twitter @MelissaWrites2
Facebook.com/MelissaMarinoBooks

www.ingramcontent.com/pod-product-compliance
Ingram Content Group UK Ltd.
Pitfield, Milton Keynes, MK11 3LW, UK
UKHW022300280225
455674UK00001B/118